VIRGIN

ROCKY MOUNTAIN STAR

DRAGONBOOKS
PUBLISHING HOUSE

DRAGONBOOKS
PUBLISHING HOUSE

Names: Fox, Virginia, author.

Title: Rocky Mountain Star (Rocky Mountain Romances, Book 2)/ by Virginia Fox.

Description: First Edition. | Boulder, Colorado: Dragonbooks, 2022.

Summary: When an injured ballerina flees her glamorous lifestyle for the Rocky Mountains, she is set upon by a dangerous stalker and runs into a former fling, setting the stage for suspense, romance, and a dash of humor.

Subjects: BISAC: FICTION / Romance / General. | FICTION / Romance / Contemporary. | FICTION / Women.

ISBN 979-8-9862800-3-5 (Paperback) | ISBN 979-8-9862800-2-8 (eBook) LCCN: 2022922107

Editor: Elaine Ash
Associate Editor: John Palisano
Cover Design: Juliane Schneeweiss
Interior Design: Jennifer Thomas

ROCKY MOUNTAIN STAR

CHAPTER ONE

CENTER STAGE IN THE SPOTLIGHT, Tyler twirled and spun to *Blackbird* played by a fifteen-piece orchestral rock band. She wore a black, figure-skimming sheath sewn with thousands of crystals that flashed like midnight diamonds under the stage lights. The sheath ended at her knees, right where the satin ribbons of her ballet shoes twisted up her calves and met the hem. A cascade of shimmering material fell all the way down her back to the floor until she raised her arms and it unfolded on the sides like a nightbird's wings.

The moment was a *prima ballerina* turn in the show and something Tyler had worked for all her life. Not bad for someone born in small-town Colorado with no connections, only talent. It had taken incredible sacrifice and dedication to master this caliber of dance, while making it look effortless to the most demanding audience in the world—Las Vegas. Show producers had decided, over time, that she was worth the risk. Difficult, diva-sue performers were the stuff of nightmares for the enormous hotels that offered blockbuster live shows to vacationers. Those million-dollar shows needed stars who arrived on time and delivered spellbinding performances night after night. No matter the personal cost. And Tyler had shown she could deliver.

The live orchestra intensified, and the music swelled. Tyler leaped into the air and took flight, like a real bird. Invisible wires lifted her so she flew across the stage and landed on the tiptoes of her satin shoes. More blackbirds swooped onto the stage, the music soared, and soon they were all whirling in the air to the music as the audience watched, breathless.

Tyler walked slowly into arrivals, her limp more noticeable after sitting in a cramped seat for the flight. Under her pants, she wore an elastic sleeve around her knee to support the ligaments. Her blond hair hung limp, and instead of walking briskly with energy, she dragged a bit. Like this, she looked small, even frail. Dancers were not large people, although she looked six feet tall onstage in a feather headdress, balanced on the tips of her toe shoes.

She was sore, very sore, and instead of being filled with anticipation at seeing her family again, as she usually was, this time she felt only dread. In fact, she hadn't told them she was coming. Just decided to hop on a plane on a whim.

For now, it was the knee that occupied her mind, much as she tried to ignore it. A little slip coming offstage the last show before a two-week hiatus, and here she was limping around like a wimp. A little ice, a good night's sleep, and it would fix itself. Right? The three-hour plane ride in a cramped seat had simply put a little more pressure on it, temporarily. Nothing worth stressing about.

Las Vegas was bursting with Cirque du Soleil-style shows like the one Tyler starred in, but only this one had a ballerina character who danced as a blackbird, and then came back in an array of costumes opposite different characters. There were many dancers in the show, but only one ballerina. Only one *Tyler Carter*.

Landing a place as the prima ballerina in a Las Vegas show was the culmination of a lifetime of dedication to ballet since childhood. Ballerinas only looked ethereal and delicate. In reality, they withstood rigorous physical training and discipline. *A ballerina*, the show choreographer was fond of saying, *requires the determination of a third-world dictator and the stamina of a polo pony.*

It was one thing for Tyler to fly from Vegas to Colorado and visit with her parents between show engagements. It was always nice to be pampered for a few weeks. It was another thing to limp back to their house at the age of twenty-three, when they were already under the impression that her career was fleeting and unstable. Tyler always wanted to put on a good front. And this sore knee wasn't a good front. No matter that it was just a slight tweak at the end of months of grueling performances. Wasn't she deserving of a few post-show aches and pains? Not to people outside show business, she wasn't.

Her parents might show support and understanding on the outside, but on the inside they'd be saying for the millionth time, *If only she'd chosen something practical.* But her plans and dreams included her own show in Vegas, one that would make her a household singing and dancing name, like Madonna, Beyoncé, or like Liza Minnelli in her Broadway days. Even Britney Spears, who had a Vegas show. Tyler hadn't gotten started on the singing part of it yet, but that would come. She was already taking lessons.

She made her way to the baggage carousel. While waiting for her wheeled suitcase to appear, she let her gaze wander. Her October visit coincided with Denver's first snow, and the airport was teeming with winter sports enthusiasts. Skis, poles, boots, snowboards— even a toboggan—circled on the carousel, waiting to be claimed. The occasional western hat and boots could be seen on a few people. This was the West, after all.

Tyler spotted her suitcase. She bent over to lift it, shifting her weight to her leg, and got jostled from the side. She stifled a groan and grumbled something unintelligible. If she had to stay around these rowdy people a moment longer, one of them would end up trussed like a turkey on the baggage carousel, Destination Timbuktu.

Rolling her suitcase carefully toward the exit, she felt for her cell phone and stopped to tap the Uber app. She could have called Paula for a ride, but her sister was bossy, and as soon as she discovered Tyler was not one hundred percent a ton of good advice would follow. If there was one thing Tyler wanted to avoid right now, it was good advice. She didn't need that on the ride from Denver to Independence Junction, the small town where she had grown up. Called Independence for short, it was high in the Rocky Mountains near the famous ski resorts like Aspen and Breckenridge. But not so near that a million-dollar price tag applied to the land. Independence was home to generational Coloradans, many of whom grew up and moved away. But everything changes, everything has a season, and now prodigal sons and daughters were returning to settle.

It was beautiful there. Clear air, a magnificent mountain panorama, beautiful trees, and warm, if nosy, fellow citizens. For a place with less than fifteen hundred people, it seemed to have everything.

Before going outside, she unzipped the suitcase and dug out a puffy parka and a pair of Ugg boots lined in fleece. No way could she board a plane in Vegas dressed in this clothing, but October in Colorado required them. The Uber arrived, and she settled in for the drive. It was eighty miles to Breckenridge. Independence was beyond that.

She must have slept, because the motion of the Uber vehicle slowing down woke her. Independence was in darkness, but Main Street glowed with lights. The Uber's tires crunched on the layer of snow on the road. Wooden storefronts had gentle yellow illumination in the windows, even though they were closed. The buildings mostly had peaked roofs, and some were painted different colors with contrasting trim. A green storefront had red trim, and a yellow one had blue trim. Tiny fairy lights bedecked potted shrubs and bushes.

Only the diner bustled with people at this hour of six in the evening. Tyler was hungry but knew that if she went to the diner, everyone would know she was home. She wasn't ready for that. Mostly, she wasn't ready for the questions.

"Up there," she said to the driver, pointing away from the diner.

The Uber squeaked through the snow for a few hundred yards.

"Here," Tyler said, indicating a sign that said "Yoga Studio" with an arrow pointing to the second floor. Tyler tapped in a generous tip for the driver on her cell-phone app. "Thanks, have a nice night." She got out with her suitcase and fumbled for keys.

Years ago, this old wooden building housed the dance school of Madame DuPont, a famous *professeur de dance* who hosted seasonal retreats for renowned dancers the world over. This was where they came to rest, got back to perfecting dance basics, and recuperated from grueling tours. As a favor to the local community, the renowned Mme DuPont taught a dance class for local children. Tyler had been one of them. When Madame DuPont passed on, she left the building to Tyler in her will.

The old key slipped effortlessly into the lock on the dark studio door. She wanted to stretch a bit at the *barre*, going easy on the leg, but still releasing stress. She was going to need a chill mood before facing the family. She pushed the door open and stepped inside, inhaling the scent of wooden floorboards and the dust of an old place.

She loved everything about it. Memories of hours spent in sweaty leotards, of the strict instructions from her teacher, and the happy atmosphere of the local girls came back. It had been Madame DuPont's wish that the dance retreats continue after her death. Busy with her career, Tyler had been unable to organize the right teacher or the accommodations for dance professionals the way Madame had. Tyler wasn't sure how she felt about resurrecting the school, anyway. No idea if she could even teach. Patience wasn't exactly her strong suit. Perfectionism, on the other hand, was. But the future of that wasn't clear.

Lost in thought, she flipped on the lights. She blinked. Was she hallucinating? Over in the back corner hung a red punching bag. Gloves lay on the floor beneath it. She looked around, but it seemed she was alone. Hesitantly, she walked over and touched the sandbag. Yes, it was real. Her eyes were not playing tricks on her. The second floor of the building was rented out right now. Perhaps those people had hung the bag here.

She'd heard about working off frustrations on a boxing bag, and the idea appealed right now. Determined, she slipped off her Uggs. Barefoot, she circled the bag a few times, then bent down and slipped on the gloves. How difficult could it be? She hopped on the spot like a boxer once or twice, only to pause with her face contorted in pain. Footwork was out, it seemed. But there was nothing wrong with her arms. Gingerly at first, she tapped a few blows on the bag. Then faster and faster, she let punches patter on the red dummy. She was so focused that she didn't even notice someone enter the room behind her.

Panting, Tyler braced herself, waiting to catch her breath. She hadn't known it would be so strenuous. And she was used to quite a bit from her own training. Slowly, she lowered her arms. She could barely lift them. Thirsty, she needed something to drink. There was a sink in the small locker room. She could drink there. As she turned, her eyes fell on someone. An image of muscular arms around her waist and intertwined legs flashed before her inner eye. Heat shot through her body. *Oh great.* She was suddenly aware of scattered strands of hair that had come loose from her braid sticking to her sweaty face.

"You!" she gasped.

"I was thinking the same thing," he answered.

Funny, she remembered the way he smelled, the sensation of his touch, but she couldn't remember his name.

"Pat," he said, as though reading her mind. "Patrick West."

"Tyler—"

"Carter. I remember."

They looked at each other, memories from the summer flooding back. Along with the dark good looks and toned body, Tyler remembered he was an architect. He was planning the restoration of a historic house in the area. Which explained why he was still in town.

He took off his jacket and sat on the floor. "I didn't know dancers could work the bag," he said.

"I didn't know either, but it's great for blowing off frustrations."

He nodded. He looked more amused than annoyed that she was holding him up and using his property. But if she was annoyed, he should be too. Fair is fair, right? No, life wasn't fair, she remembered. She should have learned that much in the last few days. Wordlessly, she turned away and went to the sink. She needed an intervention, something, anything, to give a moment to think how to handle this. She drank greedily from the tap and then held her whole head under the water. She squeezed out her hair, shook it out, and with a corner of her T-shirt, dried her face and walked back to the bag. Slooowly. The slower the better, to hide any hint of favoring the leg. She thought the wet hair would be a distraction, kind of a sleight-of-hand magician's trick, but his gaze fell to her leg anyway. She waited for a comment, but he said nothing, just waited until she slid down beside him, leaning back against the wall.

"You a boxer?" she asked out of the blue.

"A little martial arts," he answered, and didn't offer anything else.

She watched him out of the corner of her eye. Seems she'd found a topic he didn't want to talk about. They both had things they didn't want to talk about. *Touché.*

"So my dance studio is turning into a dojo?"

"You know the Japanese word for it." He looked impressed.

"I work in Vegas with dancers, stunt people, and every kind of physical entertainment professional from all over the world. Of course I know the term."

The slight, amused smile fell from his face. "If you need the space, I'll find another place."

She ducked the invitation. "I take it Jaz said this was okay?" Jaz was Jasmine McArthy, the yoga studio owner who rented the space upstairs. She was also a friend, and likely to be a member of the Carter family if and when she married Tyler's brother, Jake. Without waiting for an answer, she said, "I guess I can't be mad at her. Jaz is the reason we met in the first place."

"You remembered." Air went out of him in a sigh, like he'd been holding his breath.

They were silent for a moment. Each thinking back to a night last summer, at a music festival, when they'd left early and spent private hours of pleasure, never expecting to see one another again.

She was tempted to rattle him a little, but couldn't bring herself to do it. "It's okay. As long as you don't interfere with my training, you can stay. I don't know exactly how my plans will turn out yet."

"Thanks. I wasn't expecting that."

"Just because I'm having a bad day doesn't mean you can't talk to me."

"Now you sound more like the woman I met at the festival."

"That's good, cause I sure don't look like her." She tossed her damp hair.

"You look exactly like her. I'd know those blue eyes anywhere. Sea-blue."

She could hear heat in his voice. He was waiting for her to say something else. Maybe to give some clue to her sudden appearance in town. But she said nothing.

"I see you have a suitcase," he said. "Need a lift anywhere? If you're finished working out, that is. No rush."

Tyler had so much to say, but a thousand words couldn't explain it all, and one word felt like too many.

He spoke slowly and gently. "Should I take you to your family?"

She coughed lightly. "No, they don't know I'm here yet."

"What do you want to do, then? You're not going to stay here at the studio, are you?"

"Maybe"—she searched his face—"Maybe just take me to your place?"

He saw the look in her eye. She didn't have to ask twice.

On a snowmobile across the street, a man watched as Tyler and Pat locked up and left the studio. From the looks of it, the Vegas Twirly Girl and Mr. Fix-It were into each other. That suited him just fine. He rubbed his hands together. It had been more comfortable in the diner. But after people tried to engage him in conversation, the situation became unsafe. It was important to keep a distance from others. Normally, it was no problem for him to remain invisible. Nothing about him was noticeable. But that didn't seem to do him any good in this place. The curse of a small town. On the other hand, for the same reason, he learned many details of his victims that he would have otherwise had to painstakingly research. Maybe he had to adapt his plan to the local conditions— he would deal with that later.

The couple entered Pat's vehicle and started off down Main Street. The watcher shifted the snowmobile into drive, pulled a black ski mask over his face so only eye slits were visible, and followed at a safe distance, keeping the lights off. The couple wound up a hilly road that ended at a magnificent old house. It must have been five-thousand square feet. At least a third of it was covered with scaffolding and plastic tarps tied down against the winds that blew in over the mountains. The couple got out of the ancient Cadillac Mr. Fix-It was driving—*an odd choice of vehicle for a young guy*, the man thought—and crunched over the snow to the dark house. A sensor light went on to illuminate the way to a side entrance. The man made a mental note of that. *No dog, either.* He watched as they entered the house and disappeared.

Satisfied with tonight's results, he shifted the snowmobile into drive and drove back the way they'd come—to his temporary residence to contemplate dark plans.

CHAPTER TWO

TYLER BLINKED. Weak winter sunlight streamed in through wooden blinds. *Strange.* The sun never shone in her room in the morning. Sleepily, she turned over and encountered resistance with her hand. A large, muscular, warm resistance. Her eyes jolted open. *Déjà vu.* This was how the morning started the last time with Pat, after the music festival. Only this time, she wasn't sleeping down by the river. She was in an old house. The owner, Mr. Wilkinson, who was almost as old as the town, was staying in the bed-and-breakfast attached to the diner while Pat handled restoration.

She slipped out of bed, gathered her clothes, and grabbed her suitcase. The knee didn't feel too bad this morning. This room was located in the back quarter of the five-thousand square foot house. It had its own bathroom. But she didn't want to wake Pat. She silently backed out of the room. There had to be more bathrooms down the hall.

Walking along, she ran one hand down the smooth white wall. Even here, in the back of the house, the floor was made of burnished black walnut wood. The wood continued in the baseboards and ceiling trim. Brass sconces lit the hallway. This was a sixty-year-old house, built with the best materials of its day. The house was cold. She hoped the heating system was first on the list for renovation.

She tried the handle of a door that looked like it might be a bathroom. *Score*. It hadn't been used in a while, but it was clean and even had a dried-up bar of soap on the sink. That was lucky because Tyler hadn't bothered to pack shampoo. She planned on using whatever was in the house she bunked at, either her mother's or Paula's, and hadn't figured on staying overnight at a place like old-man Wilkinson's. The bath had an elegant old tub on cast-iron feet and a handheld shower. She grabbed the soap and opted for a shower. The water needed to run, but it got plenty hot after a minute. It would have been nice to explain how wretched she felt due to the time change, but no such luck. Independence was only one hour later than Vegas.

Her next dilemma was how to get into town without having to ask Pat for a lift. Rinsing off, she used yesterday's T-shirt to dry off, zipping it into a plastic-lined outside pocket of her suitcase, and put on fresh clothes. Back out in the hall, she found her way to the main living space of the house.

The living room, or great room, as Mr. Wilkinson might have called it, was dominated by a huge stone fireplace. Everything inside the house seemed made of wood, brick, or stone. The windows were large with deep casements, and in this room with its stuffed leather furniture and wooden chairs, the views of outside were spectacular. This morning the world was white after a snowfall overnight. A snowmobile buzzed past, the driver disguised by a heavy down jacket and ski mask pulled over his face. If he noticed Tyler at the window, he didn't wave. *Shoot*, that guy could have been her ride into town.

Her puffy parka and Ugg boots were in the entryway, where they'd been left the night before. If she went outside and waited a bit, maybe the snowmobiler would come by again. She dragged her suitcase out the front door and walked across the spacious front yard to the road. Birds were singing in the snow-covered trees. The chance of another vehicle coming by seemed remote. There was likely a toboggan somewhere around this old place. Maybe she could toboggan down the hill. It was downhill almost all the way. She could tip the suitcase on its side and hold it with both arms wrapped around it. Who was she kidding? That was the fantasy of a ten-year-old. She'd likely capsize and catapult herself off the road headlong into a tree.

The thought nagged that she was going to an awful lot of trouble not to wake Pat up when the theme song from her show sounded in the pocket of her parka. What a miracle, there was a signal. It was her cell phone, and that ringtone was Sarah, her agent.

"Hello?"

"Sweetheart, how are you? It's Sarah. Are you in Colorado?"

"Hi! Yes, I'm home." *Not exactly*, her conscience whispered guiltily.

"Everything okay?"

"Of course."

"Just calling to make sure. Yuri said you had a little slip backstage after the last show."

Yuri! That backstabbing choreographer. She wanted to growl, but instead gave a silvery laugh. "Sorry to disappoint Yuri's handpicked understudies, but I'm fine."

"Good, sweetheart. You know the producers worry at the drop of a hat."

"Maybe if Yuri kept his mouth sh—"

Sarah blew that off with her own airy giggle. "Good to check in, sweetheart. Ta-ta for now."

She hung up and Tyler brought up the show's Facebook page to see if Yuri had made the story public. There was nothing in the comments. She clicked over to her professional page. Fans were moaning about the two-week hiatus, nothing much else. She clicked into the Facebook feed with Instagram stories. Same thing. Lots of publicity pics of Tyler in her blackbird costume, and in her silver dress dancing on the moon. But nothing about her itty-bitty slip and fall.

Forget dancing on the moon. I'm living in a fishbowl, she thought. An unpleasant and unfamiliar feeling threatened to settle over her as a pickup truck with a snowplow on the front rumbled into view. The side was painted with *Joe's Snow Removal.* Tyler threw up both arms in the universal "Please, stop!" gesture. The plow grunted to a halt.

In the light of day, with a fresh layer of snow, Main Street's colorful storefronts looked like a winter wonderland. Tyler got out of the plow-pickup and handed the driver a bill. He wouldn't take it. "Say hello to your mother for me," he explained. "It's always nice to have young people come back." He pulled away.

Then Tyler heard the truck stop and back up. The driver rolled the window down and held out a card. "You need another ride? Here's my number. I'm on call."

Tyler smiled and said thank you. As though her feet were making the decision, she strolled away from the diner and enjoyed the pretty little street. It was kept in the Breckenridge and Aspen style of one and two-story clapboard buildings, nothing larger. There were still empty storefronts with room for growth, but the trend was clearly pointing upward.

Just about to walk into the diner, she pulled out her cell phone and texted her mother, Brenda Carter. *Hi Mom. In town 4 a few days. Be home in time for supper.* There, now Momma knew first. If any news escaped from the diner, her mother would already be up to speed. Being the first to know was currency in Independence.

She pulled open the big door with *Miss Minnie's* etched in the glass. The place was bustling. Red padded booths lined the walls while four-top tables with wooden chairs filled in the center. A big counter had silver stools that swiveled. For the breakfast traffic, steaming hot breakfasts piled with pancakes and eggs, toast and hash browns, sausages and bacon, came out on plates almost the size of Thanksgiving platters.

The place was run by two sisters, Miss Minnie and Miss Daisy. A bed-and-breakfast, located right behind the restaurant, was also theirs. They shared the work and were among the best-informed residents of the small town. No nugget of news escaped their ears, no gossip went unrecorded in their busy memory banks. The diner was the only restaurant in town. No one dared compete with the Disney Sisters, as they were affectionately known.

"Come here, Tyler," Miss Minnie called, and hugged her tightly.

Tyler was pressed against her enormous bosom, and no sooner had Miss Minnie finished with her than she was passed on to her sister, Miss Daisy. Both women were rather short and portly, their white hair up in buns, and they exuded a motherly caring. Tyler was shooed off to one of the red padded booths with a menu where Tyler spotted Jaz McArthy. Jaz had returned to Independence from Seattle after trouble with a boyfriend-gone-bad. With the help of her grandmother, she opened that yoga studio on the second floor of the dance school. Tyler slipped into the red-leather booth as elegantly as her leg would allow and took a seat across from Jaz.

"What a surprise!"

To Tyler's eyes Jaz had never looked better. And why not? Coming here, she'd stepped up from yoga instructor to business owner. In fact, she was probably on her way to the studio, although it was too early for the place to open. Jaz had established herself as the town's leading alternative health guru. She was also in love with a good man who was crazy about her. Of course Jaz looked good.

"How are you feeling?" Tyler asked. Truthfully, getting settled here hadn't been all sunshine and roses for Jaz. She'd been attacked last summer by thugs that the boyfriend sent to teach her a lesson for leaving him. All three were now in jail. But Jaz spent time in the hospital over it.

Jaz pushed her chin-length blond hair back before she answered. "I'm feeling pretty good." A smile lit up her face. "Good as new. A new group opened up: Yoga Rehab. Works wonders on injuries."

"Really?" asked Tyler, bright-eyed. *Someday*, she thought, *that might interest me too.* "And how's my brother, Jake?"

A diamond seemed to sparkle in Jaz's eye. "We're not engaged yet, though Jake would like that, and as soon as possible. But I'm quite content for him to live with me now."

"*Living* with you—"

"In Grandma's house. She left the place empty to stay a while with a friend and decided to make it permanent. I'm living there now with my poodle, Rambo, so there was plenty of room for Jake."

Tyler was startled. *Jake engaged? As in "to be married"? To Jaz?*

Off her look, Jaz said, "It's not so much a question of if we'll get married, but when. And whether Jake can pull off a proper marriage proposal." She grinned, the challenge in her eyes clear.

But Tyler was stuck on the ease that Jaz had with the word *marriage*. "So, the small-town sheriff and the big-city vegetarian yoga instructor found a match made in heaven?"

"Seems like it."

Breakfast arrived. Jaz had a veggie omelet. Tyler's poached eggs and dry toast came with add-ons. A platter of muffins was set down along with organic jams, jellies, and honey. Then came a platter of berries and fruit. A stack of flapjacks half a foot high.

"I didn't order all this—" Tyler began.

"Hello Miss Carter," a voice interrupted. "What brings you to West Cow Plop? Aren't you awfully far away from Sin City—excuse me, the Holy City of Las Vegas?"

It was a voice she had known since childhood. She turned to see the shrunken but still dapper form of Mr. Wilkinson, the unofficial town mayor and patriarch. He wore a wide-brimmed western hat, a string tie, and a pair of handmade boots with big heels that made him five-foot-six if he didn't slouch. The hat added another four inches on top.

And you just spent the night at his house, Tyler's conscience whispered.

Tyler knew Mr. Wilkinson loved conversational banter, and she had learned the art in Vegas. "Mr. Wilkinson! If I wasn't married to my job, you could tempt me."

"I'm too young for you, my dear. But my older brother might be interested."

Tyler's mouth fell open. She didn't have a comeback for that.

Mr. Wilkinson seized the moment. "My brother just wrote his will. It was two lines. Want to hear it?" Without waiting for an answer, he added, "Being of sound mind and body, I already spent all my money."

Tyler and Jaz set their coffee cups down. Nobody, absolutely nobody else in the world, could get away with these lines. But it was Mr. Wilkinson, beloved by all and

20

ultimately harmless. When he was on a roll, you didn't dare have a beverage near your mouth in case you spit it all over anyone sitting across from you.

"Seriously though, I'm so old the doctor can check my age by counting the rings in my wrinkles."

Tyler put her hand up for mercy. "Kidding aside, how have you been?"

Mr. Wilkinson tweaked his string tie. "Haven't you heard? My old woodpile is getting a facelift. Thanks to a friend of Jaz's. An architect all the way from See-attle."

And at that moment, like a genie conjured from a lamp, Pat appeared at Mr. Wilkinson's elbow. "Hi," he said, looking a little sheepish. His hair was sticking up in places, and he looked like he'd just rolled out of bed.

Jaz's face lit up. "Pat! What brings you here?"

"Ummm, actually," he mumbled, and extended something in a plastic bag to Tyler. "I thought you might need this."

A pregnant pause fell over the table. Tyler felt the world shift to slow motion. If underwear was in the bag, everyone would know she and Pat had spent the night together. But she'd stowed her underwear back in her suitcase and put on a fresh pair after this morning's shower. So what could be in there? She decided to gamble.

"What is it?" she said in a businesslike tone and pulled the mystery item from the bag. It was a black spandex tube, of sorts.

"What's that?" Jaz blurted.

"Same question crossed my mind," Mr. Wilkinson said, and turned knowing eyes from Jaz to Tyler.

"Nobody knows what this is?" Tyler twirled the item on her finger. "Any guesses?"

"We're in a family place, remember," Mr. Wilkinson warned.

"It's an elastic knee sleeve," Tyler stated. "You pull it over the knee to support the muscles and ligaments. Dancers wear them."

Jaz gave a hoot of relief. She pointed from Tyler to Pat. "You two know each other?" Astonishment was written all over her face.

"Not really," Tyler said.

"Since the Indie Rock Festival," Pat said at the same time.

Tyler glared at him. She balled the sleeve up and squashed it into her pocket.

"The old Indie Rock Festival, huh?" Mr. Wilkinson said thoughtfully. "So that's what they're calling it nowadays." He rubbed his chin thoughtfully. "Well, I never!"

He attracted the attention of Minnie and Daisy, who tuned their ears to what was coming next. "I'll have no hanky-panky in my house, do you understand?" he broadcast loudly.

Jaws dropped around the table.

Across the room, Daisy and Minnie thrust out their chins in agreement. They really didn't know what was being discussed, but if Mr. Wilkinson had a moral opinion on it, they agreed.

Then he lowered his voice, winked at Pat and Tyler, and said, "Now go and have fun."

CHAPTER THREE

Tyler stomped up the steps to the dance studio. She and Pat had fled the diner, but she'd said no to his offer of a lift anywhere she wanted to go and sent him away. They were both very embarrassed about the knee-sleeve incident. Pat groaned when she let him know a dozen knee sleeves were in her suitcase as backup. All that public humiliation for nothing.

At the door of the studio, she snapped an icicle off the frame and crunched it into pieces. Her mood was really not improving, and she still hadn't heard from her mother. *Nice to know I'm important.* Putting the old key in the lock, she noticed a red stain on the ground. There was no snow here under the porch overhang. Otherwise, she would surely have noticed it as she approached. She frowned and bent down. Was that blood? Carefully, she touched the wet spot with one finger. At the same time, she felt a tingle on the back of her neck. Straightening up, she looked around. She couldn't spot anyone. Tyler was about to smell the liquid on her finger when her eyes fell on the studio window. She drew a sharp breath, like a gasp.

Three jet-black feathers were stuck to the window, clotted with blood. Shiny black crow feathers. On the windowpane were more red streaks and spatters that appeared intentionally arranged. Was that blood? Who on earth did this? Was it meant for Jaz? Or was it meant for her? *Only one of us performs as a blackbird onstage in front of ten thousand people every week. A crow is a black bird.* And yet anyone could have known Jaz would soon show up at the yoga studio to see it. She had classes to teach. Perhaps the person who did this didn't care, just so long as the gruesome "artwork" got seen.

Tyler pulled out her phone and took a picture of the display. Then she grabbed handfuls of snow and wiped the window clean. She threw the feathers over the side of the porch, walked around, and packed them down with her foot so they were buried. Then she stumbled off up the street.

In a few dozen yards, she stood in front of the flower store known as Lily's. Tyler had known Lily from school. She'd always gotten along with her even though girlfriends were few because of her intense dance interest. After graduation, she and Lily lost touch.

Tyler hesitated for a moment. Did she really want to barge in unannounced? She could see Lily moving behind the counter, even though it was pretty early for the store to open. She had questions she wanted to ask but would need a reason for being here so early. Flowers for her mother or Paula? That would do it.

Lily spotted her and waved from inside. No sooner had Tyler pulled the glass door shut behind her, accompanied by a melodic chime, than Lily closed in for an embrace. "What are you doing here? I thought you were knockin' 'em dead in the entertainment capital of the world?" The dark-haired beauty with wild curls, a green florist's apron over jeans, and a blue shirt squeezed her again with delight.

"To think I was worried about you even wanting to see me," Tyler admitted.

"When did you get so complicated? Not enough fresh mountain air? My favorite thing that we have is, if one has time, she gets in touch. If the other also has time, great. If not, also good. No stress."

Tyler wrinkled her nose. "True. I just wasn't sure if the warranty had run out."

"How do you like my little empire?" Lily spun in a circle, gesturing at the store.

Tyler followed her hand and saw that the small flower store looked completely different since Lily had taken the store over from her parents. Gone were the plastic tubs of day-old flowers. The dark-brown wooden trim had been repainted a light gray and set off with metal trim. Flower arrangements alternated with blossoms arranged stylishly in tall glass vases. Dried orange and lemon slices were placed with river pebbles and sand to hold the arranged flowers in place. Houseplants were everywhere.

"I have a clientele from Independence and contracts with hotels about ten miles away from here, closer to Breck," she said, using the local slang for Breckenridge. "I still find time for Pebbles."

"Who's Pebbles?"

"My dalmatian dog. She's five months old now."

Tyler felt her anxiety move over to make room for a longing tug at her heartstrings. She didn't have a dog or a cat. She didn't even have a goldfish. Yet she loved animals, and grew up with dogs, cats, and horses.

Lily was eyeing her suitcase. "I'm home on a surprise visit," Tyler started. "Thought I'd pick up a bouquet for—"

At that moment, a van pulled up outside. "There's my cut-flower order," Lily said. "Please excuse me."

Tyler wandered around the store. What was really on her mind was asking the questions rattling her on the inside. A picture of the bloodied feathers kept popping into her mind. Even so, she forced herself to stop and look at a small arrangement or one of the gift items scattered throughout the room. She spied a small owl carved out of wood. The grain of the wood appeared to give the wings movement. Maybe she could buy it and figure out who to give it to later.

Lily returned, leading a delivery person with his arms full of flowers. She pointed him to the glassed-in cooler and returned to Tyler, who handed over the little owl. Lily began wrapping it in white paper covered with tiny pink dots.

Tyler was just about to pose her first question when Lily said, "This item was hand-carved. The architect renovating the old Wilkinson house made the figurine."

Patrick? It seemed impossible to escape him.

She continued off Tyler's astonished look. "He doesn't really sell his carvings, but I was able to persuade him to make a few pieces for me."

"Have you and he..." Tyler let the rest of the sentence trail off in embarrassment, trying to look as uninterested as possible. She wasn't really interested, either. She was just making conversation. *Yes, yes. And the man in the moon was coming for tea tomorrow afternoon.* She almost rolled her eyes as she listened to her inner monologue. It wasn't really like her to lie to herself like that.

"Good grief, no! Sure, he looks good, but I don't know. He'd be too" —Lily searched for the right word— "too quiet. I need someone to light a fire inside me." She winked conspiratorially at Tyler.

But Tyler kept her poker face on. Pat fanned her fire with ease. But she didn't want to share that with Lily ten minutes after their first reunion in years.

Lily finished wrapping the owl and handed it over. She was going to move on to another chore if Tyler didn't move quickly with a question. In desperation, she said, "Maybe I'll take one of those bouquets, too. I think it's time I went straight to Paula's."

"Have you seen your sister yet?" Lily asked. "And the girl who lives with her?"

"Not yet." Tyler made a snap decision. "But I'm going there straight from here." She caught a look on Lily's face. "Is there anything wrong?"

Lily hesitated. "For the most part, it's all good. Paula is her temporary foster mother now, but Leslie is refusing to go to school. If she refuses for too long, the children and family services people may have to put her back into the system in Denver."

Don't get sidetracked, Tyler's inner monologue warned. *Deal with this later.* In desperation, she blurted, "How are things around town?"

"Same as usual," Lily said, tearing off a big piece of paper to wrap flowers in. "Pick any one you want."

But Tyler stubbornly stuck to the counter. "I mean, has there been any funny stuff?"

Lily laughed. "Not if you don't count Mr. Wilkinson trying out his comedy routine at the diner all day long. He's staying at the bed-and-breakfast while his house gets finished."

"I already heard it."

"He gets an early start, doesn't he?"

They both smiled knowingly.

"I understand the noise and dust from the reno bothered him," Lily said. "That's why he moved to the B and B. Minnie and Daisy are giving him a room rate from 1979, and he's working the diner as unofficial greeter and comedy act."

"What I mean is..." Tyler changed tactics and forced her voice to sound light. "Any pranks? Vandalism? We get that in Las Vegas from time to time."

Lily paused and laid the paper aside. "We're lucky. Any problem kids seem to leave town as soon as they get a chance, rather than hang around and play tricks. Although the minute I say that out loud, there'll be something to prove me wrong."

"No news of other store owners getting pranked?"

"Not that I know of. Why do you ask?"

Tyler forced a chuckle. "Just making conversation. It's nice to know Independence is the same old place."

"You take the good with the bad. This is the good."

The two hugged and Lily squeezed her tightly.

"I have to go now," Tyler said.

"Sure. Tell Paula and Leslie hello."

Tyler stowed the little owl away in her suitcase and stepped outside. Both hands were full with her suitcase and the flowers. Tucking the flower stems in a side pocket of the case, she pulled out her phone and the business card for Joe's Snow Removal.

The plow moved effortlessly over back roads covered with snow that led to Paula's homestead. Homes built on eight acres or so of land dotted the landscape. At one time, Jaz McArthy's grandfather had owned all this land. But about ten years ago he'd broken it up into smaller parcels, built homesteads, and now her own sister, Paula, lived right next door to the original McArthy residence. Tyler realized, with a start, that the McArthy place might be the next one in line for a renovation update. If so, she knew just the architect for the job.

"How are things around the town?" Tyler asked Joe, the snowplow driver, casually.

"Pretty much just the way they look," Joe said. "We're getting back to normal."

"Any odd stuff going on?"

Joe narrowed his eyes and looked across the truck cab at her. "Odd stuff?"

"Pranks, teenagers trying to scare people, that kind of thing."

Joe ruminated for a moment. "There was that attack at the music festival last year. I think you know Jaz McArthy. Two guys roughed her up. They are in jail, far as I know."

"Yes, I knew about that," Tyler answered. *What were the chances that the bloody feathers were connected to those creeps? Was it blood or red paint? Was this morning's prank connected to her Vegas show?* Both scenarios seemed pretty far-fetched. She'd make a point to ask Jaz if anything weird was happening.

The snowplow slowed, jerking Tyler out of her thoughts. "Miss Paula's is right there," Joe said.

"What do I owe you?" Tyler asked.

He named a price so ridiculously low she doubled it and thrust the money at him before hopping out. Her little suitcase with the flowers sat between them on the bench seat, so she pulled it out the door.

"Say hello to your sister, too. Think you'll need a ride back?"

"Not likely tonight, Joe. But tomorrow, I might," she answered.

He drove off with a cheery wave.

CHAPTER FOUR

"HELLO, ANYONE HOME?" Tyler stood on the porch of Paula's house and knocked on the door. Her sister's pickup truck was in the yard, so she knew her sister was there. Somewhere. With eight acres of pasture, though, the possibilities were many—more than she could manage on foot. She considered putting the flowers and small gift on the bench next to the door when four dogs darted around the corner. First came the homestead's two bosses, Paula's blue heelers, Barns and Roo, who diligently helped herd the goats and kept watch over the place. A black standard poodle followed closely behind the two. If she was not mistaken, this was Jaz's dog, who went by the name of Rambo.

Following at some distance was a smaller white dog with black spots, floppy ears, and paws that were still way too big. What he lacked in speed, he made up for in enthusiasm, judging by the wild wag of his tail. She looked around for her sister. Usually she was not long in coming once the dogs showed up. But who turned the corner was not Paula, but Leslie, the girl who had been living with her sister for a few months. She gave Tyler a suspicious look.

Tyler waved. "Hi. Your name is Leslie, isn't it?" She hoped she had the name right.

Leslie didn't like visitors. Every time someone showed up unannounced, her stomach turned, afraid the unknown guest would take her away and back to where she never wanted to go again. When the stranger said her name, she relaxed a little. Cautiously, she took a few steps closer.

"I'm Tyler, Paula's sister."

That was okay, Leslie figured. She allowed herself to speak. "Paula will be here in a minute. She's still in the stable with the horses." She was about to turn and leave when Tyler called out, "Wait. I have something for you."

Leslie paused and turned around. What could Paula's sister possibly have for her? Maybe cookies? Paula's family thought she would starve here. Everyone kept bringing her food. She once asked Paula if her family didn't know that she could cook. Paula gave her a funny look and fluffed her hair. "Yes, they do, but they know I don't always have time for it. And we're firm believers in the saying 'love goes through the stomach.' It has to do with caring, with wanting to take care of someone." Leslie had lain awake late that night, realizing these people actually cared about her. A whole new concept. And here was Paula's sister, whom she hadn't even met yet, bringing her something. Curiosity brought her feet right up to the porch steps.

Tyler bent down and placed the package on the top step of the stairs and then retreated back to the bench where she sat down as casually and relaxed as possible.

Roo sat on the other side of the stairs and looked expectantly at Leslie. He was dying to do something for her. She bit back a laugh and sent him to get the small package. That way, he had something to do, and she didn't have to approach. A win-win situation for both of them. Roo jumped up, carefully took the little package between his teeth, and then placed it at Leslie's feet. She lifted it up and marveled at the wrapping paper. She suddenly had the feeling that maybe it didn't contain cookies. It was too small for that. Reverently, she unfastened the tape and unwrapped the contents. Her mouth dropped open as she held the miniature owl, about the size of a fist and intricately carved.

Tyler was watching her intently. Leslie wanted to say something, but she was speechless. She croaked, "Why?"

Tyler seemed to understand what she was trying to say with that one inadequate word and shrugged. "I spotted it when I was shopping, and it made me think of you."

"Thinking about me?" asked Leslie, visibly puzzled. "But you don't even know me."

Tyler grinned as she bent down to keep the dog at her feet from eating her shoelaces. "True. Not personally. But since my sister talks about you a lot, at least I know who you are."

Leslie nodded shyly and smiled. "Thank you."

"You're welcome. Will you take me to my sister now? I have a present for her, too." She pointed to the flowers jutting at an angle out of the pocket of her suitcase.

"Sure. Come on," Leslie replied eagerly. Her face lit up, as if transformed by the realization that so many people were thinking about her. A small spark of joy ignited inside her and burst to the surface with a giggle as she ran ahead to the barn.

Tyler followed at a pace her knee allowed. She wanted the flowers to survive, at least until she handed them to Paula. Besides, she was afraid of tripping over one of the dogs.

Around the back of the house, beside a small grain silo, a clump of Aspen trees stretched their bare limbs to the sky. Paula stepped out of the barn with a bay horse—brown with a black mane and tail. Leslie bounced up and down in front of her, pointing in Tyler's direction. A delighted smile appeared on Paula's face. She said something to the girl, who then stowed the wooden owl in a pocket of her jacket. Then Leslie grabbed the horse's rope and led him to the fence of the paddock to get a little exercise. It was obvious how proud she was to take on this task of walking him around.

"I knew it," Tyler quipped as her sister approached. "It wasn't charity, but the free labor that sweetened this deal."

Paula cast a worried glance in Leslie's direction. Tyler read from it that their relationship might still be a little shaky. The girl was suspicious enough as it was and expected only the worst from the world.

"Relax. She can't hear me." Tyler rolled her eyes.

Paula turned back to her. "Right. I'm sorry. It's just that she's only just started to trust me. She wouldn't realize you were joking. It would confirm her bad opinion of humanity in general and adults in particular."

"In that case, I'll try to keep my mouth in check."

Leslie was a runaway who had simply turned up on Paula's homestead one day. For a while, her sister had tolerated her without comment. But in the end, she had decided to offer her a home. As far as Tyler knew, Paula was anxious to prevent Leslie from becoming a pawn in the system. Tyler could well understand that. Thanks to her brother, Jake, the sheriff of Independence, they knew no missing persons report existed for Leslie. That alone was scary enough. A kid that age and no one missed her enough to register a report?

The bay horse flicked his tail and pawed at the snow. Leslie stayed gentle and patient, holding the rope. Rufus had everyone believing he was a dangerous animal. If he got away with it, he did what he wanted. If he were told in a friendly but firm manner that bad behavior wasn't an option, he turned into a sweetie within seconds. For this reason, Leslie and he were currently inseparable. Every day she practiced riding him, and he patiently made his rounds. He ignored rough or wrong aids. If she did it right, he did everything for her. In the last few weeks, Leslie had made significant progress.

"I'll probably take them out for their first ride this weekend," Paula commented. "Will you be here? You're welcome to come along."

Riding. That was out of the question for Tyler at the moment. But Paula didn't know that. So she just said, "We'll see."

Paula glanced at her leg. "Is something wrong? You seem to be walking a little slower than normal." From working with horses, Paula was used to watching the movements of animals. It was important to detect any lameness as early as possible. The habit spilled over to watching people, too.

"I tweaked it after the last show. No big deal."

"Tweaked it, huh? Have you been to a doctor?"

Tyler felt cornered by all the questions she didn't have the answers to yet. "What is this? The inquisition?"

"My, we are touchy."

Tyler held out the flowers.

"Give them here already," Paula said. "I think this is the first time in ten years that anyone brought me flowers. Thank you."

"No wonder. You usually act like you'd rather have a new broom for the barn than something as useless as flowers."

Paula held the bouquet in front of her nose and inhaled the fragrance. "They must be the last wildflowers before the snow," she said, looking over the colorful collection. "Or maybe they aren't from around here. In any case, they're beautiful."

Tyler smiled and shrugged. "Let me give you a little sisterly observation: Sometimes you use your practical nature like a shield. It can make you seem like you'd shoot anyone who dared to make a romantic gesture in the yard."

"Since there's no one in all of Independence I want romance from, that's probably for the best. Changing the subject now that you're back, Patrick West won't be leading the gossip hit list much longer."

Tyler gave her a venomous look. "I see the bush phone has been buzzing. This topic is off-limits. It's exhausting enough that he seems to be the number one news item in Independence right now."

"But now, the local star is back. That's you. Get ready for your closeups."

Tyler took a step back. "I hadn't even thought of that. Shoot." She ruffled her own hair. "What do I do now?"

"After the Vegas paparazzi, the residents of Independence should be a cinch."

"You don't have any idea. Paparazzi aren't interested in dancers. Some actor is always more exciting. But here?" She stamped her healthy foot. "I feel like I'm twelve years old again when Mom always knew what happened before I got home. How did I ever get the idea I could rest up here?"

Paula grabbed her hand. "Come on, let's go inside. I'll make coffee." Paula held the door for her. "How are you getting around?"

"What do you mean?" Tyler followed Paula through the house. It smelled like homemade biscuits.

"I mean, are you going to call Joe's snowplow every time you need a lift? Or whistle for Mister West?"

"I told you to lay off with the jokes about him," Tyler warned. "And why do you want to know?"

"Because I could loan you some transportation."

"I don't think riding Rufus is quite what my leg requires, Paula."

"I'm not talking about that. I'm talking about my ski bike."

Paula bustled to the coffeemaker as Tyler noticed a cookie sheet of golden biscuits cooling beside the stove. Before Leslie, Paula baked about once a year. Tyler held back a smart remark and said, "Your ski bike? You mean that crazy-looking motorcycle on skis?"

"It's not crazy looking. It's practical."

"I live in Las Vegas. I don't do practical."

"You're taking it. The three of us will have dinner here and before I take you back, I'll load the ski bike in the back of the pickup. You can toot all around the town on it."

"Wait a minute. I already told Mom I would be home for dinner. I haven't seen her yet."

"Didn't she tell you? Mom and Dad are at some real estate seminar she wanted to attend in Aspen."

Tyler face-palmed her forehead. "I sent a text. I didn't actually talk to her."

"We're meeting everybody at the diner later. Jaz and Jake and—"

Paula's cell phone dinged. "Oh look, it's a text from Jaz. She says she invited Pat to the diner, too."

CHAPTER FIVE

THE SUN WAS LONG DISAPPEARED behind the Rockies when Paula pulled the pickup onto Main Street with Leslie and Tyler beside her. Rambo was crosstied in the back of the truck with the ski bike, so he couldn't fall out or jump out. He was also wearing a red plaid coat, which looked rather Scottish on a French poodle. Never mind, he still looked very handsome. "Let's get the ski bike unloaded in case I'm too drunk to do it later," Paula joked.

Leslie gave her a stern look. "I've never seen you get drunk," she said.

"You're getting to know me too well. I can't lie around you," Paula said.

That made Leslie grin happily. She jumped out, unlocked Rambo and took his leash so Paula could pull down a lightweight steel track from the tailgate. It extended far enough to allow a gentle drive-off for the ski bike.

Tyler watched this operation with her hands on her hips. Calling this thing a ski bike was misleading. It was a three-wheel motorcycle, one fat tire in the front, two in the back. A ski was latched underneath the front tire with heavy-duty snow-grips on the back tires. Worse, it had a sidecar to hold a passenger. Knowing Paula, it was probably for a dog. "You could climb the Rockies on this thing during ski season," Paula said.

"My thoughts exactly," snapped Tyler. "If anybody in Las Vegas sees a picture of me on it, my career is finished."

"You can't borrow Mom's car if she's away," Paula retorted, starting the engine. "You don't tell us you're coming, this is what you get."

To Tyler's ears, the ski bike rumbled like Joe's snowplow. Only it wasn't as elegant.

"You'll be glad you have it when you're stuck somewhere and no way to get home," Paula yelled. "Besides, it's ski season with plenty of strangers in town. I don't like the idea of you not having your own ride with Mom and Dad away." She glided the bike down the steel track and onto the snow-covered street.

Tyler rolled her eyes. It was worse than she expected. The sidecar stuck out like a tumor. "Can you leave that thing off?" she asked.

"What if you go to buy groceries? Or need a place to put that suitcase of yours?" Paula parked, turned the engine off, and held out the key. "You're welcome."

Tyler took it and let Leslie lead the way with Rambo into the warm diner. Since it was already after seven, most of the dinner guests had left the restaurant. A game of pool was going on in the back.

"There they are," Paula said, pointing.

Jaz and Jake were tipping bottles of cold beer that had just been served to them. They were standing next to a vintage pool table that normally sat under a dust cover, but once supper was over, and the adult-libations-and-pool crowd came in, the old table was uncovered in all its glory. Made of mahogany, it was crafted in 1926 by the Brunswick-Balke-Collender Company of Chicago, with fancy inlay and hand rubbed to a dull finish. It had seen many fierce matches, and many dollars had been laid upon its high-speed felt. Daisy and Minnie knew a money-maker when they saw it, and felt the old table represented them, in a way. It was solid, authentic, and built to last.

On her way to the pool table, Tyler stopped at the bar and ordered a mineral water.

Jaz threw her arms around Leslie and Rambo. She busied herself getting the dog's coat off and settled in a corner with a treat and some water. The others greeted them joyfully. Jake gave Tyler a brotherly punch in the shoulder, while Paula hugged her. Lastly, she turned her attention to Pat, who was leaning casually against the wall. She groaned inwardly. It just wasn't fair. For once in her entire life, she'd had a one-night stand with a stranger, only to discover that not only was he friends with her extended family, but he'd moved here as well. Her conscience whispered, *Twice means it's no longer a one-nighter*. Jaz would probably mutter something about bad luck in karma distribution now. She could agree with that.

When their eyes met, Pat's mouth curved into a broad smile. Her heartbeat accelerated. With a knowing expression in his eyes, he toasted her with the beer in his hand. She returned the gesture. Had he always been this arrogant? Probably. Deep down, she knew she was kidding herself. He had never been arrogant with her, not last summer, and not this time. But when a man was that good-looking, it was easy to accuse him of arrogance.

Enough with the psychological introspection! She pushed these unproductive thoughts aside and concentrated on the game of pool now going on between Paula and Jaz. In a short time, Jaz was the last to sink the black eight ball and held out her open hand to Paula. "Give me the money," she said gleefully.

With a shake of her head, Paula pulled a twenty from her pocket and slapped it into Jaz's hand. "I don't believe it!"

"Have you met your match?" Tyler teased.

Paula's look of astonishment lingered. "She said she played a little with friends now and then. A gross understatement, if you ask me."

"You didn't ask," Jaz retorted. "If you had, I would have told you I wasn't working while I was in college. I was playing pool."

Jake put an arm around her shoulder and kissed her on the temple. He was clearly proud of his girlfriend. A little wistfully, Tyler looked at the two of them. Someday, she wished she could have that, too, with someone. Just not right now. She averted her eyes and caught Pat watching her. "What about you? Are you a former pool pro, too?" she joked.

He shook his head.

"Want to play?"

He looked questioningly at the others.

"No. Jake and I have already gone one round."

"So?" Tyler threw the question at Jake. "Did you at least save the family honor?"

"Yes, he did," Pat hurried to say.

Tyler grabbed a cue and began prepping it with chalk. "Then what are you waiting for?"

Pat looked at her wordlessly for a moment, then he shook his head in amusement and grabbed his cue, which was leaning against the wall behind him. "Ladies first," he said, making an inviting hand gesture toward the pool table.

Good. Tyler wasn't above taking the small advantage and got ready for the first push. She didn't want to make the mistake of underestimating him. But she was pretty sure that by the end of the game, he wouldn't be quite so generous. She grinned and let the white ball loose on the others.

Pat watched her. He had never claimed to understand women, but at least she seemed to be in a more peaceful mood tonight. Maybe a friendly game would relax her enough for them to have a drink together afterward. He watched her bend over the table and set her sights on the white ball. He grinned. Had he underestimated her?

Fifteen minutes later and twenty dollars poorer, he found that was exactly what happened. Not only had his twenty dollars changed hands, onlookers had placed bets the whole game.

"Looks like I underestimated you," he commented appreciatively to Tyler.

She laughed kindly. "It happens to most people."

"How did you get to be so good? I thought you spent all your free time dancing."

Before answering, she caught Jaz alone in the corner tending to Rambo and decided that now was the moment to ask about what happened this morning. She held up a finger to Pat, miming *just one moment*, and walked over to Jaz.

"Can I have a quick word?"

"Sure, what's up?"

"Ladies room?"

Jaz followed Tyler's lead to the diner bathrooms that had a cowboy on one door and a cowgirl on the other. The cowgirl was occupied. Without missing a beat, Tyler went into the cowboy side, closed the door and locked it.

"This sounds serious," Jaz said, even though Tyler hadn't said a word.

Tyler fished out her cell phone. "Wanted to show you something." She brought up the picture of the bloody crow feathers stuck to the window of the studio.

"What's this?" Jaz started. "Wait a minute, is that *my* window?"

"It's the window to the building where your studio is on the second floor. Technically, the first floor is vacant except for Pat's workout bag."

"You saw that?"

"Yes, it's how I met Pat yesterday."

"I hope it's okay. I was going to tell you—"

"Never mind that. Look at the photo. Has anything like that ever happened before?"

"No. What do you suppose it means?"

"I was hoping maybe some kids had been playing tricks lately."

"Not that I know of."

"I'm not sure if it was meant for you or me. Or maybe for no one. Maybe it was just a silly prank."

"Does it mean anything to you?" Jaz studied Tyler's face.

"I don't want to read too much into it. I took the picture and cleaned the window off this morning before you got there."

"I want to tell Jake. He might want to talk about this."

Tyler gave her a wistful expression. "Do you have to?"

"There's some stuff you don't know. Yeah, it's important."

Moments later, Jaz was outside, alone with Jake. The fresh air was stimulating. A couple of cross-country skiers came *schussing* down the street. They looked deliriously happy.

"Vacationers," Jake said simply. "Tell me what happened."

Jake examined the photo while Tyler spoke. After hearing the story, he said, "I take this seriously, but a whole other level of bad is required before either of you need to feel alarmed. That being said, there's something you don't know."

"What's that?" Snowflakes started to fall. One fell on Tyler's eyelash and she blinked it away.

"That night that we caught the men who roughed Jaz up for her boyfriend. You know they shot me in the shoulder."

"I heard. I hope you're okay."

"Good as new, except when it snows."

"Like right now?"

Jake batted at the light snowflakes and smiled. "Only somebody living in Vegas would call this little sprinkle 'snow.' The point is, that night, those guys said they were going to kill Rambo to teach Jaz a lesson. When they headed for the house, we knew Jaz was at the hospital by that time, but Paula was home. With Rambo and Leslie."

"That's right next door to Jaz's grandmother's house. She was staying there."

"And she still is. We're living there now. Anyway, the Independence PD were right behind those guys as they headed to the house, and they didn't want Paula to head out with the kid. She would have been a sitting duck, with no one else on the road."

Tyler wondered where this was going. A couple of late diners burst out of the eatery doors and passed them by with a wave.

Jake continued, "Paula knew we were waiting for police backup to surround those guys. But they were coming faster than we figured. And the minute they found out Rambo wasn't at Jaz's home—"

Tyler jumped in. "They'd go next door and find him with Paula."

"That's exactly right. So Paula put Leslie and the dogs in the basement, went out to the road with the shotgun, and blasted away until those guys turned around and ran straight into an ambush by our guys in the PD."

Tyler was open-mouthed. "Why are you telling me all this?"

"Because there could be a connection to your feathers, even though, in my opinion, the chance is slight. We're keeping Paula's actions that night quiet because the perps still don't know it was her shooting at them and not cops. They could try to retaliate." Jake waited for this news to sink in.

"Could those guys have left the feathers?"

"Those guys do more than leave feathers and a little red coloring. They leave bullets. And all three of them, including Jaz's old boyfriend, are in jail. They're not going to be there forever, which is why you need to keep what I told you very quiet."

"So you don't think the feathers were left for Jaz?"

"I think it's a prank. Maybe by some visitors. Something happens every season when the outsiders pour in. But I'm very glad you told me, and I want to know if and when anything else happens." He brushed some snowflakes off his face. "Now let's go inside."

They walked up the porch steps and back into the cozy diner. Suddenly, the place seemed too noisy, too crowded, too stuffy for Tyler. She walked over to where Pat was still watching the pool players.

"Can I go to your place again?"

He looked surprised, but nodded. "Ready to go?"

"Tonight I've got my own ride. I'll follow you."

The watcher followed at a safe distance, lights off on the snowmobile. He accelerated gently, so as not to rev his engine and draw attention. Thankfully, the ski bike made noise like a motorcycle and it was directly behind the Cadillac with all the windows rolled up, so luck was with him.

Up, up the hill they went to what was commonly known as Wilkinson Butte, where the great house withstood winds from the mountains as though it were made of rock itself, and the view of Independence was breathtaking. Tonight, the tarps that covered exposed parts under restoration were flapping gently, giving the impression that it had sprouted wings and might take flight at any time.

The watcher pulled the snowmobile over and hid himself behind a copse of trees as Mr. Fix-It and the Vegas Twirly Girl entered the home for the second night in a row. The two of them were getting pretty cozy, and that was good. It all fit into his plans.

CHAPTER SIX

THE NEXT MORNING, Tyler woke early. Lying next to Pat was comforting, whether it was him that comforted, or just a warm body. But it felt nice. Her eyes roamed around Pat's room. They slept in an Arts and Crafts bed with a wooden headboard and foot. A colorful handmade cotton quilt covered them. Around the room, baseboards made of black walnut wood matched the ceiling molding that ran a foot deep all around the room. The dark wood contrasted with white walls. It was a gorgeous room in an equally gorgeous old Prairie-style house—that needed a lot of work.

Tyler pushed back the quilt and moved to swing her legs out of bed. Pain shot through her knee. She pushed the cover down further to take a look. There was swelling. She was supposed to be taking it easy, and last night's bedroom gymnastics weren't exactly "taking it easy." It would be simple to blame Pat, but it wasn't his fault. She had been the one to invite herself back here, and also the one who kept answering, "It's okay," whenever Pat asked about her knee during the long and romantic night. Where was her famous ballerina self-discipline?

Pat stirred beside her. "You awake?" His eyes fluttered and zeroed in on what she was looking at: her knee. "Uh oh," he said.

"And I had plans to start dancing again today." Which might have been a tad optimistic, but optimism was currency she'd always banked on. *It's just a postponement*, her optimistic side said. *It's a red flag*, her practical side argued back.

"What are you doing for physical therapy?" he asked.

She gave him a confounded look.

"For your knee. I assume it's been diagnosed."

"I thought—"

"Tell me you've already been to the hospital and discussed the next steps with your doctor."

"As I was trying to say, I thought I could do it myself. I'm supposed to use the hotel doctor first, in Vegas. That alerts the producers and then the insurance company. It's a big *shemozzle*."

"So, you thought the smart thing to do would be just to come here and ignore it?"

"That's exactly what I thought. It works a lot. The body heals." She was getting very annoyed, but not exactly sure at what.

"There's an excellent medical center in Breckenridge."

"No!"

"Alternatively, there's a local GP just down—"

"No!"

"What then?" He was remaining calm, and she knew she was getting heated.

Why was her body choosing to rebel at this time of all times?

"You're not ready for the truth?"

"I'm not ready because it's not necessary."

"You know what they say about wishes."

"What do they say about wishes?"

"If wishes were horses, poor folks would ride."

"You sound like Mr. Wilkinson." She pulled the quilt over her swollen knee so he'd stop staring at it. "Let's go to a walk-in clinic in Breck. If I show up to the local doctor here, I'll set the bush phones off. If we go to the big medical center, I'll have to use my insurance, and that will tip off the show producers."

"Sure, let's treat it like a drug deal. Pay cash and wear sunglasses?"

"Very funny. But kinda like that, yes." She was about to try and get away without a long goodbye before she remembered her only transportation was the ski bike. It was enough to make her scream with frustration. Instead, she showed restraint. "Do you mind driving me?"

"So long as you don't mind Mr. Wilkinson's old Cadillac. He gave it to me to use while he's at the B and B."

"I've been in it twice already."

He winked. "I know, but only after dark."

Tyler thought about the monstrously ugly ski bike parked outside, shuddered, and quickly agreed. After that, she was silent and looked out the window. Her stomach was in turmoil and her palms were sweaty.

Pat gave her a quick sideways glance before taking her hand and gently stroking it. The touch was unexpected and strangely soothing. Grateful for his wordless support, she didn't pull her hand away. Small talk would have really overwhelmed her at the moment. She turned her gaze to the window and stared blankly out into the snow-covered trees.

Somewhere outside, a snowmobile started up and buzzed past the house.

An hour later, Tyler and Pat stood on the streets of Breckenridge after a short stop at a walk-in clinic. A basic x-ray and doctor's examination showed Tyler's knee ligaments on the right side strained almost to the point of tearing, and it looked like the meniscus cartilage that cushioned the knee joint had been squished a bit in the fall. The doctor had used a much fancier word, but it boiled down to "squished." Luckily, the clinic dispensed basic medications, and Tyler had been handed pain meds as well as an anti-inflammatory. "Ice it," the doctor said before handing over a cane. "Just to take some of your weight off the leg."

She also mentioned regenerative medicine and two noninvasive treatments that had great success with rehabilitating joints: prolotherapy and stem-cell therapy.

Pat and Tyler stood on the street, still deciding what to do next. Pat said, "Interesting that she mentioned there are doctors using the stem-cell method for rejuvenating the knee."

Tyler seemed preoccupied with how to use her cane. "What did she say about that stem-cell therapy again?"

"They take platelets from your own blood to put back into the knee so it can rebuild tissue." Pat paused and wrinkled his forehead. "How do you think the producers in Vegas would feel about you doing something like that?"

Tyler pulled her attention away from the cane. "Whatever gets you back onstage fast is all they care about. If it's not invasive, I might not even have to tell them about it."

"A couple of days on the anti-inflammatories with the cane might do it, too," he said hopefully.

"You wanted brunch, right?" Tyler replied in an attempt to prolong the Breckenridge visit. She was supposed to be on hiatus, a holiday.

He took her by the hand.

Tyler allowed herself to lean against him for a moment. She blinked up at him from under her long lashes.

Pat noticed that she didn't even reach his shoulder. He enjoyed the closeness and was glad to see her smile again. At least she didn't seem to resent him for pushing her to go to the clinic.

They left the old Cadillac parked where it was and strolled slowly through downtown Breckenridge. Tyler was trying out her cane, letting it take the weight of her body instead of her knee. It hadn't snowed today, and the sun warmed their faces as they walked. Pat slipped his hand into hers. She snorted and just managed to hide it under a cough. Pulling her hand away was her first thought, or at least making a comment about it being purely platonic, but decided against it. It just felt too good, and she didn't want to ruin the mood. Who was she kidding, anyway? All the reasons that had seemed so valid to her before about why she should stay away from Pat were flying out the window one by one. And for today, she had already taken a giant step by visiting a doctor and getting some meds.

She was lost in her thoughts and the pleasant feeling of Pat's nearness when he slowed and said, "What do you think of this?" He pointed to a small café across the street. The large windows were invitingly decorated with fir branches. Strings of lights twined around them.

"Sure, why not? If there's something to eat there, too?"

"We're about to find out."

There was something to eat. Sandwiches in imaginative variations alongside sandwich classics, stew, soup of the day—everything you could wish for on a cold day. Tyler bit her lower lip. How to decide?

Pat didn't seem to have those problems. "For me, please, the stew and a cup of coffee," he told the counter attendant. "What do you want, Tyler?"

She decided on the soup of the day, potato with ginger, and a sandwich with avocado, roasted ham, and mustard. Coffee, of course. They paid at the bar and took their food to a wrought-iron table for two. The place was so small, but she imagined it would be packed by noon.

"Thank you," she said to Pat.

His eyebrows shot up questioningly. "For what?"

She averted her eyes and drew patterns in her soup with her spoon. "For being persistent enough to ask me about my knee. For not being shy about telling me what you think."

"It's basically none of my business. I realize that already."

"True. Still, it was just what I needed. Even though it stings to admit it." She looked up. Her blue eyes flashed. "I was stuck. Couldn't bring myself to deal with my hurt."

Without really looking, she turned her concentration to her sandwich and crumbled the edge.

"It's normal," Pat reassured her, placing his hand on hers. "No need to massacre your sandwich."

They both chuckled over it and tucked into the food. After a bit, she posed a classic question. "Why not tell me a bit about yourself?"

"I grew up with my mother. I never knew my father. Depending on my mother's mood of the day, he was either the most wonderful man on earth, a hero who had died for his country, or a good-for-nothing, a thief and a swindler who had taken off with her money as soon as I was born. That was actually the case with all things. It swung from one extreme to the other. I never learned any reliable values to direct myself by. That's not meant to be an excuse for what I'm about to tell you. But I think it helps to know the background."

Tyler didn't want to interrupt his flow of words, so she nodded imperceptibly. He answered with a quick squeeze of her arm. She sipped her coffee and waited for him to continue. The sage-colored wall behind him almost matched the sweatshirt he was wearing. The sweatshirt that set off his shoulders. *Handsome*, she thought.

Pat continued. "Today I suspect Mom was manic-depressive. But I didn't know that at the time. Every day on the way home from school, I prayed to God that she would have a good day. On the good days, she cooked, took care of the household, and entertained me with fantastic stories. On bad days, she lay in bed and didn't move. I had to watch out for myself to get fed. No one played with me or asked about my day. If she was awake, she would mutter one conspiracy theory after another or rant loudly about my father."

Tyler's heart tightened as she pictured the lonely little boy who never knew what his world would be like that day. But she knew Pat didn't want her sympathy. Nor was now the time for the more appropriate compassion. So she remained very still and continued to listen to him.

"As time went on, it got worse and worse. At some point, she began to self-medicate, if you can call it that. Pills in various forms and alcohol were her drugs of choice. By that time, I had almost given up expecting anything from her. Still, it was a shock to me when she died."

"How old were you then?" Tyler's voice was hoarse.

"Fourteen."

"How did she die?"

"The wrong mix of drugs and a bottle of vodka. I found them on the floor when I got home that night."

Involuntarily, Tyler winced as the image formed in her mind. "You must have been so scared," she guessed.

"Maybe I actually was," he admitted. "At the time, though, I just felt a huge anger. At my mother. At God. At life itself."

"Were you religious?"

"No. Not at all. But I had this abstract idea from school that there's a God and he's pulling the strings. And doesn't seem to give a damn about how I'm doing. Which resulted in me developing the same attitude." He took a sip of coffee. While he pondered his next words, he let the hot java circulate in the cup.

"Maybe you'll find your way back to faith in time," Tyler murmured.

He shrugged. "My behavior got worse and worse, so I was passed from foster family to foster family. When I was sixteen, that was the end of it, and I was sent to a residential home for boys. Rough justice ruled that place, and I could either join or fall by the wayside. Giving up was not in my vocabulary at the time. So I adapted and drifted more and more into gang-type life. At first, that was really great for me. The things I was supposed to do, I was good at. Stealing was almost a hobby for me at that point. When my mother was sick, it was often the only way I had to get food. Fool someone? No problem. I had practiced that, too, all my life, when a concerned teacher wanted to know how things were going at home, how my mother was doing, and so on. Once I even had to convince the people at the Youth Welfare Office that my mother was just in bed with the flu and everything was fine."

"Not bad for a little boy." She gave him a friendly shrug.

Pat grinned wryly. "Practice makes perfect. My reputation got around. Those boys were the first real family I ever had. The stealing and cheating didn't bother me much. The only thing I tried to stay out of was fights within the group."

"I would have thought you'd turn into a real bully."

Across the table he could see her interested look, but no disgust in it. "I was small for my age and slight."

"But you grew up and became an architect. You started your own business."

"You only heard the first part of the story. Maybe I'll tell you the rest in the car. Are you finished with the meal?"

Tyler nodded and reached for her coat.

They returned to the old Cadillac. As Pat walked around to open the passenger door for Tyler, she heard him gasp. A dead crow hung between the front and back windows, its wings widespread in a macabre display. Clotted blood caked the breast feathers and reddened the car paint beneath. A single black feather sailed to the ground. She turned and threw up in the empty space next to the car. "Why is this happening?" she choked, as tears streamed down her face. She wiped her mouth with her sleeve and started to look around wildly. "Who did this?" she shouted. But although the lot was almost full, it seemed empty of people.

Pat's strong arms embraced her. "I don't know why it's happening, but we're going to find out."

His words penetrated her panicked senses slowly. She stopped flailing and leaned back to look at him. She let herself sink against his broad chest and breathed in his familiar scent. He let her calm down and then pulled out his cell phone and took pictures of the poor, stricken crow.

"I think we better call Jake." His eyes narrowed and his expression darkened.

Oops. She didn't know this Pat at all. "Why do you have Jake's number?"

"I live here, remember?"

It felt good to know this version of Pat was by her side. He dialed Jake and got him on the line. He saw the look on her face that still said, *Why do you have Jake's number?*

"Since the thing that happened to Jaz," he whispered.

Pat and Jake spoke for a moment. Then Pat held out the phone. "He wants to know if you have any enemies."

Tyler took it and said uneasily, "Not that I know of. Especially not right now."

"Regardless. You're a star," Jake interjected into the discussion. "Could be somebody's just trying to scare you. Was there a note? A threat?"

"No," Pat and Tyler said together.

"Is there anything we can do?" Pat asked.

"Go to the nearby shops and restaurants. Ask anyone on the street who might have seen something."

Pat cleared his throat. "Should we call the police?"

Jake heard him. "You just did." He went on, "Is it possible that you have fans who aren't happy that you're no longer dancing?"

"I check my social media. Yeah, people are moaning about the hiatus, but they're not upset."

"What about fan mail? Emails to the hotel from fans?"

"I don't know. Probably. Sarah, my agent, handles that stuff."

"Any stalkers?" Jake wanted to know.

"The usual stuff."

"What do you mean 'the usual'?"

"You know, fans hang out at the hotel. They ask for pictures and autographs. The producers encourage it."

"Why didn't you ever tell me about this?"

Tyler heaved a deep sigh. "Because I knew you'd react like that. There's nothing you can do about it. Fans are inevitable."

Pat grunted in frustration. From the way the muscles in his jaw bulged, his displeasure with the situation was obvious.

Tyler could feel her back going up. Her mood was close to the boiling point. She hadn't chosen to be targeted by some misguided person. She knew the two men cared about her. Nevertheless, she managed to keep her anger in check only with difficulty.

Jake snapped her out of her thoughts. "Do you still have those emails and messages?"

"Sarah collects all of it."

"I need the number of your agent. She should send everything," he instructed.

"No! Please! I mean, not just yet."

Jake fell silent. "Give the phone back to Pat."

Tyler handed it over.

"Ask around if anyone saw anything. Take a bunch of pictures from all angles. Then get on back here to Independence. I'm calling a family meeting for tonight."

CHAPTER SEVEN

THE SUN WAS DOWN and a chill wind was gusting as Pat and Tyler arrived at the Carter family homestead. Nothing had come from asking people on the street and nearby businesses about the defacing of the Cadillac. They'd already had a slight spat over the cane. It was hidden in the trunk. No way was Tyler appearing before her family with that. Their mood was quiet, as they knew this meeting was serious, and had no idea what might come out of it. The yard was full of cars, but Pat let Tyler out as close to the front door as possible. Then he backed up a bit to park the Cadillac so he wasn't blocking anyone.

Tyler was met by the old yard dogs, Pirate and Moss. Moss was a shepherd-dog mix with long, disheveled fur. It was obvious to her that he was getting on in years. His movements were slower, his gaze not so clear anymore. Rambo, Jaz's dog, brought up the rear of the pack.

While Pat was looking the other way to back up, a fit man in his late twenties got out of a parked car.

"Cole!" Tyler exclaimed. "What are you doing here, brother?"

"Same as you," he said. "Came home for a visit. I'm taking care of the place and feeding the animals while Mom and Dad are gone."

"You tell them you're coming home, they put you to work," she said.

They shared a laugh.

"Go on in," Tyler chuckled. "I'll be right there."

Cole disappeared into the house.

Moss let out a token growl when Pat came up behind Tyler.

"Good dog," she praised him. "Good watch, but this is a friend." She grabbed Pat's hand. Moss seemed satisfied by that. He turned and walked to his basket which was on the porch. He spun around until he settled into it with a deep sigh. Pirate, the Parson Jack Russell with the black patch over his eye, hopped up on them, even though he was already over ten years old. One high jump landed him directly in Tyler's arms. With the smaller dog in her arms, she bent down to give Moss his petting, too. The wagging was epic.

Pat returned to the Cadillac just to make sure they hadn't forgotten anything, and then strolled back to where Tyler was petting the dogs. She straightened up and turned to him. "The whole clan seems to be here," he said.

"Let's find out," she agreed.

He got to the door and held it open for her.

Everyone had already gathered in the living room. Stan and Brenda had downsized to this place once all the kids were out. The walls were finished with redwood and modern Mexican tile on the floor. Everything showed Brenda's talented touch from Ute Indian artwork on the walls to woven blankets in bright, primary colors, thrown over the wooden furniture. A bronze reproduction of Remington's classic Mountain Man sculpture sat on the fireplace mantel.

Paula and Jaz were chatting beside a crackling fire. Jake, who had called the emergency meeting, was standing near the shoulder of a stranger with a laptop on the sofa, the keyboard in his lap, typing with nimble fingers. Stan and Brenda were absent.

Pat wondered who this broad-shouldered stranger might be when Tyler ran past him, pushed Jake and the computer out of the way, and sat on his lap with her arms wrapped around his neck. Scorching jealousy ran through Pat's chest. Suddenly, he didn't know what he was doing here at all. Sure, Jaz was his best friend, but he had only been in Independence for a short time. That made him an outsider.

As Tyler and the stranger nuzzled on the sofa, he was considering leaving when she waved him over, a worried expression in her big blue eyes. He couldn't resist that look, even if he didn't know what she was trying to do with it. Was she trying to introduce him to her special friend? If so, she had a strange sense of humor. He took his time strolling through the living room. He didn't want to look like one of the dogs trotting in just because she'd called out. *Even though that was your first instinct*, he chided himself.

Despite his bad mood, he had to smile and joined the others at the table. Jaz and Paula also joined them.

Tyler grabbed his hand and pulled him closer.

His confusion grew, but then she pointed to the screen in front of him, and all the petty thoughts rolling around in his head a moment ago were blown away. Both incidents that he had photographed were blown up on the screen.

"What a sick mind," the stranger said.

"Don't you think some teenager did this?" The question came from Paula.

"Possible," the man said. Tyler was still sitting on his lap. "I don't mean this in a negative way, Sis, but your line of work attracts weirdos."

Tyler chuckled and replied something as Pat kicked himself. Sis? What a jerk he was! The fact that Tyler was in danger should have been enough for him to focus solely on her safety and well-being. But no. He'd rather get jealous and coddle his own hurt feelings instead of caring about her. When had he become so selfish? He shook himself inwardly. All this because of her brother. How many were there altogether? he wondered, before pulling himself together.

Paula appeared from a quick detour to the kitchen, bearing a platter of hoagies and giant homemade pickles made from cucumbers grown in Brenda's own garden. She grabbed a fat sandwich and took a bite. "I need to think," she announced to the room. "I can do that better on a full stomach."

Pat gave her a smile of encouragement. She held out the platter and offered it around.

"So, Miss Tyler," she said, still in her announcer voice. "I got it. The solution. As of today, you stay with me."

Pat rolled his eyes toward Tyler for her reaction. Her mouth fell open.

"My dogs aren't retired yet," Paula continued. "And my shotgun is always ready. What more do you need?" Paula looked like it was all decided. Tyler just had to say yes.

Tyler's mouth closed. To Pat, it appeared she was gathering her thoughts. "I hope the shotgun is hidden, with kids in the house and all," Tyler replied serenely. "Are you really sure you want me living with you? There's a chance I might drag some nutty fan over to visit you and Leslie at the house."

Paula put her sandwich down, like her appetite had run off. She obviously hadn't thought of that scenario.

"I categorically reject the suggestion of staying with you," Tyler stated, to drive the point home.

Paula bit her lower lip. Her face betrayed that when her sister put it that way, she suddenly wasn't so keen on her staying.

"Don't take this personally, Paula," Jake cut in. "We've never had a situation like this. If this is connected in any remote way to the guys who hurt Jaz at the festival, I don't want Tyler staying with any of us for a few days, anyway. It's too convenient."

Jaz looked crestfallen. "That means our house, I mean Grandma's house, is off-limits to Tyler, too?"

Jake nodded.

"What about the bed-and-breakfast?"

Tyler made a face. "Too public."

"She's right," the stranger on the couch said. "Stay here at Mom's, I'll protect you."

"Sure, you'll have me on a leash with Ranger!" Tyler cried.

Pat felt like this was his moment. "There's a lot of spare room at the Wilkinson place," he ventured.

Tyler glanced at Jake, trying to figure out what he thought of the idea. He didn't look too thrilled, but didn't seem to have anything better. "That might be an option," he said glumly.

"I'd have to ask Mr. Wilkinson," Pat said uncertainly. "It's still his house."

"Just tell him it's a favor for Rose McArthy, our grandmother," Paula said. "He can't say no."

"But," Tyler protested, falling silent as Jake patted her shoulder.

"You'll have to teach me that trick," grinned Tyler's brother, whom Pat still couldn't put a name to.

"What do you know about self-defense?" The stranger zinged the question right at Pat with a sneer in his voice.

"What does he know?" snorted Jaz. "The man is a walking martial-arts machine."

Pat shook his head in her direction. He didn't want the focus on himself. He could gladly do without that. Too late. The man's eyes narrowed speculatively. "Who are you, anyway? New here in Independence?"

Tyler gave him a jab in the ribs. "Stop playing the big man here just because you have a badge. This is Pat, a friend of Jaz's from Seattle. He's an architect overseeing the renovation work on the Wilkinson house. Pat, this is Cole, my youngest brother." She gave her brother a warning look as she introduced them.

But Cole didn't let up. "Then you won't mind if I check you out."

Pat gritted his teeth. Yes, he did mind. Only he couldn't very well say that now. "I'm sure Jake already did that when I was here the first time," he replied.

"That may be," Cole said, a wolfish grin on his face. "But I doubt he'll have the same opportunities I do."

"What exactly do you work on?"

"I'm a cyber specialist with the FBI."

"Better known as hackers," Tyler interjected. "Are you guys done with your ridiculous competition to see who can pee the farthest? Then maybe we could get back to who's making my life miserable and similarly unimportant things."

Cole snorted, but did not pursue the topic.

"I don't have a guard dog like Rambo, though," Pat added as an afterthought.

"Maybe we could loan her Rambo?" Jaz queried.

"No," everybody answered in unison.

"You need Rambo for your own protection," Jake warned.

"Hi," Tyler called out, waving her hands in front of both of them. "Do I get a say?"

"No," everybody answered in unison, again.

Cole's face lit up. "I have a dog."

"What? You just got here from out of town," Paula said.

"Wait here. I'll be right back." Cole jumped up and left the living room. A moment later, the door to the outside was heard opening and closing.

Tyler looked around at the others. "Did I miss something?"

Jake shrugged his shoulders. "I don't know what he means, either."

The front door opened again. The icy wind whirled snowflakes into the hallway, followed by Cole with a German shepherd on a leash. The animal waited patiently while Cole slipped the shoes off his feet, then followed him into the living room.

"Meet Ranger. A German-trained K9 for law enforcement. He is already nine years old and retired from active duty last year. Since his previous owner was killed in his last deployment, I took him over."

Ranger sat patiently on his hind paws, panting, while everyone stared wordlessly at the dog.

Cole continued. "Ranger's mother was a Czech border patrol dog. He was handpicked and trained for real-world situations on the street, and in businesses and homes. He also has the knowledge of a counter-terrorist dog and a special-operations canine. He may be retired, but he has a lot of training and experience to call on."

Murmurs of "impressive" and "wow" went around the room.

Tyler couldn't resist Ranger's brown eyes for long, settling down beside him and holding her hand near his nose. She waited for him to sniff it before burying her hand in his thick fur.

Pat watched the two of them. His thoughts wandered to the beautiful late-summer evening when they met. That evening he had been babysitting a friend's *Dogue de Bordeaux*, also known as a French mastiff. Tyler had bumped into the dog and immediately befriended the giant beast. Even then, she had charmed him. Today was no different.

"Ranger is great," Tyler sighed. "But I can't possibly take him."

"He's registered as an ADA service dog." Cole looked at her in surprise. "You can take him anywhere."

Tyler chewed on her lower lip.

"Why not? You don't have any shows right now, do you?" Cole looked at her in surprise.

"Thanks for pointing that out." Tyler scowled. "And why don't I have shows?" She pointed to her leg, which she had stretched out to the side to sit on the floor. Her leg wasn't the whole reason—she was on hiatus from the show with the whole cast—but it sounded better." I went to a clinic for my knee. That's why we were in Breckenridge. Pat convinced me to get a second opinion." She emphasized the last sentence to make sure Cole caught it. "There are two therapies that might work. I will check on them first thing tomorrow."

"I'm glad to hear you say that," said Pat.

Leslie came in from outside with Rambo, interrupting the conversation. It seemed like a good time to pause discussion and refresh plates and glasses.

"Who's ready for an adult beverage?" said Paula. "Everybody but you, Leslie. But we'll find you something *delish*."

Ranger lay down at Tyler's feet so she could reach his belly for a rub. Secretly, she wished she could take him. But that wouldn't be fair to him. Or could there be a way and she just didn't see it?

Jaz and Paula sauntered over to her. "You can't resist a dog either, huh?" she teased them as they sat down on the floor next to her.

"That's true. But the dog to pet was just a bonus. We came over because we care. About you."

Tyler blinked sheepishly. "Don't be," she defended. "I'm fine."

Paula's tone turned serious. "We just hope the surgery goes well and everything else will fall into place."

"It's not SURGERY! It's a noninvasive therapy."

"It's still a procedure to take seriously."

"I am taking it ser—"

"You NEVER take injuries seriously," Paula said. "You talk about it like it's a snap."

Jaz jumped in. "And having a stalker breathing down your neck in the process is just a minor inconvenience, too. Remember, I was in a similar situation."

"Sure. But the threat against you was much more real. From the very beginning. What's happening here seems so unreal. Sure, a bird is dead, too. I feel bad for him. But otherwise? Somehow I can't put it in context with me." Tyler stroked Ranger's ears. The feel of his silky fur soothed her.

Jaz and Paula looked at each other. *She's hopeless*, read their expressions.

Cole stepped into the breach. "The problem is we don't really know who the target is."

Jake backed him up. "We get that it's shocking, but without a direct threat, it seems more like a bid for attention. Like something a fan would do, not a hardcore criminal."

"Let me show you guys something," Cole said, transferring the laptop to a table and motioning the men around the screen.

Jaz, Paula, and Tyler huddled together in front of the fireplace. When she spoke, Tyler's voice was full of frustration. She pushed a strand of blond hair behind her ear. "What does the dog want with me? I can't even walk far enough. What about when I'm having this therapy? Am I supposed to take him there, too?"

Paula rolled her eyes. "It's a good thing you ended up onstage. All that drama has to go somewhere."

"I'll walk him, Aunt Tyler," Leslie said. For a moment, everyone paused at the sound of "Aunt" but Tyler used her performance skills to brush by it.

"At last, a solution. Thank you, Leslie," she said warmly.

"When you're in the clinic, Ranger can come to me," Jaz chimed in. "And until then, I can always take him with me over lunch when I make my rounds with Rambo."

Ranger picked that moment to lay his head in Tyler's lap and look at her with wide eyes.

"You see," Paula smirked. "He agrees with us."

Tyler sighed. "I know when I'm outnumbered. All right, then. I'll take him to my place."

"Hmm. Great. And where is that exactly?"

Tyler shot Paula a look. "Leslie, would you mind taking Ranger out for a bathroom break?" she said calmly.

"Sure."

After Leslie and the dog had cleared the room, Paula jumped in. "Now where were we? Oh yes, where are you going to stay? I'd be interested in knowing."

"There's only one place she hasn't rejected," Jaz pondered aloud. "What's the reason for that?"

"Oh, I don't know," Paula giggled. "Maybe the memory of a certain night not so long ago?"

Tyler felt the blood rush to her face. "You two are impossible."

"Right. But are we right?" Jaz batted her eyelashes and raised her eyebrows meaningfully.

Now Tyler couldn't hold back and laughed out loud. "You two, in a double act, are dangerous."

Paula narrowed her eyes to slits. "And you haven't answered our question yet, Miss Evasive Maneuver."

Tyler conceded defeat. "Yes. In part. Maybe. Oh, I don't know either!" Her gaze drifted and softened when it lingered on Pat, who seemed engrossed in a serious conversation with Cole and Jake.

"Our summer night together was really, really nice. Not just that part," she added hastily, rolling her eyes as her sister made kissing noises. "Jeepers! How old are you? Twelve?"

"I can transform in the twinkling of an eye," Paula laughed, "if I can tease you with anything."

"Ignore your sister and keep talking," Jaz urged.

"It was quite magical. Only I'm not sure the magic didn't come from knowing we wouldn't see each other again. It was liberating. I don't think I've ever had such honest conversations on a first date as I did with him. And now? Now here I am, knee banged up, a drooling fan psycho on my back—who wants that?"

"Pat, from the looks of it," Jaz said dryly.

"It feels like I'd better gather back the pieces that represent my life and assemble them into a reasonable picture before adding new pieces."

Jaz nodded in understanding. Her sister, on the other hand, almost choked on her sandwich.

"What is it?"

Paula pulled herself together and stopped laughing. "You said that very nicely, little sister. But I think it's much easier. You're just scared."

"Excuse me?" asked Tyler incredulously.

"You heard me. For years, you've been focused like a laser on your career."

"Is that a bad thing?" Tyler felt backed into a corner.

"No, not at all," Paula reassured her. "But that's gone now. No wonder you don't know where to go right now. And then, of all things, you meet an exciting man. Your focus changes. I can imagine that's scary."

Tyler gently ran the tip of her index finger over Ranger's ears. "When did you get so wise?" She studied Paula with a thoughtful look. "It must be the child. Leslie seems to be a good influence on you."

Paula stuck her tongue out at her.

"Or not," Tyler muttered. Paula was only trying to be funny and her usual obstinate self, but the longer they talked about Pat, and where she was going to stay, the more real the incident became. So far, she had successfully managed to minimize what had gone down in Breckenridge. With every minute that passed here, she was less able to do so, and fear rose in her. At the same time, anger flared. She already had enough trouble in her life. And now some creep was probably jerking off to it.

The need to punch Pat's boxing bag crossed her mind. Ranger was on the spot and nudged her, just in time, before she went into full panic mode. She crouched down next to him and hugged him.

"Kids, kids, get a grip," Jaz said gently. "Tyler, try to let go of the fear. We're watching out for you."

Jaz's emotional words hit home. Goosebumps formed on Tyler's arms. Jaz was so right. And, she reluctantly admitted, so was her sister. She scrambled to her feet. "Everyone, listen up. I'm moving in with Pat and taking Ranger with me." She looked at Pat meaningfully. "If he'll have me. If the offer was serious." She kept her gaze steady. Butterflies flew up in her stomach, the ones she'd always banished right to the back of her mind until now. This time, she let them fly and enjoyed the feeling while she waited for his answer.

CHAPTER EIGHT

PAT KEPT HIS FACE from looking shocked. Her announcement about moving in was a shocker. Something was different, only what? But his questions could wait. She needed an answer. The whole room was waiting. "I'd love to."

"Even with a dog?"

He nodded. "I like dogs. You know that." He was hinting at last summer's first meeting.

She caught it and her face relaxed.

"I think once Mr. Wilkinson knows the situation, he'll be okay with it. And Ranger is well-trained. He's not going to tear the place up. No more than I'm tearing it up already with a renovation crew."

Jake spoke up again. "I want you to check in with me or Pat every time you go somewhere alone. You're alone, too, when Ranger's around," he added as he watched his sister cast a glance at her new four-legged partner. "No saying, 'I didn't call you because of the dog.' Kay?"

"She's not going anywhere alone," Pat assured.

"I'm sorry, what?" Tyler indignantly straightened up. "You must be out of your mind! First of all, the man here has a job." She pointed at Pat. "At least that's what he claims. And second, I don't need a chaperone, Jake. I think I've done a pretty good job of that myself so far."

She grabbed her jacket, which she had hung over the back of a chair earlier, and stomped angrily into the hallway. Ranger seemed to have already internalized the holder change and followed her out. He probably sensed how upset she was. As she slipped on her boots, she felt her jacket pocket for her car keys. *Duh!* She didn't even have a car here. She was tempted to bang her head against the wall. So much for leaving in diva style. To cover her fluster, she stomped back into the living room. "Thank you for giving Ranger to me," she said.

"No problem. I've only had a little time for him. I'm sure he'll like it with you better." Cole lowered his voice a little. "Are you sure you want to stay with Pat? We can find another solution, if not."

"I'm not sure of anything," she replied. "But I'm not in Las Vegas anymore, and I can't act like it either." A sob caught in her throat.

"Pat looks at you like the wolf looks at Little Red Riding Hood. He would love to eat you right here and now."

"Really?" It was ridiculous, she knew. But she couldn't help but be pleased at her brother's words. Which surely hadn't been his intention.

Instead of an answer, Cole just shook his head. "I give up. To recap, Jake and I don't think you're in immediate danger. There's been no threat, and it seems like a fan trying to gaslight you."

"Do you think that was just the beginning? Are we going to see more of this bird stuff?"

"If you do, call Jake right away. Then call me second. And by the way, Jake vouches for Pat and says he's a good guy. But you know how I am, 'In God we trust, all others pay cash.' That's my rule."

"Okay." Tyler took a deep breath as a cold-wet dog's nose pushed against her palm.

"Ranger," she said softly. At least all the trouble had given her a great dog.

Behind her, Pat said, "Do you want to take some more of your stuff right now?"

"Stuff?"

"Things. Clothing you've left here from before at your mom's?"

She looked at him without understanding until she remembered that she lived with him from now on. She groaned. "Right. All right, then." She took off her boots again and dragged with heavy steps to the room she usually stayed in when her parents were home. She found a couple of T-shirts, sweatpants, pajamas, underwear, three sweatshirts, and three pairs of jeans. Into a gym bag they went. She also found a TheraBand to stretch the muscles in her feet and a tennis ball to put under her calves and hamstrings. The idea was to roll around on the ball and stretch the muscles out. Little helpers.

In another minute she was standing next to Pat in the snow, watching him let one snowball after another fly for Ranger. The big dog cavorted like a puppy. He caught the snowballs in midair and bit them to pieces.

"All packed?" Pat asked as she stepped up beside him.

"I don't have much here. And if I forget something, I can just go get it. It's not like I'm emigrating to the Amazon with no connection to civilization."

He smiled. "True again." He squinted against the sky, which was darkening with snow clouds. "Let's get going before the next blizzard hits."

"Cole said he still had some of Ranger's stuff in his truck. Can you go get it? It should be open."

"Sure."

Tyler and Ranger went to the Cadillac, where the dog placed himself in the middle of the back seat. Tyler got in the front and leaned her head against the cold window until Pat returned.

He glanced at her out of the corner of her eye. "It's all been a bit much today, hasn't it?"

"You can say that again. To think I came here because I thought I'd get peace and quiet."

He let out a sympathetic chuckle.

"The dance never ends," she murmured.

"I'll credit you with having a sense of humor about the situation. I don't know many women who could do that."

They spent the rest of the drive in tranquil silence. Pat concentrated on the road and the steadily falling snow. He seemed to understand that after the chaos of today, a little breather would do them both good.

Tyler was grateful to him for that. In her head, one thought chased another, and her pulse seemed reluctant to calm down. She was feeling the aftereffects of the adrenaline that had raced through her body every day since she'd landed. Thanks to her performances in front of large audiences, she was aware of the symptoms.

The old Cadillac purred along the wintry road. It was a rich midnight black on the outside and all burnished black leather on the inside. The roomy seats smelled of saddle soap and leather conditioner. It was luxe and cushy. Tyler felt like she could sink into the seat until she disappeared. Outside, snow-dusted pines seemed to offer their branches to the road on either side. In the backseat, Ranger sat alert with his tongue hanging out.

Pat turned on the headlights. "What time is it?" he asked.

"The dashboard clock says it's seven."

"I forget about these old-school luxuries. One of the great things about an old car." Pat tapped the steering wheel and looked thoughtful.

"Is there something you have to do?"

"Might swing by the bed-and-breakfast. Have a word with Mr. Wilkinson about the new living arrangements. Will you be okay in the car with Ranger?"

"With the dog, I'll be fine." Minutes ticked by as they drove. "What are you going to ask Mr. W.?"

I'm going to do just like Paula said and ask him for a favor for Grandma Rose McArthy."

A laugh bubbled out of Tyler. "The old guilt trip works for me."

Pat turned onto Main Street and headed for the diner. He pulled into the small parking area behind the diner that separated it from the bed-and-breakfast. It was a matter of a few hundred yards between the two buildings, which meant meals could be delivered easily from the big commercial kitchen to the small dining room in the B and B. He stopped and shifted the Caddy into park.

"Get your cell phone out," he suggested. "I'll have mine in my hand. If you see anything, just call me."

Tyler nodded and fished her phone out of her parka.

"I'll leave the keys. Make sure you lock the doors." He exited and crunched away, over the snow.

A lone light over the parking lot made a circle of light around the car. Tyler cracked the window and a tiny burst of cold air came in, bearing the scent of fresh pine from the hills. Out of the corner of her eye, she saw someone move from the street into a corner of the parking lot. It was a woman around thirty. She was fit, dressed in city clothes instead of sporty winter wear, and that's what made Tyler pay attention to her. She stood looking intently over the parking lot at the B and B. Her eyes flicked over and saw Tyler in the car. For some reason—later, Tyler wouldn't even be able to explain why she did it—she picked up her phone and took a picture of the woman while pretending to read a text.

The woman turned her back and walked out to Main Street, where she disappeared.

A minute later, Pat was back. When he opened the door, cold air rushed in and Ranger leaped to his feet.

"We got the all-clear," Pat said confidently.

"Anything for Rose McArthy?"

"You got it. He was in a really good mood. I think all the company around here is doing him good."

Tyler smiled. "How do you feel about not going to the house quite yet?"

He looked at her, puzzled.

"I thought we might work out a bit with the bag."

"Best idea I've heard all day."

"Let's go."

Pat insisted on getting her cane out of the truck so she could use it going up the stairs to the studio entrance. "I want you to give that knee as much relief as you can."

Once inside, Pat held Ranger by the collar and Tyler went to get something to dry his paws. No trotting paw prints across the floor. As she walked across the rich old hardwood, she thought what a lift the old place could get if she replaced the old ballet barre with a new one, painted the walls, sanded down the old floorboards and refinished them. She cast her eyes over the gray ceiling of the studio. She might have to wield a paintbrush in here if she wanted to use the studio professionally at some point.

The paper-towel holder over the sink was almost out, but she found a terry towel and brought it back. When Ranger's paws were dry, she folded the towel and laid it down next to the doorway. Ranger immediately recognized that it was suitable for lying on and trotted toward it. After turning in a circle twice on the pad, he settled down with a sigh.

"Don't worry, I'll take my boots off," Pat said. His innocent words brought a blush to Tyler's cheeks. In an instant she was remembering last summer in the trailer when the first thing they had done was take off their shoes. But they hadn't stopped there. The clothing just kept shedding. She bit down hard on her lower lip to get her thoughts on a different track.

Tyler took their footwear and placed them under the old radiators, which were slightly warm. She didn't notice Pat step up beside her. Absent-mindedly, she glanced over at him. He was pulling his shirt over his head. "What are you doing?" she croaked.

He paused briefly before pulling the garment fully over his head. "I thought we were going to train."

Tyler licked her lips. Any thought of the red punching bag in the corner was suddenly blown away.

Pat seemed to notice the hungry look in her eyes. If she kept looking at him like that, his good intentions would fly out the window.

Speaking of windows, the glass on this level was frosted. No one could see in.

Tyler took a step closer. Pat took a tiny but deliberate step back. She didn't expect that. She lifted her gaze, which had been fixed on his spectacular chest since he'd taken off his T-shirt and looked him in the eye. His brown eyes sparkled, but at the same time, he looked at her suspiciously. Very mixed signals the man was sending. Potential rejection or not, she wasn't going to wait any longer for him to make the first move. He looked scrumptious, and a distraction was just what she needed right now. So she took another step, leaning forward a little until she was almost touching his mouth with her lips. His breath danced over her skin as light as a feather. Greedily, she sucked in the air. She was reminded how safe she felt in his presence—a very welcome feeling in her current situation. Still, he made no move to meet her. But at least he wasn't moving away either.

She moved her mouth closer and nipped his lower lip. Surprised, he winced. To soften the effect, she let her tongue slide over his lips. He groaned. Her eyes grew wide as he clasped her head with both hands and pulled her in for a kiss. Not that she minded. Her hands came to rest on his chest. He felt so warm, so alive, so there for her.

Pat nearly lost his inner battle as soon as she bit his lips. He could only remember vaguely why kissing her would be a bad idea right now. Her scent rose to his nose. When she also brought her tongue into play, he pulled her toward him and kissed her back.

She tilted her head and looked at him with dreamy eyes. Conflicting emotions moved over her face. She was almost about to say something, but simply lowered her head again and rested her cheek on his chest while wrapping her arms around his waist.

For minutes, they just stood there in silence. Tyler wondered what was going through his mind. After the kiss they just shared, she didn't want to break the moment. It wasn't really in her nature to make the first move.

"This was not what we came here to do," he said.

"I know but—"

"I'm worried about your knee on this floor. Come on, let's work out." He led the way across the studio.

Gloves lay on the floor beneath the bag. Pat helped her lace them up. The last time she'd only slipped the gloves on. She faced down the bag and decided to hop on the spot with her good leg, like she'd seen boxers do. Then she landed a few taps. Gingerly at first, she tapped a few blows on the bag. Then faster and faster, she let punches drum a beat.

Pat's arms encircled her waist. "Let me take the weight off your leg," he said. "Just use your upper body for now."

She tried it. The idea worked. She was able to lean in with the punches.

Pat explained the basics of various techniques, supporting her lower body to take the weight off her leg while she tried aikido moves.

Two hours later, they lay side by side on the mat, looking up at the ceiling. She was exhausted. Under his patient guidance, she'd just had the best exercise in recent memory.

Pat let out a happy sigh. "There is a theory that accidents or traumatic experiences leave lasting shock and tension in the body."

"I thought everybody believed that," she said.

"I mean down to the cellular level," Pat replied. "Various cultures believe it, now and in the past. Scientifically, it can be considered controversial, but many medical pros think there is something to it."

She hadn't understood what he was getting at first. "And what does that mean for me?"

"Every time you make a similar movement, or in your case, lose your balance, it triggers a similar shock response to what happened at the time of the trauma. That's why they're called 'triggers.' This can have different consequences. Some people don't get rid of the fear, others are still in pain for years even though the original injuries have long since healed."

"Hmmm," she said dreamily.

"You can also talk to Jaz about this. We worked together quite a bit in that direction. A physical assault like she experienced is difficult to deal with."

"You mean Jaz did martial arts with you?"

"We share knowledge. I even do some yoga. It's not about martial arts in the strict sense. Any movement that improves body awareness can, in principle, be used for this. It's mostly about finding where those triggers are hiding and using appropriate physical exercises to change the 'programming' of your body. To use a computer example, you can't delete the information, but you can overwrite it with positive information."

A mischievous smile on her lips, she rolled onto her stomach and into Pat. Both of them were completely sweaty, but she didn't care. She laughed when she saw his surprised expression.

Ranger, who was still lying on the towel by the entrance, raised his head at Tyler's laughter. When he saw that the two people made no effort to get up from the mat, he put his head back down and closed his eyes to continue dozing.

A dreamy smile stole onto Tyler's face as Ranger started snoring.

"What are you thinking about right now?" She glanced at Pat out of the corner of her eye and felt herself blushing. Shaking her head, her long blond hair fell forward, hiding her face.

"Nostalgic feelings. It's been a long time since I've been here in the evening."

Her eyes roved across the room and she noticed that it was so bright in here, under the studio lights and so dark outside. An idea occurred to her. "Wait here a minute. I have to get something."

She got to her feet and used her cane to go upstairs. Ranger trotted to the foot of the stairs and stared up.

"Sorry, buddy. I have no idea what she's doing," Pat said.

In a moment, she was back. Ranger followed, tail wagging, glad to be back in his sphere of influence. Pat could relate to how the dog was feeling. "What did you do?"

"I borrowed a blanket and some tea lights from Jaz. Then we can dispense with the bright lighting."

"Good idea."

"And I found this." She held up a half bottle of red wine. "I have paper cups over the sink, if you don't mind getting them."

Pat got smoothly to his feet and came back with the cups. They made themselves comfortable. As if they were in their own private world.

Pat poured the wine, then raised his cup in a toast. "To you and your health."

"Let's not talk about my health."

"Guaranteed. No health talk."

They sipped without taking their eyes off of each other. Sparks flew, and for a moment, the evening was ready to go in a completely different direction. But then Pat seemed to have something on his mind.

Tyler, realizing he was having a hard time getting started, snuggled closer to him and focused her attention on the flickering tea lights. Maybe that would make it easier for him to tell the story.

Pat relaxed a little and began to talk. "Look, if Cole is going to check into my background, there's something you need to know." He looked to the side and then met her eyes directly. "I have a past."

CHAPTER NINE

"Uh huh, you have a past." Tyler tried to keep it light. "Doesn't everyone?"

Pat shook his head, a little sadly. "Remember I was telling you at school I got involved with a gang?"

"Yes."

"The boss of our gang, Julio—he was older, he was eighteen—was very pleased with me. I could pick any lock, forge all the signatures for school, read blueprints."

"Blueprints? For architecture?"

"For casing out a place before we robbed it."

"Oh."

"I made myself indispensable. I was important enough that he made sure the others left me alone, and kept me away from the more violent side of his business. I was completely in the dark about a lot of it. He didn't say anything, and I didn't ask. But I was in on enough."

"What was that like for you? I imagine it's extremely stressful, always having to be so on guard."

"I didn't know any different. So now you know. If your bro, Cole, digs up some dirt on me, it's probably true. But it was all long ago. I don't have anything to do with those people anymore. I was a kid. It was in the past. I'm an architect. I own my own business. I have a reputation based on good work, and I don't want to mess that up."

Tyler was surprised at his honesty. She touched his hand in empathy.

"I hope you will tell him to come and talk to me. I can prove I've been on the right side of the law my whole adult life."

Tyler was moved. She felt compelled to add a little of her own. "You know Vegas is very competitive."

"I can imagine."

"And I haven't said anything."

"Just tell me what you're thinking."

"I'm going over the events, and backstage before I fell, I think someone touched me."

"Pushed you? Ran into you?"

A KNOCK sounded at the door of the studio.

Pat and Tyler exchanged looks. He got to his feet in one smooth, athletic motion and walked over to it. "We're closed."

A voice said, "We saw the lights. Thought there might be something going on."

"Sorry, private workout."

"We're tourists, on vacay. Just exploring the town. Is there yoga here during the day?"

"There sure is. The owner would be glad to see you tomorrow."

The people outside moved off the porch.

Pat turned to Tyler. "Maybe it's time we went."

Tyler stifled a little yawn. "Sounds like a good idea to me."

When they got home around eight-thirty p.m., Tyler chose the guest room next to Pat's as her home base. She put Ranger's sleeping basket in there and stowed his food. The room was bright with one of those huge casement windows and a faded goldenrod-colored quilt on the bed that provided a welcome splash of color.

She kicked off her shoes and put the gym bag with her luggage next to the door. Who knew, this might all be over in another twenty-four hours and then she'd be joining Jake and Jaz, or going home with Paula. She dropped onto the bed, wanting to know if it was as comfortable as it looked. *Just ten minutes of shut-eye*, she told herself.

After half an hour, Pat began to worry. He hoped Tyler wasn't having a breakdown. She had plenty to be upset about. He listened, trying to hear if she might be crying. But everything was quiet. Even Ranger, who had always responded to her mood all afternoon, as he had observed, was being quiet on the other side of the wall. Finally, he couldn't stand it any longer and went to see. The door to the guest room was ajar. He pushed it open a crack and spotted Tyler. She was lying on her stomach on the bed, fully clothed, asleep. Sleeping was good. He went to a linen closet and grabbed a wool blanket.

After tucking Tyler in, he gently stroked a blond strand out of her face. He had never met a woman who appealed to him in so many different ways. It wasn't just her beauty. It was also her laugh and even her downright stubbornness that set off sparks.

An hour later, Tyler woke up disoriented. She blinked. The room was unfamiliar. Where the extra blanket she was clutching came from, she didn't know either. Then she heard Pat's music next door. It all came back to her. Pat must have tucked her in. Briefly, she felt guilty but shook it off. The nap had done her good. Her phone said it was ten-fifteen p.m.

She felt refreshed and not quite so rattled by events. Stretching, she eased out of bed. Ranger shifted in his basket, and his ears pricked up. Armed with fresh clothes and some toiletries, she ventured into the hallway and set off for the bathroom. Ranger padded behind, toenails clicking on the hardwood floor. Down the hall, they encountered Pat. He had changed clothes and was wearing Seattle Seahawks track pants and a T-shirt. The fabric stretched across his broad chest, and the defined muscles of his arms showed nicely. *It should be illegal to look that good in an old T-shirt*, she thought. To distract herself, she tapped the Seahawks logo on his chest.

"You should change that. You're in Broncos territory now."

He looked down at himself and frowned. "Forget it. Wherever I live, my heart beats for the Seahawks."

"Aha. We'll see," she replied. "I'm off to the nearest rest stop." She kept going down the hall.

Pat stared as she disappeared through a door and grinned broadly as Ranger settled himself outside it. Whistling, he turned and headed for the kitchen. Listening to her shower was not something he was going to do to himself. It was hard to think of anything but her naked, wet body. He forced his mind away. Now that she was moved in, he wasn't going to act too quickly. He would play it cool and wait for her to make the moves. Better for her knee that way, too. Maybe he would shower when she was done, too. Preferably an ice-cold one.

Pat didn't go to bed most nights until eleven and Tyler had just risen from a nap, so they went into a study with a TV and watched an old James Bond movie. They shared the sofa. As soon as Pat sat down with her, the piece of furniture seemed to shrink. Every time he reached for chips sitting in a bowl on the coffee table, he brushed against her leg.

Tyler tried hard not to flinch as she sat next to Pat. Goosebumps covered her entire right side, and she grew warmer. She wondered if he felt the same way. He seemed to enjoy their occasional repartee. But when she thought about it carefully, she noticed he hadn't made a single innuendo all evening. No hidden glances under heavy lids, not even a meaningful look with a raised brow. Until now, he'd never missed an opportunity to draw her attention to the pleasure they experienced together. It seemed that her moving into the guest room had a cooling effect on him. Even now, when they were sitting almost thigh to thigh next to each other, he didn't seem to feel anything. Quite the opposite for her. *Great.*

What Tyler didn't know was that Pat was managing to pull off this chill effect only by repeating all the math formulas he knew. It helped prevent him from throwing himself at her lithe curves. Curves that pressed gently against him with every movement she made. If this kept up, he wouldn't last two days. He had no idea what had gotten into Tyler, either. If he didn't know better, he'd say she was flirting with him. At least the looks she gave him out of the corner of her eye weren't scowling like they'd occasionally been the past few days, but seemed much more—yes, what, actually—seductive? Best he didn't even try to figure it out and simply stuck to his plan. *What was the plan again?* He tried to remember as her subtle scent of honeysuckle hit his nose.

Tyler looked at him questioningly from under her long lashes. In the glow of the light from the TV screen, her blue eyes looked like the Colorado sky in the morning. Yow, things had to be worse than he'd thought if he was already starting to think in those terms.

She seemed so approachable, sitting relaxed next to him on the sofa in her yoga pants and comfy T-shirt with one leg underneath her, and the leg with the knee sleeve stretched out on the coffee table. Even her facial expression seemed softer, more open somehow. The tip of her tongue darted out and all he could think about was what it would be like to lose himself in her kiss. Was he mistaken, or had she even moved toward him a bit? He lifted one hand and stroked her cheekbone with his fingertips, down to her neck, where a pulse fluttered.

The credits rolled on the Bond film and an announcer said that a second movie was about to roll. Tyler looked at Pat to see if he was interested. But he didn't seem to notice. She licked her lips—a nervous gesture—and the movement drew his gaze to her mouth. Would he kiss her? The tension between them was palpable, causing all her nerve endings to dance. Involuntarily, she tilted her head an inch toward him.

BRRINGGG!

Pat's cell phone went off, interrupting the spell. He jumped up as if he had burned his fingers on it. "This house," he complained, "you never know when you're going to get a signal. I have to take this." He blurted the words out, searching frantically for his phone.

What was wrong with him?

"Bernie," he said, answering the call. "The lumber arrived today. You can start first thing."

To Tyler, Pat sounded downright relieved to be on the call. But she could have sworn he looked guilty the moment before they'd been interrupted. What on earth was wrong with the man? Glad she hadn't given in to the temptation to make the first move, she decided to skip the second Bond movie. She fluttered her fingers at him in goodbye and moved off the couch. Ranger got to his feet, ready to follow. By the time Pat was off the phone, she'd be behind a closed door in the guest room.

The next morning, Tyler was up early. Ranger, who had been sleeping in her bed, stayed close to her heels. She wandered toward the back of the house and found a door to let Ranger out. The north-facing view of the house had a panorama of the Rockies. This morning, the sky was overcast and the tips of the highest peaks were shrouded in mist.

Ranger hunted around the vast yard and Tyler shivered in the open door until he returned. She went back to her room to grab the bag of dogfood and then led the way to the kitchen.

There was no sign of Pat. Presumably, he was still asleep. It made sense, since she'd had the unfair advantage of an early nap yesterday. The kitchen came into view, and Tyler was surprised to find it torn apart. Tools and materials were laid on every available surface. A sawhorse with a big electric cutting blade took over most of the space. So that's why Pat kept a coffee maker in his bedroom. But where did he keep the food? Wait a minute, the living room had a large bar in it. Maybe there was storage there?

Moving through the house, marveling at the high ceilings and gorgeous gleaming wood finishings, she and Ranger came to the bar. She walked around it and *bingo!* there was a fridge. Inside were meats and cheeses, sealed pouches of prepared dinners, and containers of salads and side dishes. On the bar rested a platter of fresh fruit, and a basket beside the fridge held breads, sweet rolls, muffins, and spreads including honey and marmalade.

Setting Ranger's bag of food on the bar, she read the feeding instructions. A 97-pound dog, moderately active, was supposed to eat over six cups of kibble daily. Ranger was supposed to eat twice a day now that he was retired, so she filled the bowl with what was about three cups. Patiently, he waited until she put the bowl down and stepped back. Still, he did not move and looked at her expectantly with pricked ears.

"Yes, eat," she said, pointing at his food. That was the signal he'd been waiting for. He dove in. Now that was a well-behaved dog. Since Pat had decided to keep his distance, she had gladly made do with Ranger's presence. *Pffff.* Who needed a man when there was a dog? A tug in the pit of her stomach reminded her that there were definitely a few places where a dog was no substitute. But she immediately shooed that unwelcome thought away.

As Ranger dove into the bowl, Pat emerged from the hallway. He was carrying two mugs of steaming coffee. "I didn't tell you about the kitchen," he said. "Sorry about that." He held out one of the mugs. "Black?"

"You guessed right," she said, beaming. "I found your secret stash, anyway."

"The bar fridge? Did you help yourself?"

"Not yet."

"Dig in."

Standing at the bar, they laid muffins on napkins and feasted.

"You've heard of Frank Lloyd Wright, the architect?"

"Yes," Tyler replied, sipping at her coffee.

"His daughter, Elizabeth Wright Ingraham, came to Colorado in the 1960s and started designing houses. This one is called Prairie style, and it was designed and built by one of her colleagues at the design firm she opened in the fifties."

"I love the huge windows."

"That's the style to bring the outside in."

"I'm so glad you're restoring this old place instead of tearing it down."

"You and me both. I think I may be able to get the Colorado powers-that-be to award it heritage status."

Her eyes roamed over the leather couches and mission-style furniture arranged into "conversation" areas, making the room very inviting. The soaring ceiling had hewn beams that formed an artistic pattern over their heads.

"We're replacing all the old support beams and making sure the foundation is solid," Pat said. "That's phase one—" He was interrupted as a truck pulled up outside. "There's Bernie," he said. "The rest of the crew will be here in a minute."

"Sure, do what you have to do," she said hurriedly, and turned to go. The last thing she needed was to greet a work crew still dressed in her sleep T-shirt.

As soon as she and Ranger made it back to the room, her cell phone chattered. It was an alert she'd set for herself. *Call clinic re: therapy*, it read. At this early hour the office wasn't open, but she dialed the clinic and left a request for a referral to a doctor specializing in regenerative medicine and stem-cell therapy for the knee.

Her phone chattered again. This time, it was a direct call. She answered it.

"It's Jaz. This morning is my physical recovery group. I have it at the house. Why don't you come, too?"

"Ummmm..."

"Oh, come on. Do something for yourself."

What else do I have to do?

"And Ranger can have a visit with Rambo."

"All right, then. The work crew just arrived at the house, anyway. I'm sure all the power tools will be screeching away in no time."

"Exactly."

CHAPTER TEN

TWO OPTIONS PRESENTED THEMSELVES for getting to Jaz's place. She could ask Pat to interrupt work and drive her—that wasn't going to happen. Second, she could call Joe's Snow Removal and be at the mercy of his schedule, even though he seemed pretty available. And the last option was the dreaded ski bike. Or the *Ski-Thing*, as she decided to name it. The sidecar had its own windshield, which would offer Ranger protection from the wind, but it was going to be breezy, and he had no coat like Rambo wore when he went to town.

"Sorry, buddy," she said, leading him out to the beast. What she did have was a warm woolen blanket from a trunk in her room, and a couple of heavy-duty hair clips to hold the blanket in place around his neck.

"We don't look in vogue, buddy, but we're built for comfort," she said.

There was a rattrap device on the back to hold things in place, and she reluctantly secured the cane in it. Straddling the seat, she put the key in the ignition. Ski-Thing farted uncertainly and then settled down into a putt-putt-putt. It didn't sound glamorous, but it sounded reliable.

In another minute, they were off. Avoiding Main Street, Tyler opted for an indirect route and was soon passing snowy clearings with frozen ponds where skaters circled and skidded, and cross-country skiers carved tracks through everything. It was a beautiful day, and she was quite warm in a full-face helmet and puffy parka. In spite of the occasional twinge in her knee, she felt stress lifting off her shoulders. Motorcycling in the open air had that effect. Even though the Thing was no cool motorcycle, it still had that free, open-air quality of driving. It was almost like riding a super-smooth horse.

A couple of hikers in snowshoes stopped to gape and wave as they passed by. When they caught a glimpse of Ranger in his blanket, and his tongue hanging out with delight, they fell into the snow, laughing.

"Go ahead, enjoy yourselves," Tyler said to no one. She really couldn't blame them. The Ski-Thing was an unusual sight, to say the least. The machine ate up the miles and sooner than expected, she turned into Jaz's place, the house that used to be known as Rose McArthy's. Rose still owned it, but she no longer lived there.

Now Tyler stood on the doorstep and wiped her damp hands on her pant legs, wondering if she really wanted to join a group of strangers and for some frank talk. She looked down at Ranger, who was swiveling his ears, as though wondering why she didn't go in. His blanket was gone and folded neatly in the sidecar for when they went back. At that moment, the door opened. It was Jaz.

"Hi there! Hi pup! She ruffled Ranger's coat. To Tyler, she said, "What are you waiting for? A written invitation?" Rambo pushed past her legs to greet them. Ranger looked like he was smiling, letting the younger dog have his way. Rambo was a full-grown standard poodle but in Ranger's eyes, he still had a lot to learn. Especially when it came to dignified behavior.

"How are you?" Jaz asked, pulling them in and shutting the door against the cold sunshine.

"I don't know why, but I'm as nervous as I was before my first public appearance." To emphasize her words, Tyler extended her right hand, which was trembling slightly.

"Hmm, did someone tell you that we abandon everyone who can't do the lotus position?"

This got a chuckle out of Tyler, who gave her a friendly shove.

"It is extremely unwise to mistreat the yoga teacher before the class," Jaz said affectionately.

They reached the living room, where furniture had been pushed back to make space on the floor for yoga mats. Tyler plopped down on a chair to one side. "So where are your other innocent victims, uh, students?"

"They'll show up, eventually. You're fifteen minutes early."

"I couldn't wait to get here," she fibbed.

"Guess who just called before you came?"

"I give up."

"Kat! Remember her from last summer? My friend in Seattle?"

"How could I forget? She had that big dog. What was his name? Rocky?"

"She's having trouble with her landlord in Seattle. She wants me to keep an eye out for places she could relocate to out here."

"Nice to have another friend around?"

"Definitely."

Rambo's yelp brought them back into the here and now. He was trying to impress Ranger with his toy collection by placing old chew toys, tattered stuffed animals, and other items in front of his paws. Ranger sat down next to Tyler and laid his head on her lap. Gratefully, she buried her hand in his warm fur and began to cuddle him. As always, contact with the dog calmed her instantly. Her pulse rate calmed and her thoughts became clearer. Better than any tranquilizer, this animal.

"So, what are we doing here today?" she asked Jaz.

"Did Pat tell you anything?"

"He explained a little bit of it. How you used bodywork to overcome your own injuries. Is that about right?" She looked up uncertainly at Jaz.

"Pretty much. People can come to astonishing realizations unexpectedly."

Tyler rearranged her graceful limbs in the chair. "We only scratched the surface of the philosophy behind it. He mostly made a point of me taking it easy on my knee, now that I think back on it."

"And you don't want to do that? Take it easy on your knee? Basically, that's reasonable right now, isn't it?"

"I..." Tyler paused, feeling a sudden lump in her throat. "Yes. I have to go easy on it. Doesn't leave me much choice," she admitted. "But I don't want to go easy on it. I want it to work the way it always has." The words burst out of her angrily. She realized how childish she sounded. But she couldn't fight this pent-up anger that rose to the surface so unexpectedly. She felt abandoned by her body, betrayed by Yuri. To this day, she didn't know if she'd been pushed or someone had staggered against her. Until now, she had successfully suppressed all these questions.

"That's probably why you were nervous about coming here," Jaz said knowingly. "Because you had time to think about it."

Tyler sighed. Now that she had pushed the anger safely back to the farthest corner of her mind, she was exhausted. Just great. She hadn't done a single exercise yet, and she was already pooped.

Fortunately, one by one, the other participants arrived and distracted her from her stress. Jaz called everyone together by striking a golden gong. Tyler joined the others in finding a mat to sit on. What was she supposed to do now? Just do exercises on the floor?

Jaz began the lesson with the sun salutation.

Even with this sequence of exercises, Tyler had to modify half of the movements to make them tolerable for her knee. A few others she had to leave out completely. She tried to block out the presence of the other participants. Still, her frustration increased with each exercise not perfectly executed. That was everyday life for a dancer. Until now, she always knew she would get better if she just trained enough, whereas now she was reaching the limits of her body. But she gritted her teeth and kept going.

Tyler was far from the only one with knee problems. But she was so focused on herself and her inability that she didn't even notice.

Jaz announced the various exercises and assisted each woman according to her needs. She could see that Tyler was getting more and more frustrated, and progressively more tense. Jaz decided to take it up with her after class. Few had been through an experience as impactful as hers, or an accident like Tyler's. In her case, the advantage had been that she knew where the problem was buried. She had known exactly what she needed to work on. Physical therapy and her own yoga training had restored mobility to her battered body surprisingly quickly. But the feelings of being at the mercy of others, of helplessness, still ran deep.

When Pat offered to train Jaz in aikido, she took him up on it. Aikido challenged her body awareness in a completely new way than yoga. Also, Pat deliberately incorporated elements of self-defense. As a result, she gradually regained her confidence in her own strength.

With Tyler, the case was different. She did not know the exact background of the accident. But watching her now, it seemed she was mainly fighting her own demons.

The lesson was coming to an end. After completing the last exercise, *Savasana*, Jaz went from student to student giving them praise and homework, and encouraging them to keep it up. When she arrived at Tyler's mat, it was already rolled up.

"Glad you hung in there. Will you stay for some tea?"

Tyler looked up in surprise. She had intended to get out of there as quickly as possible. The morning had been embarrassing enough. All she wanted to do was get home and curl up. Or take a hot bath to loosen cramped muscles. But Jaz looked at her so hopefully that she heard herself murmur a yes.

"Fine. Then I'll meet you in the kitchen. If you want, you can let the dogs out for a minute. Take the back door."

"Will do," she heard herself say. *How about thinking first, then speaking?* her inner voice scolded. Now it would take another hour before she could relax her tired muscles in hot water. In a bad mood, she went downstairs. Ranger and Rambo had made themselves comfortable near the fireplace, where the remains of a fire were still glowing.

"You guys are smart," she said to them. "Just lying in the house in front of the fire waiting for us to bring you food. That's what I call evolution."

At a snap of her fingers, Ranger rose. Rambo, not wanting to miss anything, hurried to follow. Tyler opened the door to the back porch and released them into the brilliant day. Rambo sniffed, caught a scent trail, and disappeared straight behind a clump of aspens growing a hundred yards away. Carried away by the exuberance of the poodle, Ranger dashed after him. When he realized Tyler wasn't following, however, he slowed his sprint. Uncertainly, he looked back and forth between Tyler and Rambo. Then he turned around and trotted back to her.

"That's nice of you to wait for me. But I'm not coming with you. Run along," she told Ranger, gesturing toward the surrounding meadow.

At last, he seemed convinced and began to scout the immediate area. Tyler smiled despite her foul mood as she waited, freezing, on the back porch. When Ranger was done, she called for Rambo. No response. The dog remained missing. She hoped he was making his usual evening rounds, and that she hadn't lost Jaz's dog, too, after her disappointing yoga performance. *That would complete the day perfectly*, she thought sourly. She returned with Ranger to the warm kitchen, where Jaz was pouring hot water into two mugs.

"I lost your dog outside," Tyler confessed, sitting down at the old kitchen table.

"That happens to me a lot, too. He usually runs after some squirrel trail that gets lost at the base of a tree, and there he sits until he comes to the glorious realization that his prey probably won't come down today."

"I'm glad about that. I was afraid we'd have to start a search operation."

"I'm sure we could have convinced Ranger to do this for us." She placed the two cups on the tabletop. "Tired?"

"As much as I hate to admit it, your yoga class really wore me out."

Jaz nodded understandingly as she blew into her tea and looked at Tyler over the rim of her cup. She looked as though she was inwardly debating how best to broach a subject. Tyler put her cup back down and asked, "What did you want to talk to me about?"

"What makes you think I wanted to discuss anything?" Jaz tried to stall.

Tyler rolled her eyes. "Why is it that everyone assumes I not only twisted my knee, but also hit my head?"

Jaz laughed. "Sorry. I definitely didn't mean it that way. But since we're on the subject, what do you know about your accident?"

Irritation rising, Tyler looked at her. "What's there to know? I had a slip and fall, lost my balance, end of story." She realized how aggressive her voice sounded, and was dismayed to see Jaz flinch. Only very slightly, but it was enough to make her rein in her emotion. "Sorry. That was a perfectly normal question, and I'm about to rip your head off." She groaned and propped her head in her hands. "What's wrong with me?"

"No problem. I still overreact with emotional outbursts from time to time," Jaz replied with a self-deprecating smile.

"Here I sit, wallowing in self-pity. Not giving a thought to what you have been through."

Jaz held up a hand and stopped her.

"Please don't. You don't have to apologize because you feel that my experiences are so much worse than yours. You can't put that in perspective. I have to deal with my experiences, you have to deal with yours. You have every right to be frustrated about it."

Tyler pressed her lips closed and thought about her words. "When did you get so wise? Is it the tea? If so, I need a gallon."

"Good distraction," Jaz grinned, "but let's stay on topic."

Tyler sighed. "The accident. I was conscious all the time. So it's not like I was missing parts of my memory."

"But maybe your memory is playing tricks on you?"

"You mean it was all very different?"

"I don't know. I wasn't there. All I know is that our brains—and bodies, for that matter—can be very selective in stressful situations. In other words, maybe you're just missing some of the information."

"And what makes you think that?"

Jaz bit her lower lip. "I hope you won't take offense to this. It's mostly a gut feeling, if I'm honest. I noticed earlier in yoga that you're extremely hard on yourself and your body. It has to be able to do everything. When it doesn't, you force yourself to keep going anyway. By the end of the hour, you were so cramped that not even the easiest exercises, or the exercises that didn't involve your knee at all, worked. Instead of allowing your knee to participate in what it could and otherwise relieve it a little, you acted as if there was nothing wrong with you at all."

Tyler swirled the tea in her cup and studied the light green liquid while she thought about what she had just heard. It all sounded reasonable, and she was able to take the criticism without feeling stung, but did it help her? "I already know I'm ambitious. It's part of being a dancer. What does that have to do with my knee?"

"I don't know. But I'm sure your ambition wasn't always so self-destructive. Otherwise, you wouldn't have gotten this far. Sure, you're no stranger to pushing boundaries. But like today? That was pretty extreme."

Self-destructive? Was Jaz right? Dazed a little bit by this, she said, "Let's assume that's true. Now what?"

It was Jaz's turn to play around with her cup. "Holistically speaking, knee injuries have a lot to do with ambition. I suspect that's one of the reasons you're struggling with your injury. You want to continue to devote yourself to dancing with all your might." She checked Tyler's reaction. Hopefully she hadn't offended with such a frank diagnosis. She cleared her throat. "Pat has a lot more experience there than I do. Maybe we should discuss when he can be there, too?"

No way. The last thing she needed was Pat watching her have another breakdown. She had her pride. "I'm glad you're here and not Pat. Please go on. You seem to have put some thought into this."

At that moment, scratching came at the back door. Grateful for the brief interruption, Jaz jumped up and let Rambo in. "See, there he is again."

Tail wagging, the black poodle ran from one to the other, happy that everyone was still there. Jaz tousled his curls. "What do you know about shamanism?" she asked softly.

"Shamanism?" Tyler hadn't expected that now. "Native Americans? Medicine men? Expensive workshops for seekers of the light?"

At the last words, Jaz snorted and smiled wryly. "Not bad. I'll try to find some terms outside our reference of Christian culture. Shamans or medicine men actually appeared in all known cultures where faith, culture, and daily life were closely interwoven. The shaman was there to keep everything in balance. He cared for the spirits of the ancestors as well as for the sick. I'm making this very simplified. I'm not an expert."

"You know a lot more than I do. Which amazes me. I thought you would be totally absorbed in your yoga world and maybe dabble in Buddhism. I hope that doesn't sound negative. I don't mean it that way. It's difficult to have a conversation about these topics."

"No problem. It doesn't bother me at all. Buddhism is actually very close to me, simply from its philosophy. Nevertheless, I grew up in a Christian culture. But my spiritual outlook is not the point here at all either. I'm just trying to give you the background on a shamanic healing technique."

"Too bad," Tyler said, grinning. "I was hoping we'd spend the next two hours talking about philosophical issues instead of my knee." She winked at Jaz.

"Not a chance. So, back to the subject. In shamanism, there is a theory that if we have a traumatic experience, the cells in our body store that memory."

Tyler looked thoughtful. "Pat already told me something similar. He left out the feathered shamans, though."

"Typical man. No sense of decoration or how to embellish a story." They both laughed. "If these memories are stored, sensory perceptions or movements can bring the feelings and memories of the trauma back to the surface. The stupid thing is that this way you're completely at the mercy of your feelings, and it's hard to do anything about them. That's why panic attacks are so hard to get a handle on."

"And now? Do I have to lie down in a sweat lodge? Take drugs or join a drum circle?"

Jaz smiled patiently. "Drums would make a nice musical background. In Hawaiian Huna shamanism, there's a theory that the actual trauma takes place at the end when you repeat and retrace what led to the trauma. That's how the information in the cells can be changed. Like the hard drive—"

"Of a computer, I know. Pat mentioned that, too. Sorry to ask this again, but what am I actually supposed to do now?"

"Isn't it obvious?" Jaz replied, "Jump."

Dumbfounded, Tyler looked at her. "I can't jump anymore!"

"You don't have to, physically. Let your mind do the jumping. Stop where the accident began. Do you remember the music you were dancing to? Which piece it was?"

"I had the solo part of *Blackbird* by the Beatles."

Jaz tapped away on her phone. "Let me bring it up for you."

Crap. Tyler was just about to say they'd have to wait until they could get the music. There went that excuse.

The opening guitar notes sounded. Sweet, simple guitar. Tyler felt her palms getting wet and her heartbeat accelerating again. What was wrong with her? She'd rehearsed this a thousand times and danced it almost as many times onstage.

"Just say out loud what you're going to do and hint at the dance."

Piece of cake. Why, then, did she feel sick to her stomach? Maybe Jaz was actually right and there was more to her accident than she had suspected until now. Maybe she would even remember more details. That would be something. She noticed how this thought spurred her on.

Tyler took a deep breath as Paul McCartney's voice began to sing and got into position.

"I don't dance at the very beginning. I come on just before the second verse."

Jaz let the music play, tapping her foot in time to the guitar.

As the familiar notes rang out, Tyler closed her eyes and let herself go with the music. Whatever happened, she couldn't give up the music. It was too much a part of her and made her blood sing. Mentally, she returned to that fateful day. She could feel her sheath dress around her body, the black crystals slightly scratchy as she positioned her arms. Quietly, she hummed along with the melody, inwardly counting the beats, tensing her body, ready to leap, when suddenly she was flooded with memories.

Backstage at the beautiful hotel theater. In the wings, muscular stagehands, all dressed in black, were tying up the invisible ropes that they had manipulated to fly her through the air. She was the last to pirouette off—a long dance move of perfect circles executed on one foot, *enpointe*. All the way across the stage, dip-circle, dip-circle, again and again. Just three more before reaching the curtain. Every muscle straining. Sweat pouring into the washable cotton lining of her headdress so never a drop could be seen by the audience.

OFF! Her foot unflexed flat to the floor and then— she lost the memory.

Her mind flashed to days before the performance. Yuri, who was never satisfied, berated them all, asking for more, more, more. He demanded endless rehearsals. The fatigue in her limbs was ever-present. The sobering realization dawned that perhaps what she had to give was not enough.

A scream came out of Tyler and she fell to the yoga mat, sobbing, sobbing. Like her heart was about to break.

CHAPTER ELEVEN

JAZ GASPED IN DISMAY. She hadn't expected this. Or maybe she had. For some reason, she had wanted Pat to be there. She shook her head, snapped out of her stupor, and hurried over to Tyler, who was shaking with sobs. Then she ran to the couch, where it was pushed back against the wall, and got her grandmother's knitted afghan off of it. She wrapped it around Tyler. "I'll be right back," she said to the blanketed form.

Hurrying out to the kitchen, Jaz made another tea, let it steep a little longer and added two teaspoons of honey. When she got back, Tyler had curled up into a little ball.

Jaz touched her gently on the shoulder. "Here. Drink this."

Tyler didn't stir.

Not knowing what else to do, Jaz set the cup of steaming tea on the floor, sat down beside it, and waited.

Tyler's voice, no more than a raspy whisper, said, "It was nobody's fault. No one. Just me, all by myself."

Jaz said nothing and let her talk. Now everything started to make sense. The harshness Tyler showed against her body. Her shame and wounded pride. But there was time for a full analysis later. For now, it was important that she calm down.

Tyler rubbed her face. Her hand was wet. Had she been crying? Still slightly dazed, she sat up. Her eyes fell on the tea and then on Jaz, who sat patiently beside her. "Sorry. You probably didn't expect such a breakdown."

Jaz just shrugged her shoulders. "When you start digging, you have to expect to find something. It usually takes a while to get to that point, though."

"At that nervous breakdown point? How nice!" She rescued the moment with sarcasm.

Jaz wisely recognized Tyler's feelings were too fresh and unprocessed for her to talk about them.

"I couldn't stay and watch the fall in my memory. I'm just not ready."

Jaz did not push her. "It's okay, you don't have to do all the work in one day." She lifted the mug of tea and pressed it into Tyler's hand. Then she helped her to the couch. For the next two hours, flanked left and right by dogs, she rested.

And then Paula called. She was on the road, coming home, and needed to talk. Urgently.

"Hello, anyone home?" Leaning on her cane, Tyler stood at the window and peered in. Ranger did the same. Since Paula's truck wasn't in front of the house, it was pretty unlikely she was inside. Not even Barns and Roo, Paula's blue heeler dogs, were here. She'd called from the road and wasn't home yet.

Paula was always out. Either in the barn or with the horses and goats in the pasture, or at the vet or the hardware store. The list could go on and on. Tyler sighed and plopped down on the bench on the porch. Late

October wasn't such appropriate weather to be waiting outside for someone. Riding the Ski-Thing in a full-face helmet behind a windshield was different. She shivered in the cold air and let her eyes wander over the adjacent pasture. Snowbanks drooped a bit in the midday sun.

Behind a group of trees, something moved. Tyler remained very still and tried to breathe as calmly as possible. Her patience was rewarded when a weasel stuck its nose in the air and sniffed before running like lightning across the white blanket of snow. She watched it go until it disappeared behind the corner of the house. A smile stole onto her face, and she exhaled deeply. She pulled her winter jacket tighter around her body.

The sound of an engine could be heard softly in the distance. Maybe Paula was coming home? Ranger also sat up straight and listened expectantly. The snow swallowed most of the sounds and prevented her from pinpointing the direction. But she was lucky. The truck that appeared in the distance belonged to her sister. It pulled into the driveway and Paula popped out.

"You won't believe it," were Paula's first words. "The Disney Sisters are fighting again. I didn't even get breakfast."

"No breakfast?!"

"No breakfast! I promised Leslie I'd go out and bring brunch back."

"Um, ever heard of cooking?" Tyler dared to interject.

"I don't have time to cook."

Tyler refrained from pointing out that now she had a child in the house, things had to change, but decided to ignore that for the time being and help with the problem Paula had called about. So she just said, "I agree with you."

"Are you volunteering for the job?"

O-o, time to retreat. That was not her intention at all. "No. But I could be persuaded to make breakfast for you while you keep me company." She offered, knowing that otherwise time would be wasted rushing after Paula if she wanted to talk to her.

"Why would you do that?" asked Paula with a frown. She let the dogs jump out of the truck. Barns and Roo greeted Ranger briefly, but soon left him standing when he made no move to follow their play prompts.

In her early days as a homesteader, Paula had often shown up at her parents' home in search of something to eat after barn chores. Tyler, who even then followed her rigorous training schedule and continually adjusted her food accordingly, had more or less taken over the cooking. She enjoyed it and it relieved the pressure on her mother, who was always grumbling about the complicated diet plans.

"What are you feeding Leslie?" inquired Tyler. Not to criticize her sister, but she just wondered.

"You mean what is Leslie feeding me," Paula corrected her and led the way into the house. As they walked into the kitchen, Leslie was beating eggs in a bowl and adding the necessary ingredients for pancakes. Flour, baking powder, salt, buttermilk. Ranger padded over and sat down next to the stove, waiting for something. Sure enough, Tyler set an egg out for him, which she put in an extra bowl. Greedily, he devoured it. Apparently, Barns and Roo didn't care for eggs.

"I'll be ready in a minute," Leslie crowed, shooing them out.

Paula led the way to the living room.

"How is everything else going?" Tyler asked. "Anything come up with Child Protective Services yet? Are you officially her foster mom now?"

"I wish. I'm still waiting for a friend of Jake's to call me back. She works for Child Protective Services in Denver and wanted to take an internal look. The lawyer I met with said he can't do anything for me until it's clear where Leslie's come from."

"Have you asked her about her parents?"

"It throws her into such fear I stopped asking." Paula's left hand traced a pattern on the couch cushions. "Honestly, I'm quite glad I haven't heard anything yet. As long as I don't hear anything, she stays with me. As difficult as it is sometimes, I can't imagine my life without Leslie."

"That was fast," Tyler remarked.

"You know me. All my strays have a place here. Whether it's a pony, a dog, or a girl. Except that I know a lot less about teenagers than I do about young dogs."

"It seems to be working out okay so far," Tyler replied.

From out in the kitchen came the sound of batter bubbling into a hot pan.

Paula's face brightened. "I think she's comfortable here."

"If you want, I can show her some breakfast recipes. I'm sure she'd be proud if she could do that for you."

"I don't know. She already feeds the horses in the morning."

"Then why don't you do it together? It's more fun with just the two of you, anyway. That way I get to know her and you don't run the risk of her talking your head off early in the morning. Afterwards, you do something else and she goes into the kitchen."

Weighing it all, Paula tapped her foot." That might not even be such a bad idea. Especially if the mood at the diner continues to be this bad. I'll try to reach either Mr. Wilkinson or Rose McArthy today. Maybe they'll have some idea of how we can reconcile the two of them."

"I'm sure Rose is a good start. Or better yet, talk to Miss Minnie and ask her how we can help."

The smell of pancakes cooking wafted under their noses.

"Better tell me what you called about," Tyler murmured. "I take it you don't want to talk about this in front of Leslie?"

"She won't go to school," Paula whispered. Her eyes grew misty. "I'm afraid if I force it, she'll run. But if I don't get her attending school, the authorities will remove her. I'm at my wit's end."

A childhood memory of Madame DuPont floated in front of Tyler's mind's eye. The marvelously calm teacher always spoke softly and made a crystal clear case for anything she wanted done by her students.

"What are you going to do?" Paula said in despair.

"I'm going to channel my inner ballet teacher," Tyler replied.

"You're what?!"

"Breakfast is ready!" came a call from the kitchen.

After eating, Tyler sat down with Leslie in the cozy living room to play with the dogs, while Paula muttered something that sounded suspiciously like "dang paperwork" and disappeared into the office. "Why aren't you in school today?" she inquired.

The girl hid behind her hair in embarrassment. "Once a week I get to stay home."

"Why is that? Why do you get to stay home?"

"When everything gets too much for me."

Tyler looked at Leslie's bowed head and thought about what had been said and what had not been said. Although she was in a situation that she would rather not talk about, she felt it was important for Leslie to talk about what "too much" meant.

"Oh? What was going on yesterday?"

"Nothing special. The usual."

This was worse than trying to find out from Santa Claus what time he was coming down the chimney. "I remember high school being pretty stressful. Do you struggle with studying?"

Leslie's head went up. Her eyes flashed angrily. "Why is it your business?"

Tyler raised her hands in surrender. "I've struggled enough times. Especially in math." Especially when she had danced more than she had studied, which was most of the time.

"Math is easy."

Maybe studies weren't where the problem lay. "Do the others tease you?"

After a brief hesitation, Leslie nodded. Restlessly, she plucked at her cuticles.

Tyler waited. With four siblings, she had learned the art of waiting. Often you learned more that way than by constantly asking.

"They're just joking and stuff. Laughing at my clothes."

Tyler glanced at Leslie's chore clothes. They weren't fancy, but they were for the homestead. Surely Paula didn't send her to school in the same jeans the girl had arrived in.

"I have some new clothes but..." Leslie made a pained face.

Tyler suddenly understood what this was all about. "But they are not the right clothes?"

Leslie looked to the side and nodded. "I'm new, wearing the wrong clothes, and I like math."

"Let's get that fixed," Tyler said. She fished out her phone and sent a text to Sarah, her agent. *Five swan tees in size small. Here's the address.* She typed out Paula's rural-route address. The T-shirts she had just ordered for Leslie were the hottest clothing item in the show store. A bird outlined in real crystals decorated a fitted cotton T-shirt. It came in five colors. Tyler ordered Leslie all five. They would look good over any jeans or leggings.

Tyler turned her phone around and showed Leslie a picture of them. The girl smiled gratefully. "I'll make sure they send them rush," Tyler said.

"Please don't tell Paula I don't like my clothes. Don't let her think I don't like it here. Spending all day here with the horses, with the dogs and the cows, it's heaven." Leslie trailed off and sighed.

Tyler decided to go for it and provoke her a little. "Then go ahead and stay home. It's not like Paula is your mother. Who needs school, anyway? There's plenty of work to do here on the homestead."

Leslie's eyes flashed again. "Are you crazy? Don't try that on me. It won't work." She jumped up and looked about to run.

"In that case, what do you want to be when you grow up?" Tyler asked.

Leslie stormed outside, slamming the door in the process.

Paula poked her head out of her office. "Now what was that?"

"Nothing. Your protégé is just suddenly acting like a typical teenager."

Paula rolled her eyes. "I hope you know what you're doing."

"It's a process. I think we made progress. It'll likely get worse before it gets better. But at least I got a few thought-provoking questions in. Let's wait and see." Dr. Tyler's sister-emergency visit was over. It was time to return to town.

CHAPTER TWELVE

TYLER LOCKED UP THE SKI-THING and helped Ranger out of the sidecar. She checked her phone. Still no callback from the clinic on a referral for prolotherapy. Eyeing the steps leading up the diner's front porch, she debated taking the dreaded cane. It was probably stupid to try and hide it. Everybody knew everything by now. She grabbed the cane and Ranger's leash.

A man pushed out the door and came down the steps. His body seemed tense, while his pale blue eyes seemed expressionless. Strange. The look didn't match his body language. As a dancer, she was used to observing expression and muscle tension. In Vegas, she wouldn't have looked twice. But in Independence, it was odd to see someone so detached. Before she knew what was happening, he stopped and put out his hand to shake hers. She fumbled, her hands were full of Ranger's leash and the cane.

"I'm sorry, don't bother," he said enthusiastically.

Do I know you? she thought. It didn't seem like a very polite thing to say to him. But if so, she couldn't think of where to place him in Independence. She tried a smile and said, "Nice to see you," while moving to go around. But he wouldn't move. An uneasy feeling in the pit of her stomach intensified. Ranger seemed to sense her tension. With a growl and ruffled hackles, he moved in front of

Tyler. The man moved aside. But Ranger made no move to calm down. Strange.

"Do we know each other?" she blurted out.

"No. Or should I say, not yet?" The man raised his eyebrows meaningfully before his gaze drifted back to the still-growling Ranger.

"I just meant because I'm here on vacation," he said. He pointed at a helmet he held in his hand. "Snowmobiling." He took another step back, away from the growling dog."

"I see." Her mind was frozen, but she kickstarted it with a cliché from Vegas. "Have a great time and stay safe." She simply couldn't think of anything more clever.

He nodded like a bobblehead and moved off.

The watcher felt so gleeful he wanted to sing and dance in the street. There was nothing so delicious as making an innocent connection with a victim, making them think he was *normal*. Sweat broke out on his forehead as he thought about the conversation. She had looked at him in wonder. That had been a wonderfully close call. It felt like he had a very private connection with her. He plucked at the cuticle of his left thumb until it bled. Fascinated, he stared at the red liquid. So beautifully red. Blood was fascinating. He stopped in front of the diner window and stared in. Maybe Miss Daisy had noticed him. Maybe a few diners were looking this way, out the window, wondering who that guy was who had held Miss Twirly Girl spellbound in a brief conversation.

No. Inside, they were all face-first in their plates of greasy food. Nothing of the sort had happened. He punched the windowsill. Really. He would have thought that by now they would treat him with the necessary respect. They would take him seriously. Well, the game wasn't over yet. If they couldn't give them the respect he deserved, he'd take it by force.

Pushing open the door to the diner, the odd, alert feeling from the encounter with the tourist outside reminded Tyler she had not done anything with the picture of the woman she'd snapped in the parking lot between the diner and the bed-and-breakfast. She let the door to the diner close while she stepped aside on the porch and fished for her phone. In a moment she texted the image to Cole with a note that said, *Saw this person looking at the bed-and-breakfast. Might be nothing, but wanted to send it.* She clicked *Send*.

Now she was more than ready for a cup of coffee. She went inside. There was a dead silence in the room that usually buzzed with activity, the clatter of dishes, and chatter. All the guests seemed to have stopped eating. Mr. Wilkinson, who was in the midst of telling a story, had paused, holding a full cup in front of his mouth without taking a sip. He looked embarrassed.

Behind the counter, the Disney Sisters faced each other with their arms crossed. Miss Minnie held a wooden rolling pin in her hand, while Miss Daisy pointedly leaned on a broom. For safety's sake, Tyler kept a generous distance from the bar and quietly sidled up to Mr. Wilkinson's table.

"What's going on here?" she whispered.

Without moving his mouth or otherwise making a face, Mr. Wilkinson replied, "Miss Daisy wants Miss Minnie to help her renovate the bed-and-breakfast. Apparently, Miss Minnie has been putting her off and sweeping a problem under the carpet for a while."

"But I thought Minnie cooked while Daisy ran the rest of the business."

"That's what we all thought."

"Isn't there anything we can do? Help her or something?"

"If only it were that easy," a voice piped up. It was Miss O'Toole. She was known to spend afternoons at the diner, tippling from a flask until she fell asleep in her chair. "We tried offering help, but they don't want to talk about it with customers."

"Don't want to talk about it seems to be a syndrome around here," Tyler murmured.

"You can't solve a problem without discussion," Mr. Wilkinson declared.

Miss O'Toole snorted under her breath. "Daisy said she didn't have anyone coming forward to bake pies for her. Why should Minnie need help?"

Tyler raised her eyebrows. "I'm sure that suggestion would have gone over well." Everyone here knew the wary eyes with which Miss Daisy guarded her pie recipes. It was a protective measure, so she could be sure of winning the annual county pie-baking contest.

"So what now? Do we wait for the showdown or what?" she added, irritated. "I'd really like a cup of coffee!"

Wordlessly, Miss O'Toole pushed a cup toward her. Tyler eyed the cup suspiciously and touched it. "That's cold."

Miss O'Toole just shrugged her shoulders.

Meanwhile, back at the sisterly stare down, Miss Daisy whipped off her apron and threw it over a stool. Then she marched out.

Mr. Wilkinson put down his coffee cup and said, "I've tried to mediate already. Nice try, but no cigar. Maybe you could wade in?"

A faint snore came out of Miss O'Toole, who now sat with her head tilted back against the booth, a mickey of bourbon peeking out of her purse.

"Come," said Tyler to Ranger. Then she got up and made her way toward the kitchen. Daisy tolerated no one in her kitchen. But since she'd just removed herself, the usual rules seemed suspended. The small-town tempest made Tyler chuckle softly to herself as she stuck her head into the kitchen. What she saw there made her stop laughing. Miss Minnie was sitting on a beverage crate, crying silently to herself.

Tyler said, "Stay," to Ranger and he flopped down one inch outside the entrance. Tyler continued into the kitchen. "Miss Minnie! What's the matter??"

The old woman wiped the tears from her face with erratic movements. "No, no. It's all right, child. Nothing for you to worry about."

Tyler raised an eyebrow meaningfully. "Oh, really?"

"It's not my fault my sister is suddenly on strike." Minnie crossed her arms in front of her chest and lifted her chin as if to challenge Tyler to contradict her.

"What did she say? Why, all of a sudden, doesn't she want to cook anymore?"

"It's so embarrassing!" Miss Minnie lowered her eyes. "We have martens in the attic. She was after me to get them out of there. I thought they'd just leave. But they didn't. There's even more of them now, and Daisy blames me. We're always so busy with the diner that somehow there's never enough time."

"Hmm. Couldn't we all help? Like we always do when someone needs help?"

"But it just feels wrong somehow," she replied, visibly embarrassed.

So there was the rub. "What if I get Paula to help me organize a relief committee?"

"Someone already suggested that. But Daisy doesn't want that either. Apparently, it's my job to get rid of the martens. As if I have any idea about that."

"Maybe there's another way to mobilize people. You could design a poster and put it in the big window by the street where everyone walks by."

Skeptically, Miss Minnie said, "What am I supposed to write on there? Marten removers wanted?"

"I have a suggestion. Just write: Help us relocate the marten family. Trap and release. Date, time, bring humane traps only, if you have them."

"It's a load off my mind," Miss Minnie said. "If this really works out, I'll be forever in your debt."

"Not at all," Tyler replied, adding jokingly, "We'll all be glad to have you back entertaining guests and Miss Daisy cooking for us." She pursed her lips for a moment. "Sisters are important. I have one too."

Miss Minnie nodded. "This disagreement has been hanging between us for so long that we just got lost. Me most of all," she admitted after a pause.

"Why don't you go after her now and tell her it's being organized? She can come back. Mr. Wilkinson and a few others out there can keep new patrons occupied with free coffee and a promise that the kitchen will be back in service in a few minutes. Would that work?"

Minnie brushed the last tear from her cheek. "That would."

Tyler gave her an encouraging smile and leaned in for a hug. "We love you, Minnie. And we love Daisy, too. I'll tell Jake and get him onboard. You'll be laughing about this when it's all over."

Minnie nodded, and another little sob of gratitude escaped.

Tyler left to walk through the dining room and collect Ranger. She waved goodbye to Mr. Wilkinson and exited. Then she crossed the street with Ranger and walked to the Ski-Thing. When they were only a few feet away, the dog got in her way and let out a low growl. Tyler felt a chill run down her spine. Not because she was afraid of the German shepherd, but because she knew he was showing this behavior for a reason. What was she supposed to do now? She scanned the area. No one was in sight. The snow muffled many everyday sounds. She tried to hear a crunch in the snow that would give a visitor away. Nothing.

Except for her choppy breathing, nothing could be heard. *Cole.* She would call Cole. Maybe he could tell her how to get Ranger to scout. She tapped his name and the cell phone started to dial. While waiting for a connection, she kept a close eye on the surroundings. The thought dawned that she should have insisted on a dog-handling tutorial. But of course, she didn't. She was the one that didn't even want the dog in the first place.

"Hello, brother dear," she greeted Cole when he picked up the phone.

"Tyler. Did something happen?"

"That's the thing. I'm not sure. I'm about to mount the Ski-Thing, but your super dog got in front of me and started growling. I suppose I could call Joe's Snow Removal for a lift, but I'd like to know why Ranger's making such a fuss. I can't see anyone. Is there any way to send the dog on reconnaissance?"

"If he's acting like that, there's definitely something wrong. You just need to signal him to go. *Go* or *run* or *search* should be enough. It doesn't matter if he doesn't know the command. He will definitely hear your agreement to go. And he knows his job in his sleep."

"Okay, I will."

"Where are you?"

"Right across from the diner. It's pretty public."

"Good, and don't forget to call Jake."

She murmured in agreement and ended the conversation.

"Run," she said to Ranger, pointing in the direction of the Ski-Thing. Immediately he ran, once around the bike, until he scratched in the snow, then sat down and barked twice. Had he found something? Uncertainly, she glanced at the phone she still held in her hand. Should she alert Jake now? It seemed unnecessary, really. It was obvious that what Ranger had found wasn't a person. Otherwise, she would see them.

She glanced over her shoulder. The diner was just across the street. Good. With diners as an audience in the background, surely nothing would happen to her there. She approached Ranger with restrained with steps. He was still sitting patiently in the same spot where he had scratched in the snow earlier, right next to the left rear tire. She still couldn't make out what it was. But right up next to him, she saw. In the snow lay a large crow feather. It stood out and glared against the white snow. Almost impossible to miss. Like it had been planted there.

As she fought an internal debate over whether or not to call Jake, the wail of a police siren startled her. Was it Jake in his sheriff's vehicle? Of course, Cole knew she might not call him. So he had called for her. Now she would get another scolding. *Just great!* Still, she felt more anger than fear. Fear was already lurking in the background. But she would not let it get the upper hand. She braced herself for the telling off she was about to receive from her big brother.

Sure enough, the black and white braked, lights flashing, and Jake came out. But to her astonishment, he walked over and simply took her in his arms without a word. She blinked back a few tears that suddenly stood in her eyes.

"Cole called you?" she asked.

Jake nodded. "Sure. Who else?"

Tyler fiddled with her cell phone, trying to ignore the situation.

"Take a picture of that," Jake said, pointing to the feather.

She did, and then he pulled out a plastic bag, bent down, and put the feather in the bag. "Were you just going to bury it under the snow?" he asked.

Guilty, she looked away.

He gave a short laugh. "You underestimate your brothers. Don't you remember burying Mom's broken glass bowl in the sandbox?"

"Oh, that."

"Those were the days, huh? In any case, I know you, little sister. I know you prefer to disbelieve potential danger."

She snorted and sighed. "Ranger was with me and did his job excellently."

"He did. He knows a feather isn't supposed to be there, and he knows he's supposed to be protecting you, so he's calling out anything out of the ordinary."

"Kinda ordinary for Vegas," she said.

"Not ordinary for Independence," he shot back.

As Jake got back in his SUV and waved goodbye, a text came on her cell phone. She gave it a quick peek. It was from the medical clinic in Breckenridge. *Please call ASAP for an important message.*

Tyler and Pat sat across from a relatively young female doctor. The minute Tyler had called the clinic, she called Pat to ask if he could possibly drive her to Breckenridge for a consultation at the medical center. Unfortunately, they had bad news. She was not a candidate for prolotherapy. The problem in her knee was beyond that.

The young female doctor introduced herself as Dr. Trent. Basically, she made a very competent impression on Tyler. But she was careful not to rush to judgment. After all, this was about her knee. And about the possibility of an operation, which she wanted to avoid at all costs until a few hours ago. But as it was, she had no other choice.

The doctor hesitated for a moment. She seemed to be searching for the right words. "We can replace the torn ligaments without any problems. But the surrounding cartilage, especially the meniscus, has also been affected. The cartilage is what cushions the pressure on the bones during high stress."

"But that's what the alternative therapies do," Tyler protested. "They can rebuild some of the cartilage and provide relief."

"That's true," the doctor said sympathetically. "But it's usually not enough for elite sports."

The painful look on Tyler's face caught Pat's eye. He looked as miserable as if the news were for him.

The doctor continued, "The pressure on the bone will remain very painful during certain movements or peak loads. Granted, our experience here in Colorado is more about skiing. But I think it's comparable in terms of demands on the body. You know the enormous strain of ballet. Even with a completely healthy knee, the hard training is extremely demanding."

Tyler sank back into her chair. Everything the doctor said sounded frighteningly correct. But until now, she had not wanted to face facts. "Why should I operate at all?" she asked. "After all, there is also the opinion that with specific training, the muscles will take over the job of the cruciate ligaments. Why not wait and see first?"

Dr. Trent was not fazed under the attack-style question. "That's your decision, of course. But in our experience, the chance of recovery is greatest if you act as quickly as possible. Often the knee doesn't stabilize despite the proper training and you have to deal with late effects. I'm sure that's something you want to avoid."

Tyler took a deep breath and plunged into the proverbial deep end. "All right. For once, let's say I decide to have the surgery. What is the procedure and the healing process?"

Pat, who had sat silently by until now, squeezed her hand encouragingly. He had not interfered once, to his credit. After he had pushed her so hard to make the appointment, she hadn't expected that.

The doctor showed her how to find an online brochure and explained the procedure. "Physical therapy is a must and starts almost immediately after surgery, once the swelling has gone down. This is a degenerative condition, and the sooner we get the joint moving again, the better. However, without overdoing it. The doctor put emphasis on the word without. I know exactly what makes you athletes tick. If it doesn't hurt, it's not good enough."

Tyler exchanged a knowing look with Pat.

Dr. Trent asked, "Like to make an appointment?"

"What, right now?"

"Or, if you prefer, call in a few days."

Relieved, Tyler exhaled. "Good, I'll be in touch." Maybe that was cowardly, but she just wasn't ready to make a decision this minute. "And thank you for taking the time on such short notice."

The doctor shrugged. "If there are no surgeries coming up or no emergencies coming in, it's not a problem." At that moment, her beeper went off. "Like right now, for example. Just check in when you're ready."

The doctor said goodbye with a professional handshake and hurried out the door.

Pat watched her go and then said in a low voice, "So, what are you thinking?"

A sigh came out of her in a whoosh. "I've hardly digested what just happened." Her blue eyes went metallic gray, like the sky before a thunderstorm.

He raised his hands in a backing off gesture.

She brushed a strand of hair from her face and tucked it behind her ear. Her displeasure faded as quickly as it had come. "It would be nice if something would move forward," she admitted. "From the way Dr. Trent explained it, I think the chance for healing is more likely with surgery. Even though the thought of it is..." She expelled a ragged breath. "Stasis or progress. Or rather, limping or being able to walk."

"Want to ask about possible dates at the front desk?"

"Might as well get it over with." She reached for her cane.

CHAPTER THIRTEEN

COLE BLINKED AT HIS PHONE. He was out driving in the snow, returning to his parents' homestead, and a text had just come in. He should really pull over to look at it. He wished he were back in Independence just for the fun of it. At least then he could curl up under the covers in the spare room and sleep for the next few hours, or even days. But he was just finishing up a day or two of paperwork before he could rest and relax.

His eyes burned with fatigue and the effort of keeping the truck steady on black ice. That's what they called invisible but very slippery conditions in Independence. The warm, dry air from the heater did the rest. He turned into the driveway of the homestead. For a moment, the tires lost traction. He took his foot off the gas and waited for them to grip again. Fortunately, the truck was four-wheel drive. Traction kicked in and took him up the driveway.

The local snowplow hadn't made it to the house yet and since his siblings all owned all-terrain vehicles, no one found it necessary to shovel the road clear on their own. He turned off the engine and leaned his head against the back of the seat, holding up his phone to see the picture that had just come in. It was from Tyler. She had seen the woman in the photo at night, illuminated by the parking-lot lights. She was checking out the bed-and-breakfast.

Cole squinted at the photo and enlarged the face. *What the*—he recognized that person! That was Avery Swiftwater, a profiler from the FBI. They had taken some courses together. He would know that long blue-black hair, a reminder of Native American heritage somewhere along the way, and exotic dark eyes, anywhere. *What the heck was another FBI agent doing in Independence?*

Cole reached for his duffel bag in the back seat and jammed the laptop under his arm. He braced himself against the cold air and got out of the car. Although the distance from the car to the house was only a few yards, the wind chilled him to the bone. He fumbled with the keys, squeezed through the crack in the door to let in as little cold air as possible, and once inside, leaned back against the door and pushed it shut.

Soon, the house was filled with the smell of burning wood from the fireplace and homemade soup with sausages. The soup was courtesy of Brenda Carter, his mother, who always had a freezer full of prepared foods made with her own hands. She and his dad were still away. Cole glanced at Avery's picture on his phone again. Maybe he should call this in to Jake. It was Jake's jurisdiction as sheriff of Independence, and he had to be careful not to overstep bounds. That being said, citizens were always encouraged to help the police with information, and Cole was still a citizen, even though he was employed by the FBI.

"Cole, what's up?" Jake took the call as soon as he saw it was his brother.

Jake was sitting with his assistant, Polly Miners, who had once been a police officer. Now, at sixty-seven, she no longer worked active duty. But Polly was not cut out for retired life. Two weeks after retiring, she had shown up at the police station with the words, "Either you give me a job here again, or you'll have to lock me up in that cell back there soon. For premeditated murder."

Jake suspected Polly's failed retirement had something to do with being at home all day with her also-retired husband, Fred. He rehired her on the spot. Not because of the dramatic threat, but because he would no longer have to deal with so much tedious paperwork. Polly was worth her weight in gold in that respect. The only thing she couldn't do was make coffee. As a former policewoman, she made a brew that was just as undrinkable as the rest of the troop's.

Today, Polly was poring over a stack of letters that had overnighted from Tyler's agent in Las Vegas. Links of various social media boards had come in via email, and Polly was busy cross-referencing anything that looked promising.

Jake turned his attention to Cole's call.

"Are you using a profiler on any cases, by chance?"

Jake made a face into the phone. "No, why?"

"There's one in town. A very good one."

"Suppose there's a chance she's on vacation?"

Cole gave a sarcastic laugh. "Like me, you mean? Just in little old Independence for a sightsee?"

Jake gave his own rueful laugh. "What are you getting at?"

"We already suspect these Tyler incidents are connected to her show. The show is in Las Vegas. Those guys who shot you in the shoulder last summer were mob-connected to Vegas."

"We already figured this latest stuff isn't their style. They'd have installed some lead air-conditioning into whoever they're after by now."

"Yes, that's what we said. But now there's an FBI profiler in town."

Jake looked at Polly who was on alert that something was happening with this phone call. "You said you know this profiler? Why don't you ask her?"

"I could do that unofficially. Just don't want to overstep into your jurisdiction, bro."

Jake gave a sigh of relief. "I appreciate that. Find out what you can. Do you even know where he's staying?"

"She. I assume at the bed-and-breakfast."

"Good place to start. While I've got you..." Jake put the phone on mute for a moment. "Polly, have you found anything?"

Polly had a short stack of printed emails from Tyler's Las Vegas agent in front of her. She was making notes.

"Nothing, yet, Sheriff," she said. "A couple of the emails I found significant but none of them really fit with the black-feather incidents in Independence."

Jake clicked the phone off mute. "If only we had a profiler, huh? What do you say, Polly? Would a profiler be helpful?"

On the other end of the line, Cole heard perfectly. "Ten-four, big brother. I'll report back."

The watcher kept his eyes trained on the police station. Good. They were paying due attention to his actions. It had started snowing again. But he didn't notice the cold. Feverish excitement gripped him. He needed to go back to the diner where there was Wi-Fi. Where, hunkered over coffee at the least desirable table, he could fire up his tablet and edit the images he had already collected online with the video he'd shot in Breckenridge. Everything was ready. Now all he needed was Internet reception. With a cold glint in his eyes, he turned the snowmobile around and drove away.

At the Wilkinson house, he pulled to one side and surveyed the house. The Cadillac was gone, no workmen were here at this time. He pulled the keys out of the snowmobile, leaving it partially hidden in some trees. Then he walked across the road and up to the side of the house where heavy tarpaulins heaved and sighed in the air currents. He felt around and loosened a tie on the tarp. Then he slipped through the side. A plastic cover over the open window casing was easy to slip through. That was it. He was in.

The watcher gently slid his feet to the floor of the bathroom and listened. He heard nothing but the sounds of an empty house. His bar of soap had been used. By the Vegas Twirly Slut. For some reason, Mr. Fix-It's bathroom wasn't good enough for her. But his was, imagine that!

He picked up the bar of soap and smelled it. There was nothing of her left on the bar. Disappointingly, she had rinsed it off after use. Miss Blackbird was using *his* shower. He felt like one of the three bears after Goldilocks intruded.

A few hours later, Cole heard back from the unofficial inquiries he'd sent out. There was no reason for an FBI profiler to be working in Independence. He'd even gotten a pal in HR to confirm that Avery Swiftwater was on a well-deserved vacation. This called for the old bull-by-the-horns approach.

The bed-and-breakfast had a common room where fresh drinking water and coffee were always laid out for guests. When Cole entered, Mr. Wilkinson was chatting with a few tourists. They were full of questions about Independence, and Colorado in general. The old fellow was only too happy to oblige. At one break in the conversation, Mr. Wilkinson noticed Cole.

"Hey there, son. Aren't you a Carter?"

"Yes, sir, I am. Good to see you. I was wondering if I could ask a question."

"Anything. Shoot."

"Just unofficial, you understand. I'm not here on any business..."

Mr. Wilkinson had a gleam in his eye, Cole noticed. The old fella didn't know what was coming, but something was coming by golly!

The tourists let themselves out and were on their way.

Cole pulled out his phone. "I wonder if you happened to see this person in your travels." He showed the old man the picture of Avery snapped right outside.

"Hmmm, well now," Mr. Wilkinson stammered.

It wasn't like him to hem and haw. Cole's antenna went up immediately.

"My eyesight isn't so good anymore these days," he continued. "Got something a little more—"

"Yes, he's seen me," a voice rang out.

Cole looked up. Avery Swiftwater stood there in the flesh. Long, blue-black hair, a reminder of her Native American heritage, exotic dark eyes and full lips. She was tall and slender and had made quite an impression on him a few years ago. That impression was flooding back right now in a big way.

"I remember you from Quantico," she said. "But I don't recall your name. Wait, yes I do, it's Cole."

Mr. Wilkinson looked relieved.

"Do you want to tell him why I'm here?" Avery said to the older gent.

"I don't mind if you don't," Mr. Wilkinson said. "I suppose now is as good a time as any." He gestured at a couch and some overstuffed chairs. "Take a seat, Cole. Help yourself to a cup of coffee. Avery and I have quite a story to tell."

At that moment there was an odd scratching and squeaking over their heads.

Cole jumped to his feet, ready to act.

"That's the marten family," Avery laughed.

"It can't be. There's no second floor on this place," Cole answered.

"It's a family of weasels. Martens. In the attic. That's what Daisy and Minnie are having their argument over. They're looking for help to trap them and relocate them to a new home."

Cole let go with a surprised laugh.

"There's a sign-up sheet at the diner," Mr. Wilkinson urged. "Do it before you leave."

"I will."

Avery took a seat next to Mr. Wilkinson and took his hand. "Tell him."

Mr. Wilkinson enclosed her hand in his. He smiled into her eyes tenderly.

Cole could hardly believe his eyes. Avery and a man three times her age? When did this happen? *How did this happen?*

Mr. Wilkinson turned to Cole with his hand still entwined with Avery's.

She had a slight blush in her cheeks, with her eyes downcast.

Cole felt a lump rise in his throat. The strong reaction took him by surprise.

When Mr. Wilkinson leaned over and gave Avery a peck on the cheek, it was all Cole could do to keep his face from falling.

"Avery is my long-lost great granddaughter," Mr. Wilkinson announced.

If Cole hadn't been sitting down, he might have fallen on the floor.

Mr. Wilkinson continued, "My son was estranged. He passed away years ago. I never knew he had a child. And then his child had a child. I've been sitting up in that old house alone for many years since my wife died. I heard about those DNA sites that match you up and decided to try my luck. Who knew who might show up? Well, Avery did. I am so happy to have her in my life."

Well. Now Cole knew what an FBI profiler was doing in Independence. Nothing to do with police work of any kind. Not wanting to interrupt family matters, Cole made some small talk about the martens, Mr. Wilkinson's renovation, and the weather. Then he excused himself. Outside, he noticed a marten leap gleefully out of the dumpster behind the diner, skip over the yard to the foundation of the bed-and-breakfast, and disappear.

The Next Morning

"Tyler!"

Pat's voice rang through the house. Tyler was immediately awake, rather disoriented, and jumped out of bed in one leap. *Ouch*. Her knee did not appreciate the cold morning start. Ranger was faster, barking at the door like a maniac. Should she try to calm him down? Better not, she decided. As long as she didn't know what was going on out there, it was better to sound like she had a bloodthirsty beast in the room. Vaguely, she remembered that Ranger had been acting strangely last night. When they came home, he had growled. She'd entered the old house with an uneasy feeling. But there was no one they could find, even though the dog had led Pat all over the house. They chalked the dog's tension up to their own.

Surgery was scheduled in three days. That would give them both time to join in on helping Minnie and Daisy with their problem in the attic before Tyler had to be admitted to the hospital.

After searching the home, she and Pat had settled down and forgotten about it. Ranger, on the other hand, had not been able to rest properly at all. Again and again she had called him to her, half asleep. After a few hours he had jumped on the bed and laid down next to her. But he had not relaxed immediately. For a long time he stared vigilantly at the door with pricked ears. She must have fallen asleep at some point.

At that moment, the door flew open, interrupting her drowsy train of thought. Pat rushed into her room, wild-eyed and clad only in his boxers. Tyler shrieked. She had no pajamas on! Not so much as a sleeping T-shirt. As much as she wanted to enjoy the feel of Pat's bare skin on hers again as soon as possible, she felt uncomfortable without clothes on.

She frantically reached for her blanket to cover herself in and promptly got tangled up. Head first, she fell against Pat's chest. He caught her, and she found herself pressed stark naked against his equally naked chest. Before she could stop herself, she sank a little more against him and took a deep breath. She just couldn't get enough of the way he smelled. Slightly of sandalwood, of Pat, and a little of just-woke-up. Heavenly. Only slowly did the rest of her senses start working again. That's why it took a while for Pat's voice to get through to her. He held her like he never wanted to let go, murmuring something into her hair.

"What did you say?"

"I've never been so happy to see you as I am right now!"

Assuming that his statement was nothing more than a reaction to her unclothed state, she rolled her eyes. "The next time you feel the need to see me naked, why don't you try a simple 'please, undress now'? Or better yet, 'kiss me.' As we know, there's a high chance that I'll lose my clothes sooner or later in the process." Spoken out loud like that, it sounded a little embarrassing, but didn't change the facts. "No need to rush into my room, Tarzan-like. It upsets my dog."

He leaned back a little to look her in the face. He stroked a strand of hair behind her ear. Fleetingly, she thought about what her hairstyle looked like. But then she decided that at—she turned sideways to glance at the alarm clock next to her bed—seven in the morning, she didn't give a hoot. Her hand was still on his chest. Only now did she notice that his heart was still beating much too fast. She met his gaze.

"What's wrong?" she asked, suddenly serious.

Instead of answering her, he exhaled deeply and pulled her back into his arms. "Jake called."

The seriousness of his voice sent a shiver down her spine. She pushed against his chest with her hands until he released her. She kicked aside the bedspread on the floor and grabbed a sports bra and black leggings from beside the bed. Clean socks and a Colorado Avalanche sweatshirt completed her outfit. Ranger, calm by now, squeezed past Pat, who was standing in the doorway. Pat just stood there silently, watching her get dressed with a worried look on his face, as if he didn't dare let her out of his sight for even a second.

"Coffee?" he said.

"No," she answered more sharply than intended. A bit more friendly, she added, "Otherwise, I'm imagining the most horrible things. Is everyone all right? Is something wrong with my family?"

"Everyone is fine," he hastened to assure her.

"Why wouldn't I be fine?"

Pat pulled out his phone. "Jake sent me the link for this. It's not a pretty sight."

Her stomach contracted.

"Click play," Pat instructed.

Over a midnight background, the first guitar notes of *Blackbird* started up. Still photos from her very first show flashed past in a slideshow. It was all beautiful, nothing was out of place.

"It's very nice," she said,

"Keep watching," he answered.

The theme song ended and there was the sound of nails scratching on a chalkboard. Tyler winced. Up came a video of a Breckenridge parking lot. The camera zoomed in on an old Cadillac, and then on a bloody crow spread-eagled on the window. The video showed everything from Tyler's arrival, to the car, to her gruesome find, to when she threw up afterward. It was all there.

"That's sick. Where did Jake get this?"

"It debuted on TikTok, then it got banned. Then it got picked up by alternative sites and fans caught wind of it. It went viral even though it's going up, getting banned, and taken down."

"It just pops up somewhere else, you mean?"

"Yeah, like that."

"Does Jake know who made it?"

"Likely the same person who did the dead crow in the first place."

"Is it possible some teenager saw it and filmed it, like everyone films everything now, and then posted it online to look cool in front of his buddies?"

"Possible. Jake's having Polly Miners look into it."

"Why is this happening?" Tyler whispered angrily. She brushed away a tear. "I have to call Sarah. She's going to be so mad at me! How could I bring this down on the show and everyone?"

Pat watched with wide eyes as she ran for her own phone and then dialed in front of him.

"Do you want me to leave?"

"No. I need you beside me."

Sarah picked up on the first ring. "TYLER!"

"Sarah, I'm so sorry—" Tyler could imagine her agent in the New York office, staring out over Manhattan.

"Darling! The video is selling tickets for us like they're ice cream on the Fourth of July! Did you post this, you clever little thing?"

"No, I—"

"We've been communicating with your brother, the sheriff. Sending him icky fan mail, that sort of thing. The story's developing into a whole 'damsel in distress, star in turmoil' thing online."

"What story? Oh no!"

"Isn't it wonderful?! Look, it's awful, I know that. But there's still no threat being made to your personal well-being and safety, as the sheriff points out. It's the best of both worlds! All this lovely publicity!"

"He wants us to take every precaution, but he wants you to go on living your life, too. Isn't that what you want?"

"Yes," she choked.

Pat whispered, "Surgery? Tell her about the—"

"Sarah, I have to go," Tyler said abruptly, and cut the line. "Not yet," she said to Pat. "I can't face that with her right now."

"Coffee, then," said Pat, and led her back to his bedroom where a freshly brewed pot waited.

Tyler stayed silent as Pat poured two mugs.

"I need to get my mind off everything for a little bit," she said. "Can you divert me?"

Pat made a face. "Divert you?"

"Tell me a story. Tell me anything, maybe about yourself. Just to get my mind off it?"

"You want to get your mind off it," Pat ruminated as he sipped at his steaming mug. Tyler took a seat on the edge of the bed and patted Ranger into a sitting position.

"I'm going to tell you a happy story," he said. "So, after my troubles were over from my younger days, they sent me from Brooklyn to Seattle. An unofficial foster father, a guardian, was there. Dante was Italian, and he'd spent a lot of time in Asia. He took one look at my puny physical appearance and shook his head while muttering something about a lot of work. You can imagine my excitement."

"O-o. Not exactly a smooth start, was it?"

"You can say that again. Dante kept me busy with kitchen duty, helping around the house, checking my homework, studying with me for school, and training with me. He was a master in aikido and made it really clear I was not a master of anything. I would stand in his dojo at five-thirty every morning and curse him."

Tyler was listening intently.

"There was a problem with stealing at school and I was blamed. Kids were being pickpocketed. Dante was warned by the principal that if it didn't stop, I would be punished for it. To his credit he stayed calm and every morning he still gave me lunch money. I keep getting my pockets picked, too. And finally he gets called to the school, and the principal wants to kick me out. So Dante just asked for one thing before that happened. He asked if the class could show him their money. The principal didn't know what was up, but he was okay with it. So the kids pulled out their bills and coins and put them on their desks. Dante pulled out a little flashlight, it's a black light, and he walked around shining the light on the bills and coins. You see, he had marked my money every day before giving it to me. And sure enough he got to one kid, a real slippery little liar, and a message showed up. It said: 'This money belongs to Patrick West.' The principal was astounded 'cause this kid was one of her favorites. She'd been played. The whole time, Dante was very polite. He didn't raise his voice once. That was the moment I decided to give this thing with Dante an honest chance. As soon as we were outside, he put me in a headlock and whispered in my ear, 'You better always be telling the truth. If not, then you'll really get to know me.' From then on, I trained hard and studied for school. In time, we became best friends."

Tyler blinked at him. "It probably wasn't easy, though, was it?"

Pat flashed his handsome smile. "Dante had a big heart and strict principles. Aikido helped me channel excess energy and use it constructively. My thoughts became clearer and my heart didn't feel so heavy about my wrecked family and my wrecked past." Pat grimaced. "How corny that sounds when I say it out loud."

She moved closer and put an arm around him.

"All I know is I'm glad you told me."

"Feel better now? Got your mind off problems for a minute?"

"Yeah." She slid her arm off his shoulder. "I think I'll make an appointment as soon as they can take me."

"For surgery? Wow."

"And since that won't be today, let's go to the B and B to relocate the marten family."

CHAPTER FOURTEEN

THE BED-AND-BREAKFAST BUILDING stood two hundred yards from the diner, built into the hillside. It was a wooden house with a barn-shaped roof and a big, glassed-in common room for guests in the front, decorated with carvings, artwork, and textiles from Colorado's storied past.

At ten a.m. Nate Bale, the local vet, arrived at the bed-and-breakfast with humane traps. Pat was there to show him possible exit and entry places where the martens were sure to pass by and notice the trap. A selection of local people and tourists with kids staying at the B and B had gathered to help out.

"All we need is some delicious bait to lure Mr. and Mrs. Marten in," Nate said.

"And what bait might that be?" Miss Daisy asked.

"Chicken gizzards, liver, anything from a fish," Nate answered.

"Yuck!" Leslie exclaimed.

"Comin' up," Miss Daisy answered, and bustled off to the diner kitchen in search of just the right items.

"Once we get these traps set, all we have to do is leave them and check back now and then. We can keep the family at my animal hospital and relocate them as a group."

"But will they be safe?" a young tourist said anxiously.

Nate nodded reassuringly. "They'll be taken to a new home with plenty of natural food. It will probably be healthier and fresher for them than eating out of the diner dumpster."

"It looks like there's nothing else to be done," the young tourist added.

Well, Miss Minnie has the coffee on and a platter of goodies set out in the common room. Why don't we go inside and socialize?" Ned looked from face to face.

"Ned, why don't you tell us about martens?" someone said helpfully.

Everyone filed inside and Ned stood at the front. "A pine marten is a weasel about the size of a cat. They normally live in trees, so the attic of the bed-and-breakfast just feels like a super-roomy treehouse to them."

A chuckle rippled through the crowd. They were drinking coffee and nibbling pastries, waiting for the action to start. The marten rescue was the best show in town.

"Martens even have fur on the soles of their feet," Nate continued. "It keeps them warm and has a snowshoe effect so they can scurry across the top of snow. It's like they're wearing snowshoes."

"How do you think they got in the attic?" a boy asked.

"Females give birth in late March and April. They can have up to five babies called kits. Mama found an entrance somehow and since they like to live in trees, made her way to the attic."

Pat chimed in, "As soon as we're sure all the martens are out, my crew will be sealing all the possible entrances and exits to the building, so this doesn't happen again."

And with that, there didn't seem to be much else to say or do until one of the traps activated. But Mr. Wilkinson was not one to let a good audience go to waste. He strode to the front of the common room and swept off his big western hat. "My great granddaughter is here visiting, and she is half Ute Indian. Would anyone like to hear a bit more about the Ute tribe right here in Colorado?"

Cheers went up.

Avery shook her head. "Grandpa, no."

"You're precious, Avery. There are less than 10,000 Ute people left in Colorado and Utah. We want to hear what you have to say."

Pleased, Avery smiled at the people in the room. She shyly joined her great grandfather. "The Utes were hunter-gatherers who roamed, fishing and hunting all over this region and into Wyoming, Oklahoma, and beyond. My ancestors on my mother's side were skilled warriors known for daring maneuvers on horseback."

She pointed to a nearby portrait of a chief and his family on the wall. "In fact, I see Minnie and Daisy have some pictures of the Utes in this room." In the picture, two babies were swaddled in deerskin papooses so their mothers could carry them on their backs. "The Ute people fasted, participated in sweat lodge ceremonies, and painted their faces and horses with symbols that had spiritual meaning."

THWACK!

The sound of a trap door closing right outside interrupted Avery's fascinating talk.

"I think we got our first marten," Nate said.

The children present got up and rushed to the window to see what they could see. Sure enough, one little marten was in the trap, enjoying a tasty snack of fish guts.

"Hey, a pine marten looks a lot like a cat," one of the kids said.

"Look at his little ears," another said. "He's got a face like our Tibby. Let's go pat him."

"That's true," said Nate. "But you can't treat them like cats because they're not tame. They're wild animals and they bite."

"He looks like he has soft fur, though," the child said wistfully.

"True, buddy. Very soft fur. Very sharp teeth."

By late afternoon, six martens had been humanely captured and taken to the vet hospital. From there, they would be relocated as a family several miles away on forested land with plenty of wild food.

Minnie and Daisy arrived to send everyone home or back to their rooms with bags of take-out food.

Pat promised to show up the next day for a final inspection. Paula and Leslie left with Ranger since Tyler was going in for surgery the next day.

Back at the Wilkinson house, Pat and Tyler sat on the floor in front of a big oak coffee table and dove into the bag of food. Neither of them wanted to remind the other that by tomorrow morning Tyler would be in surgery. They ate lasagna and salad in silence. When they had finished, Pat moved closer. He felt an urgency to be close to her. To feel that she was alive, that they were both alive and had a new chance. He put all his feelings into his touch, his kiss. She let out a soft whimper of pleasure as his teeth dug into the sensitive skin at the nape of her neck.

Breathing heavily, he instantly let go of her, thinking he had hurt her. "Wait, your knee! We shouldn't."

"Yes! We definitely should," she replied, looking at him under half-closed lids before grabbing him by his shirt and pulling his lips to her once more. This felt so good. But she needed more. She wanted his skin on her skin. To feel his body sliding over hers. She needed him so much that she almost forgot to breathe.

"Are you sure?"

She nodded. She had no time to speak. The velvety skin over his collarbone was too tempting.

Relief flooded through him. Of course, he would have taken her condition into consideration and stopped. But he was very glad that there was no need to do so.

"Then do it properly," she said.

With one fluid movement, he lifted her up and carried her into the bedroom.

I could get used to this, Pat thought, as Tyler slipped away from him an hour later. He watched her hop into his bathroom with her bandaged knee and actually manage to keep her composure while doing so. Something had been different today. He felt closer to her somehow. Not just because of the wonderful start to the night. How she had snuggled up to him afterwards, trusting him. He had the feeling that they had been heading for this point for quite some time. Or at least he had. He wasn't so sure about her. *Just ask her*, his inner voice said knowingly. *Yeah. Sure.* For once, he had to agree with her. That would only be reasonable. How else was he going to find out? But the fact was, he was afraid of her answer. What if she didn't feel the same way? He had learned a long time ago not to ask questions where he wasn't sure he wanted to hear the answer.

And what if she returned his feelings? Would he simply say, "Honey, of course I love you. Now pack your things and come with me wherever I go while I pursue my dream job?" He could imagine how that would go down: not well at all. If he were honest, he didn't want that either. He wanted her to pursue her dreams and be happy. Sure, preferably with him. But he wasn't so presumptuous as to think he could make her happy with his mere existence alone. *Crap.* Why was everything always so complicated?

At that moment, Tyler stepped out of the bathroom. Wrapped only in a scanty towel, she managed to drive all the dull thoughts out of his head. Suddenly, it no longer seemed important to him what projects he would be working on. As long as she was there to share his life with him, it just felt right.

THE NEXT MORNING

No breakfast, no coffee. Tyler's hair was tucked into a bonnet and she lay on a gurney at the medical center, ready for the operating room. Pat had dropped her off and would be back when visiting hours started. She had been given a pre-anesthetic, and all that was left was for the anesthesiologist to do his number and put her out. While she waited, Tyler thought about her time in meditation at Jaz's house. She had cut off the memory of her fall right after the dance, hadn't allowed it to play out. But if someone had pushed her, that's where the memory would reveal that person.

Her phone was the last thing they were going to take away from her. She still had it on the gurney with her. She searched for the *Blackbird* song and pressed "play."

The opening guitar notes sounded. Sweet, simple guitar. She felt her palms getting wet and her heartbeat accelerating again. Paul McCartney's voice began to sing, and she felt herself get into position to enter the stage in Las Vegas.

As the familiar notes rang out, Tyler closed her eyes and let herself go with the music. She could feel the sheath dress around her body. The black crystals shimmered as she positioned her arms. A little shake of her head set the shiny black feathers of her elaborate headdress quivering. Quietly, she hummed along with the melody, inwardly counting the beats, tensing her body, ready to leap, when suddenly she was flooded with memories.

Backstage at the beautiful hotel theater, muscular stagehands all dressed in black tied up the invisible ropes that they had manipulated to fly her through the air. Tyler was the last to pirouette off—a long dance move of perfect circles executed on one foot, enpointe. All the way across the stage, dip-kick-turn, dip-kick-turn, again and again. Just three more before reaching the curtain. Every muscle straining. Sweat pouring into the washable cotton lining of her headdress so never a drop could be seen by the audience.

OFF! Her foot unflexed flat to the floor and then she was out of sight of the audience. She ran toward the arms of her dresser, who would remove the headdress and accessories and whisk her into the next costume. As she hurried forward, she felt something click in her knee. A little glitch. And the next thing she knew, the floor was under her hands. She immediately popped back up. It had happened in a split second.

"Whoopsie," she called out in a stage whisper, keeping her voice very light and nonchalant. A stagehand rushed to where she had slipped and examined the place. Another followed with paper towels and they rubbed at the area to make sure it wasn't slippery. Even a few drops of perspiration could make a spot on the floor dangerous for the cast.

Nobody pushed me, said Tyler's own voice in her head.

A nurse popped into the room and began wheeling her out toward the OR.

"Nobody pushed me," Tyler said again, out loud. Overhead, the hall lights were whizzing by. She could feel her eyes drooping.

"I have to push you, Miss Carter," the nurse said, misunderstanding. "It's the only way I can get you to the surgeon."

"I have to tell Jake," Tyler said as loudly as she could.

"Tell him all about it when you wake up," the nurse said soothingly.

"I'm not the target, Tyler said. "It was an accident."
But by this time she was in the OR, a mask was over her
face, and she was being told to breathe deeply.

"I'm not the taaarget," she moaned as sleep came. *But
who was?*

Whistling, the watcher pushed a mop down the hall
of the hospital. It was easy getting in anywhere when you
were dressed like cleaning staff and pushing a mop. He
had hidden a special souvenir in his left sleeve. When he
thought about what he was about to do, he got all excited.
There was really nothing more satisfying than fooling an
archenemy. If he could use the Vegas Twirly Girl to do
it, all the better. Threatening letters. Fan mail. *Pfft.* Who
was interested in a second-rate dancer with a bum knee?
He certainly wasn't. His goal was quite different. He
chuckled with amusement. The risk on this part would
be a bit greater than before. But it was worth it.

Friendly, he nodded to a nurse hurrying by. Clueless,
she gave him a smile. Her name tag said, "Linda."

Maybe he could leave Linda one of his special gifts
next. No, he sternly called himself to order. That wasn't
in his plan. He was pursuing bigger goals. But tempting
it was, he thought, as he watched Linda's vanishing rear
end. He blinked as if waking from a daydream and
focused his concentration on the room numbers. They
really didn't take the safety of their patients too seriously
in this small hospital. When he had asked for Tyler's

room number at the front desk, the nurse on duty had given it to him without a second thought. She seemed almost annoyed that someone was asking about this patient again. Without looking up, she had rattled off the number and pointed vaguely in the direction of the visitor elevator.

When he reached the room, he had an idea of what might have been the cause of the nurse's bad mood. The small room was packed with flowers and gifts. Every free surface was crowded with something. Tyler appeared to be asleep. He had feared they might allow her stupid mutt in the room, but there was no sign of him. Probably hospital guidelines prevented that.

He felt sweat on his forehead. He didn't like that at all. Nervously, he tugged at his collar. Suddenly, the whole clinic seemed like a trap. What should he do now? Retreat quietly, hoping that no one had spotted him yet? No. Press on. He just had to play his ace. Step by step, he approached the bed. On the bedstand was a water glass. Originally, he had planned to place the black feather decoratively inside the glass. This would have guaranteed her attention. But it needed a special touch. So, he poured a touch of liquid from the flask into the water, turning it red. Blood red. That gave it the macabre quality it needed. He pulled out a cell phone and snapped away.

The glass and feather.

The glass and feather beside the slumbering Tyler.

This was going to look terrific in the next video.

The danger of being discovered sent adrenaline coursing through his veins. He could hardly breathe. But it was time to mop his way back down the hallway. Only when he was in the safety of the rental car did he allow himself a cry of victory. "Yes!"

INDEPENDENCE POLICE DEPARTMENT

Jake and Cole looked up from the desktop they were hunched over as Avery Swiftwater entered. She was holding a file stamped with the department logo.

"Thanks so much for coming," Jake said. "Especially since you're on vacation."

"I'm glad to help," she said. "Hi, Cole. Nice to see you."

Cole tried not to smile too broadly at the attention. "I told Jake you might lend a little unofficial help, just like I'm doing," he said. "Neither of us is in an FBI capacity."

"But I'm very grateful for both of you lending a hand." To Jake, profiling was a very exciting field, but it was more or less superfluous to his work. His policing did its job reliably, even without psychological bells and whistles. What he'd heard about Avery and her profiling work, however, was interesting enough to impress him. "I see you got the file Cole dropped off. He already sent you a link for the video. Did you watch it?"

"Several times," she said. "I've already done some homework,"

"We're all ears."

"From what I can tell between the video, the file, and the anecdotal evidence you both provided, this perp is socialized. He can move in society without attracting attention. But he won't get involved anywhere. He won't participate in any club, won't contest any relief effort."

"Or maybe we haven't asked the right person about it yet," Jake concluded.

"That's what I wanted to bring up. I understand the subject of this video and pranks is your sister. Is that right?"

Jake nodded.

"Has anyone dug into looking at her boyfriend?"

Cole and Jake looked at one another. A meaningful, horrified look passed between them.

"You mean, Pat?" Cole said slowly.

CHAPTER FIFTEEN

An hour later, and still well before visiting hours, a nurse woke Tyler to check her vital signs.

"Hello," Tyler said somewhat sullenly. It was no fun being wakened from a deep sleep. Especially when she felt this bad.

"Good afternoon, Miss Carter," the male nurse said.

Tyler turned her head away. She felt like something the cat had spit out. Stupid anesthesia. She hated that feeling. But she knew there was no point in getting upset about it. She wouldn't feel better until she could take her first shower. Briefly, she considered getting up and brushing her teeth. But just the thought of walking all the way to the bathroom made her sink powerlessly into the pillow. "I need gum, something for my breath."

"Not quite yet, Miss Carter." The man finished looking at her blood pressure and straightened up. "Now you can go back to sleep."

Her eyes roamed groggily over the flowers in the room as the nurse exited.

Water, she needed water. Her eyes turned to the bedside table. As if hypnotized, Tyler stared at it. A black feather. Sitting in a glass of blood.

"Take it away. Take it away," she screamed. Her pulse spiked and the machine standing next to her bed, constantly checking her vital signs, began to beep frantically. The nurse rushed back into the room.

He saw what Tyler was looking at but didn't understand the significance. "We can do without that," he said, snatching it up. Marching into the bathroom, he poured the red water into the toilet and flushed it away with the feather. By the time he came out, the pain medication kicked in again full force and Tyler could only whimper. In another few seconds, it carried her away completely.

A while later, Pat snoozed in a chair beside Tyler's bed in the hospital. The door to the room creaked open and Pat straightened up, all his senses immediately wide awake.

Jake stuck his head in. "Hi. Is my sister asleep?"

Pat nodded. "Has been for a while." He nodded to where Tyler slumbered.

"That's okay. I was hoping to find you here."

"What's up?"

"Some new stuff has come to light. I just wanted to ask you a few questions."

"Why do I have the feeling Cole checked into my background?"

"Is there anything you want to tell me before we get started?"

"Sure, I've got something to say," Pat said calmly. "I told you up front that I had a past. I was a member of a gang, but all of that has been expunged because I was a minor."

With Tyler's vital-sign machines whirring and clicking in the background, Pat quietly told his story. "For a year or so, my life as a gang member went well. The gang leader was Julio. He was eighteen and taught me how to pick any lock. I was good at forging signatures for school, too." Pat ventured a glance at Jake to see how the story was going so far. It was impossible to tell. He was inscrutable, so Pat continued. "I take it that you found my name as a state's witness in a case."

"That's right," Jake said. "A sexual assault case."

"Funny that for once I was doing the right thing and that's how you found me in your database. But anything you found is old. It was all from when I was a kid."

"That's true," Jake said. "You don't have anything to be nervous about."

Pat made a face like he didn't have one hundred percent faith in that statement, but kept talking, "Then, Julio recruited another kid who wasn't big either, but he was up for anything. And he was mean. He was already on the streets for a long time. He knew all the tricks and almost never went to school. He liked spreading fear and terror. The fact that he couldn't get close to me drove him crazy. Thanks to Julio's protective hand, he never dared to attack me directly."

Tyler sighed in her sleep and Pat paused talking.

"Tyler?" Jake asked, but he got no answer.

"One day," Pat continued, "I heard William bragging at school that he was really going to give it to Tamara, the music teacher's daughter. Until that day, I didn't know there was such a thing as a conscience. But Tamara getting hurt really bothered me. Fortunately, William was also a loudmouth and liked to announce his plans days before he put them into action. I listened to all the things he wanted to do to this girl. At first, I just found it disgusting and didn't want to know anything about it. But the more I heard about his plans, the more I couldn't look the other way. This time, I had to choose between loyalty to the members of my surrogate family and protecting the girl. Maybe it also had something to do with the fact that Tamara was very pretty. I was a little bit in love with her."

"Then what did you do?"

"Found out as much as I could. Then I made an anonymous call to the police. But my confidence in the system was pretty much zero. So I couldn't be sure that the police took my call seriously." He checked Jake's face for a reaction, but there was nothing he could read. "I followed William after school. He was waiting for her behind the gym where she always went to have a smoke. He was so sure of his plan that he'd even unzipped his pants." With a shudder, Pat thought back. "That detail saved me from prison later. That and Tamara's testimony. When the police arrived, William and I were brawling and the girl was in the middle of it. The officers didn't take long, grabbed us, and hauled us off to the station. My version of the story got zero interest. For the cops, the situation was clear: Two social cases known to the police and an innocent girl."

"Sometimes, there's bias."

"And sometimes it's well-founded. But sometimes it's not. Tamara testified that I helped her. They also ran my anonymous call through a voice recognition program and I was cleared."

"But you made yourself an enemy?"

"Instant enemy to William. It got so bad I was relocated from Brooklyn to Seattle. That's a story for another day."

"Any chance William is trying to hurt you through Tyler?"

Pat swallowed hard. "It never crossed my mind. But if you can't rule out any other angle, I guess William coming back to take revenge is a pretty good one."

As Jake got to his feet, the leather holster on his hip creaked. "Come with me. We need to go to PD headquarters. We'll join Cole and Avery."

"Why?"

"For your own safety. I hate to tell you this, but another video was released with new pictures."

Pat grimaced. "What pictures?"

"Pictures taken inside the Wilkinson house. In the last twenty-four hours."

"You mean inside the house where we're living?"

"Like I said, it's time we went back to the PD," Jake replied.

INTERROGATION ROOM, INDEPENDENCE POLICE DEPARTMENT

The gray interrogation room had a metal table and a video camera, no windows. Pat sat on one side and Jake on the other. They were both seated in metal chairs and the camera was pointed in Pat's direction with a glowing red light on the top. A trickle of sweat started between his shoulder blades and ran down his back. Jake was cool, but underneath, he was angry. Pat could see that.

"Can you explain to me how pictures could have been taken of you both inside the house without noticing? Without you waking up as someone entered and exited the house? Your ninja skills must have failed you," Jake sneered.

"I remember that the dog was restless sometimes."

"Ranger was restless."

"Yes. But Tyler often had him in her room. And you know she has a tendency to hide stuff that the rest of us would raise a red flag over. Plus, I'm working so hard I sleep like the dead."

"You don't remember seeing or hearing anything? No strange behavior?"

"One time, he may have been growling when I got home. But everything seemed fine."

"Didn't you even manage to stay near her for half a day?" asked Jake, visibly annoyed.

"I'm not her guard! She likes to remind me of that fact."

Jake looked like he was desperate to contradict him. Or strangle him. But Pat was telling the truth. The whole truth, and there was nothing to uncover or find out from his side.

Jake drew himself upward and then his shoulders collapsed forward. "Jaz reminds me of that, too," he said. "She calls it my protector complex." He turned his head toward the door. "Polly!" he called. "I think we're through here."

On the well-traveled road into Independence, Paula and Leslie were headed to pick up the Ski-Thing with Ranger. Fine flakes fell from the sky and danced over the hood of the pickup as they drove. The plan was to pick up the vehicle since Tyler would have to be chauffeured around for several weeks from now on. It was parked behind the Wilkinson house with the keys in it, waiting for them to arrive. Ranger had been with them ever since they'd left the B and B after the marten rescue. Ranger couldn't stay in the hospital with Tyler, even though he was a registered service animal.

The day was not without drama already. Leslie was with Paula in the car because she had refused to go to school. Again. Their deciding argument had to be delayed as the demands of the day outweighed even school.

Paula looked at the flakes coming down and made a mental checklist of the survival kit in the car: snow chains, a shovel, a flashlight, blankets, some supplies, and a few water bottles. That way, if need be, they could sit out a blizzard. But today she probably didn't have to worry about that. The sky was already clearing in the west. A little sun could turn the whole area into a magical winter wonderland.

The truck strained up the hill to Wilkinson Butte, as the property was called. It wasn't really a butte, but it was a steep hill with ten acres cleared at the top and woods on either side of the road leading up to it. Paula pulled into the big circular driveway of the home.

"Pat's car isn't here," Paula noted.

"You mean Mr. Wilkinson's Cadillac," Leslie corrected.

"He had to leave early to drop Tyler in Breck for her surgery. Maybe he's not coming back, just staying there for the whole day. Hard to say."

They got out of the pickup. Ranger jumped out with them.

"Look!" Leslie yelled, and pointed to the side of the house where the heavy duty tarpaulins were rippling and moving, as though there was something underneath.

"That's funny," Paula said. "No workmen were supposed to be here today so Pat could be at the hospital."

A man in ski pants and a hoodie emerged from underneath the tarp. He was holding a phone, as though he were in the middle of either filming or taking pictures.

"Hey!" Paula shouted.

Startled, the man froze. Then he ran like a rabbit for the road and trees on the other side. He was getting onto a snowmobile parked a little out of sight in there. The snow was slippery, and he fell.

Paula threw her phone at Leslie. "Call for help!" She narrowly avoided cursing. She would never be able to run down a snowmobile in the truck—not up here in these snow conditions.

"There's no signal!" Leslie hollered.

Paula's shotgun was behind the seat in the pickup with a trigger lock still on. Paula tore open the truck, wrestled the lock off the trigger and fired a shot into the air. "HALT! I'm making a citizen's arrest. Get on your knees, hands behind your head."

The intruder was back on his feet, doing no such thing, but the shot rattled him and he had trouble getting the snowmobile started.

Where was the ski bike? "Keep moving to pick up a signal!" she yelled at Leslie.

As the snowmobile spluttered and resisted turning over, Paula ran to the back of the house. There was the Ski-Thing! With keys in it!

Paula threw the shotgun under the rattrap on the back to secure it. She could never drive and shoot at the same time. The ski bike started on the first try. She heard the snowmobile whine and got to the front just as the intruder took off in an opposite direction from the road leading off the hill. Ranger got the idea that this was a pursuit and bounded after the fleeing man. It was taking the snowmobile time to accelerate, and in fifty yards, Ranger was actually catching up. The dog took one huge leap and caught the back of the man's hoodie in his teeth. *RIIIIIP!* Off it came, and the snowmobile surged ahead. No question, the ski bike was slower. But Paula revved in pursuit anyway.

Leslie was desperate. She needed a cell-phone signal, and fast. She could waste time traipsing all over the butte, or she could get down the hill fast where she knew reception was. But how could she get down? Paula would never want her to get in the truck and try to drive, she knew that for sure.

Leslie looked around wildly. Trash bins were out by the road, covered with dome lids. Coming from poverty, Leslie knew how to use them. She ripped the lid off the nearest can and ran to the middle of the road. She threw it down, jumped into the saucer-shaped lid, and kneeled down as the lid began moving. It took off like a shot and rocketed down the hill. Holding onto the sides, she knew it could be steered by leaning left or right and pulling each side of the lid. The lid sped along, trees went by in a blur. Leslie began tacking right and left to slow down a bit. Just as she was about to slide right into the road, she yanked the lid hard right and threw herself into a snowbank.

SMACK!

The lid clipped a tree as Leslie rolled into soft snow. In the distance, she could hear a motor coming down the hill, buzzing like an angry hornet. Was it the ski bike? Or was it the snowmobile?

She felt in her coat to see if the phone was still with her. It was. She knee-walked to the biggest tree closest to the road. She tapped *Camera* from the phone apps. As the snowmobile rode past, she got a clear angle of the rider's face.

CLICK!

Leslie got the shot.

Paula returned to the house just as Leslie struggled over the crest of the hill. Paula had lost the intruder, but Leslie seemed triumphant about something. She was waving the phone. Before Paula could stop him, Ranger ran for the house.

"Ranger, COME!" Paula yelled.

He wiggled under the tarpaulin on the side of the house and disappeared.

A short while later, Jake arrived with all sirens blazing. Cole and Avery were right on his tail. A moment later, they stood with Paula and Leslie in a hidden room on the far side of the house.

"Ranger led us here," Leslie explained.

"Nice work with the cell phone," Jake said. "We put that picture to good use. Just for the record, Pat is no longer a suspect." He went quiet and joined the others in surveying the room. There was a sea of evidence. A tablet for editing with slideshows of Tyler in T-shirts to sleep in, Tyler wearing only a towel fresh from the shower. Pat with his shirt off. Outside the window on the sill lay two dead crows. Frozen solid. Inside, there were clear plastic containers of dark red liquid that looked like collected, congealed blood.

Avery stepped forward to get a better look. Her eyes widened. "We matched the photo Leslie sent with a mugshot from a sexual assault case featuring William Vermont."

"Who is he going after, Pat or Tyler?" she said.

"Hmm. My guess is that Pat is the target," Jake answered.

Avery pointed to where pictures were shifting on the tablet. "Look how he kept capturing Pat's facial expressions at critical moments." She pointed to a fresh image. "Here he used red effects to mess up Pat's face."

Jake's phone blipped. It was Polly.

"Boss, you need to hear this," she said. "Nate's on the phone. Nate Bale, the new vet."

With an uneasy feeling in the pit of his stomach, he told her to patch Nate through. "This is Sheriff Carter. You wanted to speak to me? This better be something a little more urgent than the martens."

"Thanks for taking my call, Jake. My office was broken into over the weekend. My supply of ketamine is missing."

Jake pricked up his ears. "You're thinking about substance abuse?"

"That's just it. I don't think it was drug dealers. The only other things missing are some syringes. The rest of the meds were not touched."

"When did the robbery take place?"

"This morning before we opened up."

"Okay, thanks for the info. If you don't touch anything, I can send a deputy out to dust for prints." He stayed away from saying, *If this is Tyler's stalker, he's more dangerous than we thought.*

"No problem," Nate replied. "The practice will be closed today, anyway. I'll lock everything up here and then come see you."

"Thanks. See you soon."

Avery took a last look at the room. It was creepy knowing someone had been doing this in her great grandfather's house. She shuddered imperceptibly, but then tightened her shoulders and left the room right behind Jake.

Nate Bale met Jake right outside the Wilkinson house. When Paula saw him arrive, she stalked out right behind Jake. Nate seemed relieved at seeing him.

Jake walked and held out his hand. "Thanks for coming. Normally we would do this at the station, but we're pressed for time."

Paula piped up behind them. "Because of him, Tyler is probably lying in the snow somewhere now on drugs, if not worse."

Jake ignored her. "Please tell me exactly what happened."

"He—" Paula interjected.

"And you stay out of it!" Jake said to Paula. He felt stress begin to throb behind his temples. Poor Nate. Jake saw the confusion in his eyes, wondering what he had done to Paula to make her so eager to claw his eyes out. Nate didn't understand Paula wanted to claw *everyone's* eyes out. She just needed an excuse.

"I'm so sorry to hear your sister is in danger. My medicine cabinet was well secured. The door to the practice took hard work to break open. As far as I can tell, both locks were expertly picked. I didn't have the money for a more sophisticated system. But I can't help but feel complicit. Is there anything I can do to help?"

"You've *helped* enough, don't you think?" Paula hissed at him.

"Paula, behave!" Jake's nerves were stretched to breaking point. He really had no time to worry about an argument between her and the vet. "Where is Ranger?"

"He's already in the truck waiting," she countered.

"Good. Then you're coming with us to the hospital. I'm going to have Polly meet us here before we go and take Leslie to the police station. She can play video games in my office while she waits for you."

Avery walked over to Paula and put an arm around her rigid shoulders. "Come on, let's go inside. Is Cole still here?" She was glad to have another capable agent in the current situation, which threatened to escalate at any moment.

With difficulty, Paula swallowed her anger. "Cole? His car hasn't left. That means he's still here."

Avery knew perfectly well where Cole was. She just wanted Paula away from Jake and Nate.

CHAPTER SIXTEEN

"HELLO, TYLER," Lily's voice sounded cheerfully from the door of the hospital room. She had a beautiful bouquet in her hand. "I hear you're awake?"

Tyler was more than awake. She was dressed, hair braided, hat on, and ready to go.

"Lily! I've been waiting for Pat to come back. I'm supposed to be discharged. Can't wait to get out of here." What she didn't say was the pain meds had given her nightmares. *A black feather in a glass of blood.* The sooner she could get away, the better.

"Have you heard from Pat? Is he on his way?" Lily put the bouquet down.

"The nurse said he and Jake were here first thing, but they left. Pat's phone seems turned off right now."

"Or he's out of signal. You know how it can be around here."

Tyler made a face. True enough. "I know he'll show up eventually, but he's probably right at home working on the house. I don't suppose you could give me a lift?"

"Of course!"

Tyler rose from the bed with difficulty and reached for the crutches leaning against the wall.

Her friend eyed her from head to toe, watching as she slowly moved forward.

"How long are you going to be on the sticks?"

"The doctor thinks six weeks. Half that time is also enough. You know doctors. My cane is probably enough."

"Careful you don't overdo it. Better to walk on poles a few weeks longer than for the rest of your life."

"How wise," Tyler replied, winking at her.

Lily replied, "Call the nurse and ask her if you can go. Then I'll drive you."

"That would be wonderful." Tyler limped back to the bed to press the red button.

"No problem," Tyler grunted, trying unsuccessfully to pull a sock over her foot. She couldn't bend the knee, and the muscles and ligaments were so tightened up she couldn't reach the foot. Great. So now she needed a chambermaid, too. A feeling of helpless hysteria rose inside her, but she squashed it. That was not going to help her get out of Dodge right now.

"Give me that," Lily said. "I'll help you with your socks."

Reluctantly, she handed the stocking to Lily. She had barely finished dressing when the nurse came into the room with a bag in her hand. "I still have some tablets here. Take one in the morning and one in the evening with some water and especially after meals. If you're still in a lot of pain, they can increase the dose."

"That stuff gives me bad dreams," Tyler said simply.

The nurse looked around for Tyler's bag and spotted it on the bed. She put the pills in a side pocket and then held the bag out to Lily. "Here. Tyler will have enough to do with her crutches and knee. Meanwhile, I'll get a wheelchair to take her out to the curb." The nurse eyed all the flowers, balloons, and gifts in the room. "Maybe two wheelchairs. That will make things easier."

At the curb, Tyler thanked the nurse and took a deep breath of the fresh air as she stretched her face toward the sun.

"You'd think your last few days were spent in the dungeon."

"That's about how it felt," she admitted.

"I'll leave you with your stuff and go get the VW bus. Sorry that it's not a more comfy car, but it has enough room for the dog, your bag, and the seat can be pushed way back so we can get your leg in."

"Sounds good to me."

By the time Lily returned, there were still two wheelchairs sitting at the curb. One was filled with gifts and flowers. A bag sat beside it on the sidewalk.

The other wheelchair was empty.

One Minute Earlier

William was excited. Now it was about to happen. Before he landed his big coup and took revenge on Pat, he would have some fun with Linda, the nurse. He said the name aloud and enjoyed the way it rolled over his tongue. This time it was strictly for his own pleasure. It would be the main rehearsal before the grand finale. How fitting that he planned to give a star his big performance. The blood sang in his veins as he thought of how her blood would look on the snow. He took one last look at the clock on the dashboard. Almost eight o'clock. Now she would show up in a minute to start her shift.

Thanks to his excellent preparation, he knew that Linda preferred to use the main entrance instead of the side entrance for employees. He suspected it had to do with a certain young man Linda liked to waste time with by flirting at the front desk. Each time, she had stopped by and wasted a few minutes bantering with him. At first, William felt jealous. But then it dawned on him how stupid that was. In the end, Linda would be his. Later, maybe the young man too. He'd have to ponder these details.

He worked in comfortable silence to make sure he had everything he needed. Good timing was everything. He had to catch her before she reached the main entrance if he wanted to avoid anyone spotting him. But he wasn't too worried. Ah. There she was already. He quickened his pace until he saw something that made him stop abruptly. Despite the icy wind, sweat broke out on his forehead. Out on the curb sitting in a wheelchair—what was Tyler doing here?! He looked from one woman to the other. On his left was Linda, on her way to work on time. To his right, a little farther away, Tyler. His main prize was sitting pretty, as if waiting to be scooped up. A quick decision was needed.

Was fate trying to remind him of his real task? Linda came closer and closer, her head lowered against the strong wind, eyes fixed on the ground. Seconds passed and felt like an eternity. Linda walked past without noticing him. He expelled the air he had been holding. It was decided. There would be no dress rehearsal.

With grim determination, he gripped the hypodermic needle in his hand tighter and started moving. Out of the corner of his eye, he watched Tyler. She was completely focused on watching for her ride and paid no attention as he approached her at an angle, outside her peripheral vision.

Surprised, Tyler looked up. The tourist from the diner! What was he doing here? She hadn't seen him in Independence for days. She noticed the grim look around his mouth and strange posture. Her surprise turned to suspicion. Adrenaline shot through her veins. Too late. He grabbed her by the braid, which was hanging out from under her wool cap, and brutally pulled her head back. "Don't hurt me," she tried to yell, wanting to scream. But the unnatural position of her head meant that nothing more than a croak came out. Something sharp stung her hand, followed by a burning sensation. This time, she cried out loudly in pain.

"Shut up. You'll spoil everything," he hissed, and slapped her face.

That hurt. Her finger burned like fire. Desperately trying to keep a clear head, she struggled to get out of the chair. To fight back. To strike him a blow with her crutches. But little by little, strength left her, and she slumped. Her thoughts slipped away. The world around her blurred into white static.

Jake finished marking off the room with crime-scene tape. "Anybody here heard from Tyler? Paula, you?"

"No. I thought she would need the day to recover at the hospital."

Cole said, "Let's call. Try her cell phone, too." He pulled out his phone.

"What about Pat?"

"We left him at the PD," Avery replied.

"Call there and tell them he's no longer a suspect. Tell him we'll meet him in Breck."

"Tyler's not answering," said Cole, holding out his phone.

"Call the hospital direct," Jake ordered.

As Cole punched in the hospital's number, he tried unsuccessfully to reassure himself that, yes, cell phones weren't allowed. But after two sentences and a minute-long wait, he said into the phone, "Tell this again to the sheriff, please," and handed the phone to Jake.

Jake took the phone to hear a professional medical voice say, "The Breckenridge police are already here. Tyler Carter is missing."

Paula was speeding along the road and hit the turn signal at the parking lot turnoff to the hospital. Avery had taken Leslie back to the police department building, the safest place for her right now, so Paula was alone in the truck with Ranger. She had been informed that Lily was with the Breck police, helping them with everything she could. Paula was warned not to interfere with the police investigation, but she still felt she could be helpful.

Especially with Ranger in the car. Ranger knew Tyler. He might sense where she was when humans couldn't.

Paula flipped up the hood of her parka. The wind had picked up again. She prayed they had a little time before it started snowing again. The snow would make tracking almost impossible. But dark clouds were already hanging low in the sky. She pulled the pickup into a spot and got out. Ranger, who had waited patiently beside her until now, pulled on the leash. "Where are you going?" she asked him in surprise. She gave him more leeway and let him roam.

On Cole's advice, she had replaced the regular leash with a ten-foot length of lightweight nylon rope. This allowed him to move more freely, and there was no danger of losing him. Knowing this was an incredibly long shot, she grabbed Ranger by the collar and sent him forward with an encouraging, "Find Tyler." He lowered his head, spun around twice with his nose just above the ground, and then abruptly took off in the direction of the clinic. She hoped he was actually following Tyler's trail and not some raccoon that may have made a detour across the parking lot during the night. But after a hundred yards, she had certainty. At that moment, she would have preferred the alternative of the fox a thousand times.

Tyler's crutches lay on the ground in the snow. The packed snow showed footprints. A few yards ahead Tyler's cap lay in the snow.

Ranger pulled on the leash again. He wanted to go on. Paula made a circuit around the crutches and the trampled ground, so as not to destroy any tracks. In the meantime, the dog had arrived at the woolen cap. He barked twice briefly and then sat down. Paula hurried over and praised him. Her jacket pocket had some crumbled horse treats in the bottom. She crouched down next to him and gave him pieces as a reward. Was that the right thing to do? She had no idea how police dogs worked. Ranger certainly seemed to appreciate it.

What now? She gestured at Ranger to stay where he was and moved closer to the cap. There was something under it. She pulled off her right glove and lifted it slightly with a pointed index finger. A syringe. Didn't Nate the vet say he was missing syringes? The needle at the end was bloodied. Horrified, she staggered back a few steps and pressed her fist to her mouth.

At that moment, Jake's car turned into the parking lot, blue lights flashing. With frantic hand movements Paula motioned him over. Suddenly, Ranger quickened his pace, nose focused on the ground, and moved in another direction. After a helpless glance in Jake's direction, she followed Ranger. He changed direction twice and trotted between parked cars. In front of an empty lot, he stopped and repeated the bark he had used to indicate the first two finds. The parking spaces were not visible through the snow. But from the cars present, she concluded that there had been a car there until recently. William Vermont's car, perhaps? A vehicle he'd rented? Her pulse quickened. She praised Ranger for his efforts and handed out another crumb from her pocket. Then she rose and looked around. There was a dark spot in the snow across the lot. Blood? Her stomach turned.

Tyler came to with a pounding headache. Her hands were secured behind her back with zip ties. As she tried to sit up, a wave of nausea hit her. At the last moment, she rolled to the side and vomited on the bare floor. Tears streamed down her face and she began to shake uncontrollably. She was so cold. Realizing she couldn't move any further, she lay still. Her eyelids blinked rapidly to glimpse something in the dim light.

"Wakey, wakey," said a man's voice. "Very good. I can begin preparations for the ritual now." With a few flicks of his wrist, a fireplace flared with light. At least she could see her surroundings clearly now, and maybe it would get a little warmer.

The man stood up and came toward her, smiling. Was this what madness looked like? She squeezed her eyes shut when she realized what he had in his hand: two dead crows. "Fresh kills," he said proudly. He settled down beside her. As his breath brushed her, Tyler shuddered in disgust.

He laughed softly. "That's it. Always play your part."

At these words, she opened her eyes again.

"You're a star. Hard to believe in the state you're in now, though. Tonight I'm going to give you the performance of your life." With a flowing motion, he cut the head off one of the birds, dipped his fingers in the blood, and stroked the still-warm liquid across her forehead.

Horrified, she tried to wriggle away from him.

"You're not going anywhere," he giggled, nudging her injured leg with his boot.

Fireworks exploded before her eyes. She slipped back into darkness.

Pat drove Paula's pickup while she sat in the passenger seat with Ranger. He and Jake's detail had caught up with Paula and planned a strategy, which was why Pat was driving. Based on Avery's advice that William would likely leave clues to draw Pat to him, no one was surprised when a call came into police from William demanding they send Pat and that "crazy woman" west on a certain route and for them to "look for the crow." Pat and Paula had volunteered to go ahead while they were followed at a safe distance by Jake and Cole, and backed up by a Breckenridge PD detail. It was clear that William would like an audience for his performance, and he was willing to let them find him. It was their best chance to save Tyler.

Next to Pat in the passenger seat, Paula was clenching her teeth. Ranger sat on the floor at her feet. "There's a crow," she exclaimed, pointing ahead. This one had been nailed to a fence post. The snow underneath was blood red. "I know where this route goes. It links up eventually with the Old Shawnee Trail." She reached for the police radio sitting between them and informed Jake.

"We're a mile behind you. Wait for us," he replied.

Paula gave Pat a sidelong glance. *Wait?* Pat's expression was grim determination. To Jake, she replied, "Sure."

Ten minutes later and another dead crow down the road, Paula reached out and touched Pat on the sleeve. "Look there."

He gave her a questioning look, but stopped the car. "The beak seems to be pointing at this turnoff."

"Should we take it? Jake said to wait."

Pat returned her gaze without blinking. "I'm not going to wait for the cavalry." He gunned the pickup around the turn.

CHAPTER SEVENTEEN

WILLIAM BENT OVER TYLER. She was only vaguely aware of him and blinked before letting her heavy eyelids fall shut again. Chills kept zinging through her, but otherwise, her body was strangely numb. She couldn't even feel her knee properly. *Is this what it feels like when you're about to die?* The man's muttering and big hunting knife left no doubt. Yet somehow this fact did not seem as frightening as she always imagined. There was something immensely peaceful about this slipping into darkness. Only one thing she regretted: she'd never told Pat how much she loved him. And now it was too late.

Pain coursed through her head as the stalker abruptly jerked her head back. "Look at me when I'm talking to you!" he ordered. "Your viewer is about to come." That got her attention more than his abuse, and she widened her eyes. Her viewer? Did he mean Pat? Was he coming here?! Desperately, she shook her head as if that might keep him from coming.

"That's where you open your eyes. I see you guessed right. Your greatest admirer is about to walk through that door."

He let her head fall back onto the hard floor. Unlike the last time, she fought with all her might to stay conscious. Suddenly, death didn't seem like such a good idea. *Stay away*, she repeated in her mind like a mantra.

"I'm going to have to leave you alone for a minute. We don't want our visitor to feel unwelcome." The blade of the large knife glinted in the glow of the flames as he walked past. A cold breeze brushed her, then she was alone. Her eyes roved the room. The walls of the rustic log cabin were smeared with blood. Each side was defaced with a skewered bird. But there was nothing near that could serve her as a weapon. She tried to sit up, but her limbs were so stiffly frozen and numb that they disobeyed. Without the help of her arms, she couldn't even push off from the floor. When her face landed in her own vomit, tears welled up and she let herself sink down, exhausted.

Pat approached the shack cautiously. His only hope was that William was busy inside and would not notice his arrival. About thirty feet from the house, that hope was shattered when an arm wrapped around his neck. Pat struggled and tried to break away when he felt a blade against his neck. He stopped struggling and froze. He hated knives. The risk of getting sliced was too great. Dead, he would be no help to Tyler. He had no choice but to play along for now.

"William," he said in an attempt to distract, "long time no see."

"So you do remember me." A satisfied smile played around William's lips.

Pat heard the smile in his voice. He would have loved to smack it off the guy's face. *Later,* he told himself.

"Welcome to my demonstration. I think you'll like it. Your girl will be a star. And a real one this time. She'll have hundreds of thousands of admirers on the net as soon as tomorrow." He seemed genuinely pleased at the prospect.

Pat felt sick when he realized how deep the madness was rooted in this man. His face must have betrayed something of his thoughts, because William increased the pressure of the blade on his neck until a few drops of blood came out. This seemed to lift the kidnapper's spirits. "Blood red. I knew you'd be a good choice. You fit right in with the theme of the evening." His maniacal laughter died away in the snow.

William dragged Pat the rest of the way to the shack and pushed him through the door. His eyes took a moment to adjust to the new lighting conditions. A fire blazed in the center of the room. In the back of the cabin, a window stood wide open, presumably to let the smoke escape more easily. When he saw the lifeless bundle on the floor and recognized Tyler, his heart almost stopped. Was she already dead? Impulsively, he tried to get to her. But with the knife at his throat, William had a firm grip on him.

Reluctantly, Pat let himself be led to a rickety chair while his brain desperately searched for a solution. He was about to launch an all-out attack when he noticed movement through the open window. What was it? His heart leaped with recognition. Paula. Time for a diversion. If Paula made it to the cabin unnoticed, there was a better chance of overpowering William. So he allowed himself to be tied to the chair.

How could he distract William? His mind raced. "Really good how you got us to the cabin using the crows. That was a smart idea."

"Yes, wasn't it?"

"You always were smart, William. I'll give you that."

William beamed. "I thought it would be a nice setup for the transformation fairy tale that's about to reveal itself to you."

"Transformation fairy tale? Tell me about that." Discussion with this sick puppy was an exercise in madness, but keeping the conversation going was a safety measure. As long as William was babbling, he was halfway distracted.

"This girl here," William said, walking over to Tyler and pulling her up, "is going to go through the transformation to stardom. Just like her crow sisters."

"You know she's innocent, right? She never did anything to you. What did the crows do to you, by the way?"

"Other than they're ugly and sound awful, the crows did nothing to me. But your girlfriend, on the other hand, the one who dresses like a crow onstage, the more I hurt her the more I hurt YOU. That's the point."

With effort, he dragged Tyler in front of the fire. She groaned. Pat's heart contracted as he heard the agonized sound. But at the same time, he could have cheered. She was alive.

Out of the corner of his eye, he saw that Paula had almost reached the cabin. She disappeared behind a tree and stopped there.

Pat felt himself vibrating with adrenaline. What could he say next? "What's with the knife? Does it have a special meaning?"

William looked flattered and held the blade into the fire. Over and over again, he raised it high above his head while muttering some kind of incantation.

Outside in the frozen snow, Paula and Ranger surveyed the cabin. Ranger seemed to understand the need to remain quiet. From where she stood, Paula could see only part of the room inside. Pat was tied to a chair. The stalker had his back to the window and was wielding a dangerous-looking hunting knife. Tyler? Didn't see her anywhere. Paula wondered what she was supposed to do. Wait for help to arrive? Intervene? But how? Her eyes fell on Ranger. His entire focus was on the cabin, as if he knew what was happening inside. Could she sic him on the man? She didn't doubt that Ranger could do the job. She just didn't know if he would understand the way she said it.

Cole had said Ranger originally trained in Germany. Did the dog know German commands, too? Paula knew only one command in German: *fass*. It meant *attack*. She guessed it was worth a try. With one last look at the dog, she made her decision. She grabbed him by the collar and whispered, "FASS." Then she let him go.

Ranger shot across the snow, taking yards with each stride. He blasted through the window with a record-breaking leap and jumped William from behind. William stumbled forward in surprise and fell face-first into the fire.

"AAHHHHHHH!" William screamed.

Paula rushed through the door as Pat tore at his bonds attached to the chair. He threw himself backward, smashing the old chair and sending pieces flying in different directions. Then he was on William, pulling him out of the fire. Ranger grabbed onto William's clothing and helped pull.

A quick glance was enough to see that there was no longer any danger from him. William had fallen on his own knife. The fire had distorted his features into a grotesque mask. Pat put two fingers on where he thought William's carotid artery might be and discovered a faint pulse. *Still alive.*

Gritting his teeth, Pat put William on his side so he would not choke. That was all he could and would do for him. Next, he hurried to Tyler. Ranger was already licking her face. Pat crouched down next to her and was overcome with emotion as she managed a weak smile. She didn't seem to understand his words, but the tears spoke for themselves. Meanwhile, Paula joined them and pulled Ranger away a bit, calming and diverting him with the remaining cookie crumbs from her jacket.

Tyler's head was buzzing. She coughed and tried to form words.

Pat saw that her hands were tied. He whipped out a set of keys with a multi-tool fob and cut through the zip ties.

Outside, headlights flashed. Jake and his company had arrived. Tyler gave Pat's hand a weak squeeze before she lost consciousness again. The look on her face said she knew she was safe.

CHAPTER EIGHTEEN

A WEEK LATER, BRECKENRIDGE MEMORIAL HOSPITAL

Pat bent over Tyler, tenderly stroked a blond curl from her face, and kissed her on the cheek. She woke from her light sleep and smiled.

"Hello, Sleeping Beauty. Happy to get out of here today?"

"Departure day? Oh goodie!" She peeked at herself under the sheet. Unfortunately, no fairies had shown up during her power nap to style her look. She was still wearing sweatpants and a worn-out T-shirt. Embarrassed, she pulled the sheet over her head and mumbled from under it, "I'm sure you need coffee. Go get one in the cafeteria and take your time. Lots of time."

"Sure. Coffee. Urgent." He patted the bed and left.

A moment later, Paula and Leslie poked their heads around the hospital room door. "We're here! Mom and Dad are just parking."

Tyler threw off the sheet and sat up.

"Hurry up. It's not too late to take a shower."

"Is that a subtle hint that I stink like a cougar?"

Leslie giggled before covering her mouth in fright. Tyler gave her a reassuring wink. Paula laughed out loud. "Of course you don't. But Mom is in a bit of shock over everything that's happened. You want to look your best for her." She raised an eyebrow suggestively.

"Point taken," Tyler said, easing her legs over the side of the bed. "Meanwhile, Leslie, would you please take Paula outside before I run her over with my wheelchair?"

Paula protested, but let her enthusiastic protégé pull her out of the room.

"Close the door behind you," Tyler called after them.

Paula poked her head into the room one last time. "I almost forgot. William succumbed to his injuries this morning."

Tyler didn't know what to say to that. All she felt was a great wave of relief, followed by a fleeting, very fleeting, attack of guilty conscience.

"His heart stopped," Paula said matter-of-factly. "I think she regained consciousness for a short time yesterday, but then had to be sedated again because he was trying to get up. He was cursing the whole time. Two hours later, he was dead." When Tyler said nothing, she asked gently, "Maybe I shouldn't have told you?"

"Yes, of course." Tyler raised her head. Her face was sad. "I'm glad that guy's not alive anymore. I know that's not something you say or wish on anyone, but I'm still glad."

Paula came back inside and hugged her lightly. "Me too," she whispered, "me too."

Pat was returning to Tyler's room with two coffees when he saw her wheelchair disappear down the hall. Jake was pushing her, while her mother and father were on either side. Paula, Leslie, and Jaz followed. Pat figured Cole was likely outside behind the wheel of a waiting vehicle.

They were leaving without him.

On one hand, he knew there was a lot of excitement going on, and Tyler was tired, overwhelmed, and medicated as well. But on the other, it was a clear signal that he didn't belong to the group. It was almost as if he hadn't even been there.

At Brenda and Stan Carter's home, Tyler and Ranger got settled into one of the two extra bedrooms for visiting kids. Cole was occupying the other one. All afternoon, the parents had been brought up to speed on the latest news. They weren't thrilled that their adult children hadn't told them the whole truth about what was going on while they were away, but they admitted there was very little they could have done to help. So they accepted being kept out of the loop temporarily.

Around four o'clock, everyone disbursed, and Tyler went for a nap. Ranger prepared to sleep on the floor. Tyler looked over the side of the bed and said, "Come on up, big guy. No nurse for miles."

Without hesitation, the German shepherd jumped up and made himself comfortable next to her. With a sigh, he laid his head on her thigh and closed his eyes. Tyler put her hand on his flank and closed her eyes, too. The physical therapy she'd had earlier in the hospital had exhausted her. But she accepted that it was unreasonable to demand high performance from her body while it was busy recovering. Fortunately, her knee had not needed any further surgery. They had only punctured the skin and pulled out accumulated fluid. The knee had worked better since then, even though every movement was hard work.

Just rest for a moment, was her last thought.

By the time she woke up, Brenda was out in the kitchen putting on potatoes. Tyler walked in as a pan of garlic cloves bubbled away. The garlic was turning golden brown in generous amounts of butter.

"Hi, darlin'," Brenda said. "Sit down and catch me up." Her auburn hair was pulled back from her attractive face. She was a woman who looked comfortable with herself.

Tyler took a seat and told her in short sentences that she had injured her knee more than once, up until the fatal slip backstage where both cruciate ligaments tore and part of the meniscus splintered off.

"And that's what they operated on?" asked Brenda. She set the pan of garlic butter aside to cool. When the fat solidified again, it would make an exquisite spread.

Tyler glanced uncomfortably to the side.

"What's that face about, sweetheart?"

"They say the cruciate ligaments are not as flexible as they were before. Mobility might be restricted afterward because the place where the ligaments are patched up becomes very firm. Then again, that's just an opinion. I just have to see how it goes."

"That's the attitude. Now, get your mind off it. Dinner will be ready in a minute. If you want, you can tell your dad to wash up while I finish the garlic bread."

She cut white bread into thick slices, spread them with the garlic paste, and then put them in the oven.

Tyler was glad to pass the first question period. She knew her parents expected answers sooner or later. But at the moment, she had more questions than answers herself. What she didn't say out loud was, *My life got saved, Mom. I'm grateful. But how am I going to live?*

Back at the diner, Miss Daisy was waiting for Pat out in front of the bed-and-breakfast. She was wearing her uniform, a modest dress with a spotless bib apron over it, and her white hair up in a bun. She stood beside an attractive white sign painted with black letters. *Bed & Breakfast, Owners Daisy and Minnie Disney.* Daisy wore a contented expression, likely due to the fact that the marten family had been humanely moved out and the successful operation had restored peace.

Unexpectedly, Jake pulled up in his sheriff's SUV.

"Sheriff Carter," Daisy said with a twinkle in her eye. "You're a sight for sore eyes this mornin'. What can I get you?"

Jake tipped his hat. "Nothing right now, Miss Daisy. I am here for a favor, however."

"Anything. What might that be?"

"There's going to be a lot of talk about what happened, especially now that Tyler is out of the hospital." The tall lawman paused and looked at her meaningfully. "I'd appreciate it if speculation were kept to a minimum."

Daisy looked a little confused.

"What I mean is, we don't need to scare off tourists and ruin the season by talking about one bad apple that got into our barrel. Loose talk can lose money if you get my drift."

Daisy's expression changed. She got the message. "Why sure, Jake. I think that's a sensible thing to do. You got it. I'll tell Minnie straight away."

"I'd appreciate that," Jake said. "I've already had a word with the Independence Weekly." He gave her a winning smile and got back into the SUV.

As soon as Jake disappeared, Pat pulled into the lot in front of the B and B. Daisy waved. To Pat's eyes, the wooden building looked pretty good from the outside. The exterior had been painted in the last few years. The paint looked fresh and showed no signs of weathering. Pat parked, got out, and turned his smile on Daisy, who was obviously waiting for him.

"Miss Daisy! How nice to see you. How are you?"

"Fit as a fiddle, Pat," she replied.

Pat was here to do a follow-up on the B and B, and even though it didn't pay, it served to distract him from his worry about Tyler. He was waiting for a call—he'd expected one yesterday. *She's resting*, he told himself.

Miss Daisy showed him around the obvious spots where the martens had gained entry, and Pat inspected the job his men had done at patching. An extra trap had been left outside and also in the attic to catch any last holdouts. The traps would be checked twice a day. Pat felt his men had done good work. He stopped, looked, tapped, and pressed on the structure here and there. Satisfied, he noted that the house was in good shape.

"Everything okay with the plumbing and electrical?" he asked Miss Daisy.

"I think so. That was done a few years ago."

The couple of years was probably about twenty, if Pat guessed correctly. He asked her to show him the fuse box, so she led him inside. He breathed a sigh of relief when he saw that the wiring was reasonably up to the latest safety standards. The boiler in the basement was due for replacement at some point, but for now, it was okay.

"Is that all, then?" he asked, looking over at her. "Anything else I can check while I'm here?"

"Behind the house, the stairs to the terrace are dilapidated. But goodness, that's got nothing to do with the martens."

"Why don't you show me, and then we can decide together how much of an effort a repair would be."

She took a deep breath, tightened her shoulders, and led him to the patio door at the back of the house. "Here it is." She looked embarrassed to show him the less-than-good side of her establishment. It was obviously her pride and joy.

Pat bent down to survey the damage. One of the steps had caved in and the railing was wobbly. An unnecessary liability hazard. Again, he took out his tape measure and noted the necessary measurements and the wood used. He frowned. "Do you remember who built this deck?"

"Yeah, sure. An outfit came up from Evergreen five years ago in the summer and did some smaller jobs in the area. We were one of those jobs."

Pat pointed to the broken stair tread. "Second-rate wood was used for this. It probably wasn't stored properly." He grabbed the stair railing and rattled it. "This is sloppy work."

Her brow furrowed at his words. "Really? But it cost enough, I can tell you that!"

He shrugged his shoulders. "I'm sure it did. I'd be happy to call them and try to recover the cost of the repair. But chances are probably slim."

She pressed her lips together into a thin line. "Don't bother. Just make sure you never employ this company for your own projects." She broke off as someone called Pat's name.

"Sounds like my crew is here," he said.

"You're going to have some civilian helpers, too," Daisy replied. "Some good people from the town offered to pitch in."

"Pat?"

Jake opened the front door to the bed-and-breakfast. All around him, the walls were getting a fresh coat of paint. Laughter and the usual curses heard at construction sites could be heard from upstairs. He poked his head in the common room.

"Pat," he called out again. He poked his head into the hall leading to the guest rooms.

"Hi, handsome!" Jaz greeted him, standing on a ladder in an old shirt and jeans already smeared with paint and a paint roller in her hand. "While we were at it, we decided to freshen up the place."

He smiled and took a moment to enjoy the sight of her and the pleasure it still gave him.

"You're the beautiful one of the two of us," he replied, approaching her.

She laughed. "And what are you?"

"Big, strong, handsome, manly," he quipped, flexing his arm muscles.

She made a defensive motion with her paint roller. "No, don't come any closer. I know that look."

Undeterred, he came closer.

"You'll get paint on you for sure," she protested, just before he wrapped her in his arms.

"I so don't care," he said after kissing her.

She beamed. "You'll care if I paint your nose."

"Saucy wench," he returned affectionately. "Do you know where Pat is?"

"I think he's in the attic. He's inspecting the wiring, making sure the martens weren't snacking on it."

Jake shook his head. "You know the miracle in all this?"

"You mean so many volunteers came to help out?"

"That, yes. Also there were no angry activists protesting the treatment of the animals."

"Why do you suppose that was?"

"We invited them to the party."

Jaz laughed. "Just think about it. Paula would be on a protest line for any animals she thought were being unfairly treated. But because she was here with Leslie and got to see how we were doing this with complete transparency, there was no issue at all."

"I think that makes you a genius," Jaz said.

"Yesterday, it would've been common sense. Today it's considered genius. I'm going up to the attic."

Jake walked into the hallway and mounted the ladder to the attic. He liked animals, no question. But with martens in his own house or car, the fun definitely stopped. Where else did they live? In the forest? He thought they were wonderful there. Jake made it up the ladder and stuck his head through the hole in the ceiling.

Paula and one of Pat's workers were having a heated argument about the pros and cons of trapping wild animals. The fact that they were on their knees and cramped into the roof space didn't seem to add any restraint to the conversation. Pat was wisely staying out the discussion and checking wiring to see if the ravenous critters had done any damage.

"Sorry if I'm interrupting for a minute," Jake spoke up. "Pat and Paula, you guys coming down?"

Paula frowned. With her spiky hair and fierce expression, she looked plenty formidable. She was not happy about having to interrupt the discussion.

"I'm coming," Pat answered. "The wiring is still intact. Nate Bale says we can keep furry visitors off the wires by spreading a little dog hair up here. The sight and scent will put martens off."

At the sound of the vet's name, Paula stopped talking and made a face. Jake knew she had a disagreement with Nate every time she visited his office. Not that she didn't think he was a good vet. Paula just liked to argue over her animals' care.

Pat pulled himself away from a few wires and moved toward the ladder. Jake's head disappeared as he made room for Pat to descend.

As Pat stepped off the last rung of the ladder, he looked at Jake and said, "What's going on? Is there a problem down here?"

"No, as far as I can see, it's controlled chaos down here."

"That's a success in my book."

"I told myself the same thing," Jake replied. "Moving on, I'm a little concerned about security at the Wilkinson house. You're still staying there, right?"

"Yeah. You don't think there's any danger, do you?"

"None. Other than you're sleeping alone in a house that's very easily penetrated through tarps and plastic wrap. We saw how that turned out last week."

"I see what you mean."

"Would you move in here at the B and B temporarily? I can ask Minnie to find you a room. I'm sure both women are grateful for your help." Jake slapped Pat's arm in an affectionate way. "You're really all right, Pat. You fit right into this little town."

Pat was pleased to hear these words from Jake, a man he now considered his friend. However, Jake was also Tyler's big brother, and he realized that if Tyler was cooling the relationship, Jake might cool too.

"I never really realized you were thirty-three already," Jake said, seemingly out of the blue.

"You read my file too closely," Pat replied calmly, although he could imagine where this conversation was going.

"You know you're ten years older than my little sister?"

Pat lowered his voice. "Listen, I know. I didn't know in the summer, though. We met and hit it off. Then we saw each other again." He stopped, not sure how best to phrase it. After all, he hadn't even talked to Tyler in the last twenty-four hours. "I've gotten to know her better, and with every bit I've learned about her, she's—she's special." A hint of despair showed in his face.

Jake's face turned to stone. "I still don't like the age difference." He waited until Pat's shoulders slumped. Then Jake grabbed him and slapped him on the back. "Gotcha!"

Pat looked at him numbly.

"Lighten up. It's a joke. You're part of the family now, bro."

Pat forced a smile and hid his discomfort. *Part of the family, huh? Had Tyler gotten the memo?*

CHAPTER NINETEEN

TYLER WENT TO THE WINDOW of her mother's house and checked the weather. Fine flakes fell from the sky and covered the yard with icing. She peered into the white drift and considered just staying put. But that was not an option. Her knee would never get better that way. Today was the day she would resume her dance training. Just a little bit of work at the barre. No more working the punching bag.

After a hot coffee and a quick chat with her mother, she got permission to use the SUV, and set off for the studio. She'd made a convincing argument that her left knee did not have to be involved in driving. Brenda needed a reminder that doctors were adamant it was important to move. It kept the joint from stiffening.

Tyler had purposely left Ranger behind. It was time to pull on her big-girl pants, give him back to Cole, and get refocused. It was so early in the day that Joe's Snow Removal had not yet reached them. The main roads were always cleared first. Thanks to her mother's SUV, that was no problem. There were almost no cars on the road. She loved the early morning hours, always had. There she had peace and could devote herself to dancing. Without disturbing brothers and sisters. As tedious as she found the interference of family members, she had to admit that the familiar surroundings did her soul good. The

Rockies were a constant and solid symbol of the land and the good people here who lived in its shadow.

For the first time in days, she felt something like confidence. Of course, her subconscious immediately presented her with an image of Pat. She snorted, as dealing with him wasn't something she was quite ready for yet. They had caused each other quite a bit of trouble over the last while. She had been a tool for Pat's enemy, and Pat had nearly come to a horrific end when he jumped in to rescue her before the police got there. When he wasn't there for her discharge at the hospital, she saw the writing on the wall. He needed distance. She'd gotten the message. And respected it.

She had to admit, though, that a part of her was always on the lookout for him. Maybe she could run into him by chance at the diner. She wrinkled her nose. *Go ahead*, she laughed at herself. Fool yourself into believing it would be just a chance meeting. She focused on the road again.

Turning onto Main Street, she saw tourists were out in full force. Kids were having a snowball fight in front of the diner. Not wanting to get out and take a snowball in the head, she decided to let the kids play themselves out and return in a little bit. She drove on past the fierce warriors in warm hats and mittens, and cruised by the studio. A few storefronts later, she passed Lily's. She could see Lily inside in her green florist's apron and her curly hair tucked behind one ear. She was moving flowers around, arranging a display for the shop.

Suddenly, memories of being back in the hospital flooded Tyler's mind. She hit the brake too hard and skidded on the slippery street. She ended up sideways in the middle of Main.

Back up! Pull over, her brain commanded. But her body wouldn't move. She was frozen. Her mouth opened to cry, but she couldn't make a sound. In her mind, she was back on the sidewalk at the medical center, back in the wheelchair with flowers and gifts beside her. And then a car pulled up and a whole rush of horrible images brought the memory of abduction back.

Inside the flower shop, Lily saw the SUV brake hard and stop crosswise in the street. It looked like Brenda Carter's vehicle. Perhaps it had stalled out in the winter weather. Lily grabbed a coat and threw it over her shoulders as she hurried outside. When she got to the driver's side window, she realized it was Tyler driving. She was alone. Tears rolled down Tyler's face, and her mouth was frozen in a silent scream.

"Don't worry, I'll get help," Lily shouted.

That seemed to bring Tyler out of her shock. "No, don't," she yelled. Her hand found the automatic window button, and she rolled it down. "I just need a minute. Please, Lily."

"Come inside then," Lily said, and opened the driver's side door gently. She helped Tyler out and gave her the cane that was sitting in the backseat. Leaving the SUV where it was, Lily helped Tyler inside the shop and got her seated next to the glass-front flower refrigerator. Then she hurried back outside and drove the SUV out of the street and parked it properly.

By the time she was back inside, Pebbles, the dalmatian, had wandered out of the back to see what was going on.

"How about some good, strong coffee with a touch of Irish Cream in it? Lily suggested to Tyler, who was leaning down to pet the dog. She had calmed a bit and seemed to be sitting comfortably.

"That sounds nice," Tyler said. She even managed a small smile.

Lily prepared the hot drink and handed it to her guest, who sipped and sighed with pleasure. A sweet, creamy drink with alcohol was just what the doctor wouldn't order, but it seemed to be doing her good. Lily saw signs of Tyler's body relaxing.

"I didn't get a chance to thank you," Tyler began. "All your help with the police."

"Shush, let's not talk about that right now," Lily said. "You had a shock and there's no need to bring up bad stuff."

Tyler nodded. "I thought I could just go back to life. Such as it is." She wiped another tear that had suddenly appeared. "I just wanted to go out for a drive and visit the diner. But I got so afraid."

"Panic attack?" Lily asked.

"Something like that."

The two women chatted away in the warm shop. Tyler felt a realization dawn. She was the girl who learned to dance through sheer force of will. She was the girl who struck out on her own and conquered Vegas. The entertainment capital of the world found a place for her. A place where she was needed. And now she couldn't get out of her own mother's SUV for a trip to a diner. If it wasn't so awful, she'd cry over it. But that wasn't how Tyler Carter got things done. "Please don't tell anyone, Lily," she requested. "This will pass. I don't want people to think I'm sick or crazy."

"What about your mother?" Lily said. "Will you tell her?"

"Let's just talk about something else for a minute. It makes me feel better." She took a long pull of the spiked coffee. "Tell me what's going on with you."

Lily shrugged. "I've had my hands full, as you know."

"Your mother and father passed, I heard. I'm so sorry."

Lily shook her curly head. "It was hard to lose the two of them so soon after each other. But you know, Dad just couldn't be without her. I'm sure they're sitting on a cloud somewhere now, having the time of their lives." She bit her lower lip.

"Do you feel alone?" Tyler couldn't imagine what it would be like without her siblings and parents.

"Sure. Especially when I think of something I really need to tell Ma or Dad, and then I remember they're not here anymore. But you know the people of our little town. No way they're going to leave you alone for even five minutes to feel really lonely. I don't think I've had to cook for almost half a year. Everybody brought me food, including your mother. She was so incredibly sweet to me. Now my talent is in letting my parents' business grow. It's mine now, and it's a way of honoring them."

Tyler set her cup down. "That's beautiful. I want to honor my parents, too. I want to get past this knee and that crazy idiot who is now wiped off the face of this earth. I want my life back."

"That's the spirit," Lily said. "But remember, it's a process. Don't push too hard."

Tyler was already gathering her cane. "One day at a time. I can do this. Thank you so much, Lily. Thanks for everything."

"You're welcome. Can I help you back to the car?"

"No, I can do it myself."

Lily watched as Tyler made her way back to the SUV. The wind was coming up, and she had to pull her parka closed with one hand while navigating the cane with the other. "There's a reason she made it to the top in Las Vegas," Lily said softly, before turning back to her work.

Pat walked his duffel bag up to Room 6 of the bed-and-breakfast. A small sign on the room door said *Cattle Rustler*. Oh, the irony. So much for paying his debt to society and expunging his past. In Independence, he was forever branded. The door opened easily, and he was glad that the wood felt solid and heavy, not flimsy. A pair of Angus cattle horns were mounted on the wall over the four-poster bed. The quilt had a horseshoe pattern. Burlap curtains hung at the window. This was yesterday's

Independence. It felt comforting. Pat put his bag down and sat on the bed. The mattress didn't complain, and it felt comfortable, so he stretched out.

Before leaving the Wilkinson house, he had given it one last look-over. The crew were going to speed up the work that caused the need for tarps to be over open areas. The mission was to secure the house as soon as possible. Then Pat could move back in as the rest of the job progressed. The old place was slowly returning to its stately splendor. This was what had fascinated him about restoration from the beginning. Reviving architecture from times long past. Preserving a piece of history.

Pat could imagine looking specifically for more projects like this. It would probably mean traveling a lot. He wasn't particularly comfortable with that idea. Had Tyler already made plans? He suspected she wouldn't be particularly enthusiastic about moving like a nomad from one project to another. Maybe he should sit down and rethink his plans for the future.

The last time he thought about his career and life, he was still in Seattle. He'd sold the company to his business partner when it became clear that they were pursuing different goals. Jaz, who had just moved to the Rockies at the time, had raved to him about the region and told him about this project. She knew full well he would not be able to resist such an assignment. So he'd spontaneously decided to spend half a year here. There never was a plan to stay forever. He liked it very much in Independence, but Seattle also had very nice neighborhoods. Except Tyler wasn't there.

He hadn't counted on Tyler being here. Tyler, who had stolen a piece of his heart during the summer, and the rest in the meantime. Tyler was here, now. Not in Seattle. *But where was she?*

Pat hung a few things in the closet and decided to head to the diner for a bite.

This time, Tyler was determined to behave like a normal, healthy person and have a cup of coffee at the diner counter. She would park the car and walk in as she'd done a thousand times before. She would speak to people she knew, and have a cheerful word with Minnie and Daisy. Knowing the people here, they likely wouldn't grill her about "what happened." Everybody knew William Vermont was dead. The knee and the cane would likely pause them on conversation that dug too deeply.

Step number one was parking her mother's SUV. The snowball fighters were long gone, and she got a spot right outside the diner. Making her way with the cane over the few yards to the restaurant, she was drenched in sweat. She hoped that was mostly the after-effects of the general anesthesia and not a reflection of her actual fitness.

Miss Minnie helped her out of her jacket, leaned her cane against the wall where she could easily reach it again, and brought her a cup of coffee without being asked. "If you need anything else, just holler, honey."

Amazing how tactful the usually talkative Miss Minnie could be when she wanted. Or maybe Tyler had it written across her face in big letters: *Attention! Patient about to keel over.* Because that's how she felt. *This, too, will pass*, she told herself stoically. This forced break was giving her the opportunity to take care of her life. True, she urgently needed to have a talk with Yuri and Sarah. She still hadn't called them back. Until now, she had successfully suppressed all thoughts about her agent and choreographer, just like the questions about her career. But now that she'd had the surgery, it seemed time to deal with it.

Tyler looked outside and watched people stroll along the Main Street stores or stop to talk to friends. This was the first time she'd felt clear-headed since the surgery. She was grateful, since there were a lot of stories about people who had problems with concentration after a general anesthetic.

Miss Minnie stepped up to her and refilled her coffee. Tyler nodded thanks, hoping to avoid a conversation. But the Disney Sisters were not known to be put off by subtle signs. After all, they would never find out that way. That's why Miss Minnie held onto the cup when Tyler tried to reach for it. "Not so fast, sweetheart. How are you feeling?"

Tyler tried to answer the question evasively and reached for her coffee again. Miss Minnie pulled the cup back a bit more. So she had to give her something.

"Tired. So-so."

"And here I was thinking it had something to do with our new resident at the B and B. That delicious architect."

Tyler groaned loudly and let her head sink toward the counter. What had she been thinking coming back to

Independence? She must have been mentally deranged. Oh, that's right—there was nowhere else to go to lick her wounds in peace. But the peace and quiet seemed in shorter supply here than in Vegas.

"What is it?" Minnie asked, as Tyler raised her head with astonished eyes. "I'm old. Not dead."

Rather than give Minnie a dirty look, Tyler stared at her cane with deathly contempt.

"Really hate that stick, huh?" Minnie, the mind-reader, said.

Tyler nodded in agreement.

"There, there," said the patroness, patting her hand soothingly. "It can't be that bad. Here, drink your coffee." She handed her the cup as if that hadn't been an option all along.

"Your architect is staying with us at the bed-and-breakfast now. Did he tell you?"

Now Tyler was glad she had waited to take a sip. Otherwise, she probably would have spit the coffee across the diner. Miss Minnie's news was a shocker. She took a deep breath, turned her attention to the hot drink in her hand, and tried to hold in her anger. But then she slumped a little on her stool. Miss Minnie had pretty much hit all the sore spots that were there. Pat hadn't called. She was already receding from his life.

Better to leave the diner before it occurred to Miss Minnie that she hadn't answered any questions. Tyler pulled a couple of bills out and placed them next to the coffee mug. On the way out, she made an extra effort to not limp.

Pat made it in through the back door of the diner just in time to see Tyler go out the front.

"I told her you were here," Minnie said.

"Did you tell her I was staying in the *Cattle Rustler*?" he asked anxiously.

"She didn't ask." Minnie shrugged.

For a moment, he thought of letting her go. Then he jogged through the diner and burst out the door after her. "Tyler!"

She turned. Pat caught up to her and put a hand to her cheek. The tender gesture almost made her cry, and she knew she had to stop it at all costs. If she completely collapsed now, she hadn't the strength to get back up and collect all the pieces. "Please don't," she whispered.

He scrutinized her and seemed to recognize the fear lurking in her pleading look. His hand reluctantly pulled away.

Now she'd done it. She'd shown him her problems were much bigger than they appeared. Not to mention the horrible-looking sight she was by now.

"If you need more time, I'll give it to you gladly. I'm just so glad to see you," he said. "If you need me, you know where to find me. Anytime."

She nodded. Not trusting her voice. After a brief clearing of her throat, she managed a "thank you." She didn't dare hug him goodbye. It felt like she might break into a million pieces right there in the street.

Back at her mother's homestead, with Ranger snoring beside her on the bed, Tyler placed a call to Sarah, her agent.

"Darling! We were so worried when we didn't hear from you." Sarah had a forced tone to her voice, as if conflicting emotions were all hitting her brain center at once. "How is everything?"

Tyler imagined her office-in-the-sky in Manhattan. The agent sat with the world at her feet. How many calls did Sarah make and take in the course of an average day? *About three hundred*, Tyler figured. She decided to make this short. "I've had a procedure on my knee. I have physio scheduled so I can be back with the show when it opens."

"Ah yes, we saw the notice from your insurance. You've been through quite an ordeal." Sarah sounded as though she were hinting at more. Wanting to go into the crime, the gruesome stuff.

"Stuff happened, Sarah. I don't want to go over it right now. In fact, I don't ever want to go over it. A bad guy disrupted my life. He's dead. I'm alive. Ring down the curtain and on with the show."

"Yuri has something to say to you." Sarah passed the phone over.

"What a coincidence you're right there in the office, Yuri," Tyler said. It was easy to keep sarcasm out of her voice. The raw truth didn't need sarcasm.

"We care about you, Tyler. Don't punish us for that." Yuri's voice was sad and full of emotion.

Tyler imagined his bald head and strong face expressing a touch of tenderness. She melted a little. "Thank you."

"I always ask myself, 'What would Martha Graham do?'" He was referring to the dance legend, born in Pennsylvania, who took the world by storm with her modern choreography by the 1920s and beyond.

"Martha would get back to dancing as soon as possible."

"Exactly. I have an idea for you."

So many questions raced through Tyler's head she couldn't answer. She just stayed still, breathing. And listening.

"The Internet knows all about the crime. The discussion boards are full of it. Maybe the outside world doesn't care so much, but Vegas cares. People are asking when you're coming back. I could have you back onstage in two weeks."

Tyler sputtered. Much as she'd love to go for it, that was a physical impossibility. "How? How?" was all she could manage.

"You dance a solo in a wheelchair. Just imagine— the black sheath dress shimmering under the lights. You extend the satin ballet slipper on your good leg as you wheel across the stage and turn in circles to the music. We'll put glittering wings on the wheelchair. We'll get the music customized, we'll get designers to put crystals all over the chair. We can triple ticket prices—"

Yuri's voice was silenced as Tyler felt herself sliding. She let out a desperate, despairing cry and let her body go all the way to the floor. The phone went flying into the fireplace, where it smashed into a dozen pieces. And then she wept to the sound of her own heart tearing in two.

CHAPTER TWENTY

BRENDA CARTER EASED her husband's car into the drive of their homestead. She was driving Stan's car because she'd given her SUV to Tyler to drive. Today, Stan would get dropped off and picked up whenever he asked as repayment for his sacrifice. Brenda noticed that the SUV was parked, so Tyler was home. Cole was out somewhere, and so Brenda had taken Ranger with her grocery shopping. With his ADA service dog status, he could travel just about anywhere.

At the door, Ranger scratched to get in. When it opened, he took off like a shot and seconds later gave two quick barks. Brenda had her arms full of groceries, but didn't take the time to set them down. She glanced into the living room and saw a sight that would make any mother's heart skip a beat.

Tyler had collapsed on the floor. Her cane had gone flying. Her phone was smashed against the fireplace stone. Her arms and legs were akimbo and her hair had come loose and was spread wildly over her face and chest.

Brenda let out a strangled cry, "Tyler!"

"Mom," Tyler moaned. She pushed herself upright. Then she started to laugh.

Brenda didn't know what to make of this. She rushed to Tyler's side.

"Ahhh, ha ha ha!" Tyler sucked in a great breath and then started to cry.

"Get up honey, let's move you to the sofa."

"Oh, oh, it's too funny!" She sobbed harder, but let herself be helped up. "Mom, they want me to dance in a wheelchair."

"They what, honey?" Brenda helped Tyler hop to the couch where she flopped in a heap.

"Th-they, Sarah and Yuri, ha-ha, they want to make me a poster-victim. What did they used to call those people in the old circuses? Curiosities. They want me to be a curiosity."

Brenda straightened Tyler's clothes and brushed her hair back from her face.

"They don't care if I get better to dance my old part. As long as they sell tickets."

"Did you hurt anything when you fell, sweetheart?"

"I slid."

"Did you bang your head at all?"

"The only thing that got hurt was my phone."

"I can see that. I'm going to have to sweep that up."

Tyler stopped laughing and crying. She stretched and yawned. "Maybe I'll just stretch out here and have a little nap."

"You do that. Ranger is going to have a nap right along with you."

"Ranger..." Tyler let her fingers trail alongside the couch until she came in contact with his soft coat. A cold nose nuzzled into her hand.

Out of Tyler's earshot, a soft knock came on the front door. Brenda hurried to it and found an unlikely pair on the doorstep. Her son, Jake, and Rose McArthy had arrived at the same time.

"Goodness, what a surprise!" Brenda exclaimed.

"I heard there was trouble in River City," Rose said in her characteristically frank fashion. She handed over a bag full of jars of preserved fruit. Her specialty. "Tyler will heal in a jiffy if she gets lots of ice cream with my sweet fruit over top."

In her seventies, Rose was the future grandmother-in-law of Jake if he married Jaz. Rose was still as petite as she had been in her youth, and she wore her long silver-gray hair twisted up and tucked under a purple cashmere *cloche* hat. Rose McArthy was as colorful as her wardrobe. She also possessed a great deal of common sense that was necessary to run a farm for forty years, as she had with her late husband. Jaz and Jake were currently living in that house.

"Hi Mom," Jake said. "This is a chance meeting. We didn't plan this."

Brenda took the fruit and led them into the kitchen. "Tyler's just napping on the sofa. If we keep our voices down, she can't hear us. Are we okay sitting out here?"

"Absolutely," Rose said. "Now what's going on?"

Brenda explained the latest developments to Jake and Rose.

When she finished, Jake sighed heavily. "I'm glad the phone is broken," he said. "Tyler can't take any more calls from those crazy entertainment people."

"I'm afraid for her mental well-being," Brenda said. "She had a laughing-crying jag after that call."

"There are two things I'm concerned about," Rose said. "Tyler was thrown off first by her injury. Then she suffered an attack which I'm still not one hundred percent clear on, by the way, but your son says the details should go without attention for a while. So I'll stick to Tyler. Now she's looking at her career being thrown off course and herself made into something she doesn't want. That's enough to shake anybody."

"But what should we do for her?" Brenda asked? She looked at Jake, who was listening intently.

"She was doing pretty well with the injury and surgery. Is that right?"

"Yes, that's true. Pat, the architect restoring the Wilkinson house, became a friend. He was a bright spot in her life while she was hurt."

"Where is he now?"

Brenda and Jake looked at one another.

"He hasn't been around for a few days."

"And she gave up Ranger, too, you said. Ranger wasn't with her this morning."

"True," Brenda said. "She gave him back to Cole, and Cole left Ranger with me while he went about some business."

Rose tapped the counter with her forefinger. "If I recall your daughter, Brenda, she was always very driven. She's probably pushing too hard, maybe even trying to ignore events so she can get her old life back."

Brenda looked almost fearful at those words.

"Now don't fret. In my opinion, you should insist she take back the dog and get that friend Pat back into the picture. Let rest and healing take care of the situation. This will right itself, you mark my words. But Tyler needs support at the same time as she needs to feel she can be an independent woman."

Brenda and Jake just looked at one another.

"I've said my piece and I'll be off. Do you have an ice-cream maker?"

"Somewhere here," Brenda mumbled. She looked stunned.

"My fruit on top of some homemade ice cream is just the ticket. You should have some too, young man," she said to Jake. "Now, I'm off." She gathered her keys and hat. "If you need me, you know where to find me."

When Brenda went to the living room to check on Tyler, she had already gone to her bedroom and was sleeping peacefully with Ranger at her feet.

"Well, well, well, what have we here?" A familiar, feminine French accent filled the room like a soft breeze of sound.

Tyler sat up in bed. The lighting in her bedroom was beautiful, but strange. Everything had a purple cast to it. Out of a violet shadow stepped Madame DuPont. She looked only fifty years old, possibly less. The age she was when Tyler met her as an eight-year-old.

The voice continued, "The artist has a damaged instrument. The artist is you. The instrument is your body. Every dancer faces this moment at some time, either through injury or age. This time is now yours."

Madame DuPont," Tyler whispered. "You came back..."

"Temporarily. I'm visiting you in a dream so I can help you."

"Madame, they wanted to put me onstage in a wheelchair. I can't, I couldn't—"

"That's because you are clinging so tightly to who you thought you were. You are no longer that person, you no longer have that instrument."

"Can't I get it back?"

"You can do so many things, a million things, but no, you can't get that back exactly the way it was."

Madame DuPont's voice was getting fainter. She took a step back toward the shadows.

"No! Don't go!" Tyler cried frantically.

"You know," Madame DuPont said, as she took a final step and was swallowed completely by the shadows, "Martha Graham would have taken that wheelchair. She would have rocked the stage so hard the audience would never forget it."

"But I'm not Martha Graham!"

"That's the point, darling. You are *you*. Think about it."

Five Years Ago

Calls for casting, Las Vegas! Register and submit to local acting, dancing and singing projects now! We want headshots and a simple video of your talent demonstration. Top show producers are waiting to see what you can do NOW!

Tyler was so excited. In less than twenty-four hours after registering online at the Calls for Casting site, she had an audition.

Landing at McCarran airport at night, she had taken a bus to one of the discount hotels downtown. Driving down The Strip was breathtaking. The bus took a circuitous route and headed to the very southern end of The Strip to drive past the iconic Welcome to Las Vegas sign. It had been there since the 1950s, with its perpetually exploding star cluster at the top. The sign symbolized all the excitement and promise that Tyler felt in her heart.

From there, the bus did a U-turn and headed back up Las Vegas Boulevard, or "The Strip" as everybody called it. In the distance, the Mandalay Bay hotel loomed. Out front, a sign boasted of a show based on the life and dancing of Michael Jackson. Just the thought of so many dancers working in one place made Tyler's heart beat faster. The bus rattled past miles of neon—Luxor, MGM, Planet Hollywood. A replica of Paris's Eiffel tower sparkled and flashed in welcome. Bellagio's dancing waters went up in a spectacular geyser as the bus passed by. The Wynn offered luxury far beyond Tyler's means. *One day, maybe.*

Finally, the bus deposited her downtown. This was the older section of the city with old-school gambling dens like Binion's and the Golden Nugget still operating as if it were seventy-plus years ago. For twenty-five dollars a night, this is where you could get a little "hole in the wall" room plus coffee and a breakfast danish in the morning. Tyler stepped off the bus and shivered with anticipation. Was there a place for an eighteen-year-old ballerina in Las Vegas?

"My name is Yuri," the formidable Russian man said at the front of the rehearsal hall. He was muscled like a classical ballet dancer and dressed in all black with a shaved head. He gestured at the room. The walls were covered with mirrors and a barre ran all the way around the room. "Nobody is going to pay money to see you hop around like a jackrabbit. Coordination please! You are the elite. Act like it."

Tyler was lined up at the barre with ten other ballerina hopefuls. They had been called out of a waiting room of tumblers, trapeze artists, tap dancers, and high-flying aerialists to take their turn in front of Yuri.

Tyler flexed in her pointe shoes. She was wearing a simple leotard and her hair slicked back in a bun. Not a big doorknob bun—those were sneered at in the ballet community—but a demure bun, well-pinned and covered with a hairnet to capture flyaways. Her pink satin pointe shoes had been broken in just that morning via a tortured ritual of custom stretching, pulling, cutting and heating them with a blow dryer to make the changes permanent. Parts of the shoes she'd resewn, and it was Madame DuPont who, many years ago, taught her to sew with dental floss instead of thread. It was stronger and held longer.

Before putting the shoes on an "ouch pouch" went over the ends of her bare toes to provide cushioning. Her makeup was light with lots of powder to catch sweat. No blush on the cheeks—dancing was hot and sweaty work. A pink flush to the face would happen naturally. And plenty of powder on the ears. No red ears!

Tyler had a number stuck to the front and back of her leotard in five-inch tall numerals that corresponded to a printout in Yuri's hand, so he could easily find the names and look up the full application if he wished.

"What you want to achieve today," Yuri said, his bald head shining in the overhead light, "is not to land a dancing role in a show. You want to land a spot in our database of talent. If you bring something unique, a role may be created for you. It might be just a small cameo. But it's a great place to start."

Who could have known that Yuri, a fledgling choreographer from the Russian ballet corps and fresh off the plane from Moscow, would rise up the ranks like a juggernaut? "It's not enough to be good," he told her. "You must be able to sustain ten shows a week."

The rest was history.

"I have an idea, Tyler!" Yuri enthused. You will dance on the moon! In a silver dress, yes? First, you will play with it like a big round ball on the stage, dancing around it, playing. And then you will fly on top of it."

"Fly on top of it?" Tyler laughed and covered her mouth. "How am I supposed to fly?"

"We will have a custom harness made for you. Invisible under your dress with tiny wires that will lift you as you jump and soar. You will take a little leap and the stagehands holding wires offstage will lift you onto the ball. The lighting will change. The stage will go all black. But you and the moon will glow as you rise, your silver dress fluttering like gossamer as you dance on it. The moon rises twenty-five feet in the air and then it moves across the stage as you fly around it, land on it, and dance on it."

"Wow," Tyler exclaimed.

After a lot of work, an *unbelievable* amount of work, it happened just like that. Every night and matinee for ten shows per week, Tyler danced on the moon.

Present Day, Carter Family Homestead

When Tyler rose from her long nap at her parents' house, she could hear voices. It sounded like the house was full of people, all talking in low voices. She rummaged through her suitcase and got out the best clothing she'd brought with her. Granted it was only leggings with a T-shirt and hoodie, but the clothing was brand new and "Vegas cool" which meant both items had sparkly trim and were made of quality materials. She combed her hair out so it fell down her back in a blond fall and applied lots of mascara. The woman staring back from the mirror looked like she had it together. And in a way, she did. Out she went.

Her brothers and sisters and various add-ons like Jaz and Leslie were evenly divided between the kitchen and the living room. Dips and snacks and appetizers were everywhere, along with beer and wine and soft drinks. When Brenda saw her, she dropped a spoon in the bowl she was mixing and splashed salad dressing all over her front.

"Tyler! So nice to see you, honey. You're up!"

Tyler smiled, kissed her, and said, "I am up. In more ways than one. I've made a decision and I have an announcement."

Mopping at the front of her shirt, Brenda said, "Why don't we all go out to the living room so you only have to say this once."

"That's a good idea, Mom. Let's do it."

Without a word, they all filed out silently and spread themselves around as the fireplace crackled. Tyler looked from face to face. Her mother and father radiated concern. Cole and Jake had their professional stone faces on, preparing for any eventuality. Jaz was a little wide-eyed, and Paula was watching carefully, with her arm around Leslie.

"Over the last few weeks, we've been through the wringer," Tyler said in her clearest voice. "And I've been full of concern about my future with the show. It took some thinking to get here, but I've made two decisions I feel good about."

Tyler looked at her mother, who smiled encouragingly.

"My first decision is to keep Ranger by my side if Cole will let me."

Cole looked pleasantly surprised. "That can be arranged. Happy to do it."

"My next decision is a little different." She shifted her body a bit, unconsciously balancing her torso as though she were about to go onstage. "Some dancers work a lifetime and never get to a main stage in Vegas. I'm twenty-three and I've danced on the moon. Literally. I've come to the decision that I'm going out on top. I'm sure Mom's told you that this afternoon I was offered a cameo, dancing in a wheelchair. I think that's an incredible thing for a disabled person to do, but that's not an option for me. I don't know what the future holds. I could dance professionally in a less-demanding role. I could teach. I could choreograph. I have time to decide while I heal and take physical therapy. But for now, all my fear about going back to the show is over. I'm leaving. I'm going out on top, and that's final."

Sighs and gasps of relief went around the room. Brenda stepped forward with her arms wide. "Baby. I'm so happy for you. Happy, sad, relieved that you know what you want."

Her father, Stan, gave her a big kiss. Paula and Leslie wrapped her in a big hug. Everyone took their turn supporting her.

Tyler put her hand up for one last word. All heads turned in her direction. "Before we eat, has anyone heard from Pat?"

It was the end of the night at the Carter homestead. Holding the remains of a slab of chocolate cake, Jake came up by Tyler's elbow and said, "I understand you lost your phone."

"I didn't lose it, it got smashed in my meltdown this afternoon. But thanks for putting a soft filter on that lens."

"I didn't know we were swearing on the family bible," Jake joked.

"We're not. I just need to keep things very clear in my head right now. The only way I know how is to be honest. Even if it's ugly."

"Your phone is still gone, no matter how you frame it, though. So how are you going to get through to Pat? Or how can he call you?"

"I guess he could call me on Mom and Dad's home phone here. I don't have his number anymore since it was stored on my cell."

"Sure, I have the number. I'll let him know. Glad you got your mojo back, little sis. Proud of you." Jake kissed the top of her head. Tyler hugged him back. Everything was going to be okay. All of a sudden, the future looked real. Like it was still there, at least. All she had to do was imagine it.

An hour later, before he went to bed, Stan Carter turned the ringer off on the kitchen phone. They all needed a good night's sleep without worry and should an emergency happen, his cell phone would still pick up calls.

Early morning, inside the *Cattle Rustler* room, Pat's phone buzzed on the nightstand. With a sleepy grunt, he turned over and groped for it. "Yes?"

On the other end was Bernie, one of his crew at the Wilkinson house. "Boss, we have a problem at the house."

"What's wrong?"

"The storm knocked down the scaffolding and blew off the tarps on the west side. Snow is coming into the house."

"Crap." Pat glanced at the analog clock on the nightstand. Six a.m.

"I'll be there as soon as I can."

He jumped out of bed with the phone and pushed open the burlap curtains. There wasn't much to see in the dim light outside the B and B, but it appeared that the snow had stopped. "Thanks Bernie. Start sweeping out the snow already. I'll make some calls and see if I can speed up delivery of the new windows. See you later."

He hit the "end" button on his phone. Checked for messages. There were some, but none from Tyler. He had worked up the decision to call her and left a first message yesterday afternoon. Now, there were three messages waiting for her, all from him.

At the house, it had also stopped snowing, but a bitterly cold wind whistled down from the Rockies. They loomed like mist-shrouded peaks in the background. Pat had spent the past two hours sweeping and mopping the first-floor rooms. Now he tried to persuade the company that was to deliver the new windows to drive out here today. But they refused. Truckers were in short supply and deliveries were wait-listed. An unbeatable argument.

He gave two short whistles through his teeth. Bernie and his cousin came around the corner.

"What's up, boss?"

"No windows. That means we need to board up the casements with particle board as soon as possible before the next snow comes. After that, we need to secure the scaffolding."

"Dismantle is probably the better option."

"I think so, too. Let's get to work." He looked at the clock on his cell. Ten in the morning. It was a decent time to try Tyler again. He went straight to voicemail.

This is Tyler. I'm not here right now, but I'd love to hear from you. Please leave me a message. But instead of a beep and the expected recording time, another message came on. *This mailbox is full. Please try again.*

Full? Why hadn't Tyler cleared her messages?

BRIING! Like magic, Jake was calling. Pat dove after the call like a drowning man lunging for a life preserver.

"Jake! Tyler's message box is full. She's not answering my calls."

"I'm sorry, bro. Phone accident. She wanted me to give you the number for Mom's place. Call her on their house line. I'm sure she'll get the cell phone replaced. If she orders one online, it should arrive in a couple of days. Mom has a computer she can do that on."

Pat felt relief slide off his back. "Whoa, it's great to hear from you."

"Doing okay?"

"Working it off, Jake."

"Call her."

"I hear you. Will do."

Pat called. He called and called. He left messages. He heard nothing back from Tyler. Nothing.

No matter what Jake thought, and Pat believed he was telling the truth, it was more likely that Tyler knew his past history with William had brought this ordeal into her life. He was radioactive with a bad past. It would be just like Tyler to come to that conclusion privately and then not tell anyone else so as not to poison his relationships with others around her. His shoulders drooped as he thought, *Might as well read the handwriting on the wall and get used to it.*

The morning came and went. Tyler tried not to hover over the phone because, like the proverbial watched pot, it just wouldn't boil. Or in this case, ring. On the kitchen counter, her mother's cell phone lay abandoned. "Mom," she called, "can I use your phone to call Jake?"

"Okay," came the distant call from a far room.

Tyler picked it up and found her mother's contacts list. Jake was right at the top. Number one son, as always.

He answered before the first ring was finished. "Mom?"

"It's me, Tyler. I'm using Mom's phone."

"What's up?"

"Did you call Pat?"

"Yesterday. He said he'd call the house."

A pain shot through her heart. "He didn't call."

Jake was silent for a moment. "He seemed anxious to call you."

"So anxious he didn't get around to it."

"What can I say? Give it time."

"Okay, thanks." She hung up.

She called right back.

Jake answered on the first ring. "Mom? Tyler?"

"Give me his number, please?"

He gave it to her.

There was a pause as she swallowed. "How did you know Jaz was the one for you?"

He made a sound she couldn't quite interpret.

"Forget it," she said. "It was a stupid idea to ask you. I'm sure your girlfriend will be more helpful there. Though she might reconsider if I tell her you couldn't think of a reason."

"Ouch. All right. I'll try to answer your question." She heard the sound of him fumbling with the phone.

"I'm glad I'm not the only one with a communication problem. Must run in the family," she murmured.

"It's possible," he admitted. How Cole and Sam handled communications, he wasn't sure. But he couldn't imagine either of them wearing their hearts on their sleeves. Cole was an FBI agent and undercover all the time. What about Paula? Paula was happy if she didn't have to talk too much. From that point of view, it was probably a stroke of luck that Jaz put up with him at all. When his thoughts stopped racing he started to speak. "Jaz intrigued me at first, the way beautiful women do that to men. But before I knew it, she was the first to come to mind when I wanted a first opinion. The first I wanted to see after work. Before long, I couldn't imagine my life without her."

Tyler remained silent. She had never heard her brother speak so passionately. Yet he was calm. As if he had arrived at exactly where he wanted to be in his life. She envied him for that. One last question was on her mind. "If Jaz had wanted to go back to Seattle, would you have gone with her?"

Jake ran a hand through his hair, thinking about her question. "It probably would have taken me a while to get used to the idea. Bottom line, I would have followed her anywhere."

"What if it turned out you weren't happy there?"

"Would I be happier if I stayed in Independence without her?" he countered. "You never know whether you'll be happy with a choice. I don't think that's what your question is about. It's about whether you dare. Dare to trust the other person."

That was a convincing statement. It confirmed her own conclusion. Up until now, she had been cowardly. She chewed her lips and made a mental note to buy lip balm.

"Thanks," she said.

"Don't mention it. That's what big brothers are for."

She hung up again and called out with an up and down lilt to her voice, "Mo-om."

A distant voice answered again, "Yes, dear."

"I'm taking your phone into my room. I'm calling Pat."

"I won't disturb you," Brenda answered.

Ranger followed Tyler into the bedroom and curled up on the floor. This time, he seemed to understand she needed privacy. Tyler dialed the number Jake had given her and went immediately to voicemail. *This is Patrick West of Westward Architects. Please leave a message so I can get back to you ASAP.*

Tyler cleared her throat. As she started to speak, Stan Carter started up his snowblower right outside. She continued leaving a message, anyway. "It's Tyler. I guess Jake told you I have no phone. Forget calling. Just come out here as soon as you can. Please. I can't stand not seeing you, not having you close." She shut her eyes. "And I hope you feel the same way." She pressed *End Call.*

Up on Wilkinson Butte, Pat came in from outside. He had been scouting the windows, making sure the new protective particleboard and plywood over the casements was secure and watertight. The minute he got back inside the house within signal range, his cell phone pinged with a message. It was from a strange number, one he didn't recognize. Maybe a new client? He played the message back. All he got was white noise and static. Dang telemarketers.

Annoyed, he blocked the number.

CHAPTER TWENTY-ONE

Six Years Ago, Quantico, FBI Training Center

As Avery watched, Cole Carter flew through the air, thrown by one of the other recruits in training. Cole smacked the ground chest-first with a *thud!* The kind of impact that bruises and takes your breath away for a good long while. Avery's turn was up next, probably with a partner she was not even a match for. But that's the way training went at Quantico. It never progressed exactly as you expected.

Back on the training field, Cole struggled to get upright. Avery caught him looking around to see if she had witnessed his defeat. She lowered her eyes. No sense rubbing it in. Cole Carter was no pushover, and this was only a temporary defeat. He was smart, solid, fit, and had a good brain. He was going somewhere. And she'd caught him twice looking at her. But a romance between FBI recruits was not just a terrible idea, it could be a career destroyer. During training, nobody could afford such distractions.

Getting into Quantico meant competing and winning against thousands of FBI wannabes in a rigorous application process. It was taking countless hours studying ethics, investigative techniques, learning operations, intelligence investigations, and like today, pushing their bodies to physical limits.

Still, *the heart wants what the heart wants.* The quotation floated into Avery's mind. If only she and Cole had met some other way, at some other time. Avery straightened her cap and prepared for her turn at combat training. Everything and everyone else was going to have to wait.

Present Day, Independence

Cole pulled up in front of a house painted all-white with green shutters and trim. The trimmed bushes out front were lit with soft white lights, and the path to the front door also had gentle lights illuminating the way. It looked very inviting.

"Believe it or not," said Cole, "this is a restaurant."

Avery peered out the window of his vehicle. "It looks very sweet. How did you find this place?"

Not wanting to credit his brother, Cole said mysteriously, "I have connections."

"I get it. Your brother told you," Avery said.

Cole threw back his head and laughed. This wasn't a date. It was a thank you to Avery for loaning her professional profiler services to assist the Carter family. That was the way Cole phrased it when he asked, and it must have been right, because Avery accepted.

She waited until Cole got out and walked around to open the door for her. She knew this wouldn't happen very often in Seattle. But Independence was different, as her new relationship with her great grandfather was teaching her. For the occasion, she was wearing a simple, body-skimming wool dress with a bolero jacket in a Ute Indian print. Most striking was a necklace of dyed turquoise quillwork adorning her neck like a collar. Slim black ankle boots with kitten heels looked fine with the outfit, but she had nothing but a parka to go over the top. Since they were right outside the house, she debated whether to just leave the parka in the car and brave the weather for a few yards.

As Cole cracked the door open, she said, "Mind if I leave my coat in the car?"

"I don't care, but won't you be cold?"

"It's only a few yards. I'm not a fan of the parka-and-dress look."

"Sure. Afterward, I can bring the coat to you if the weather gets worse. We'll have had a few drinks by that time."

"You're right, nobody will care. Least of all me!" She put a note of laughter on the end of that, and Cole was completely charmed. To know her was to love her—correction—to know her was to like her a lot. As a friend and colleague, of course.

She popped out of the car and took Cole's arm so they could scurry down the short walkway. Cole leaned in to get the door and in a split second they were inside the house, bringing a wave of cold air with them. The living room of the house had been converted into a small fine-dining room. Four white-clothed tables had small vases of flowers and candles glowing. Only one table by the window was vacant. As they waited, a man wearing a chef's apron appeared and greeted them.

"A sight for sore eyes!" the man said with a theatrical flare. He shook Cole's hand enthusiastically. "The Carter men bring the most beautiful and interesting women in the state here. Tonight is no exception."

Before answering, Cole looked for Avery's reaction. She seemed to be taking it okay. Frank was a "personality," a transplant from the big city where he had learned to cook international dishes that won awards and got rave reviews in gourmet magazines. But he and his wife Gail had exchanged the glitz and glamour for a simpler life, one infinitely more interesting and connected to a meaningful community than the lifestyle they left behind.

Cole said simply, "Avery, I'd like you to meet Frank, the proprietor and host."

Frank took Cole's coat and graciously ignored the fact that Avery wasn't wearing one. He gestured at the empty table next to the window. "Allow me." He pulled a chair back and looked at Avery, inviting her to sit.

She gave him a genuine smile. This warm man knew how to make people feel welcome. Maybe he was a bit larger than life, but no one could say he wasn't trying his best.

A beaming, dark-haired woman appeared at the table and clasped Frank's arm. "The asparagus for table two is ready, darling," she said. As Frank hurried off, she said, "I'm Gail, the other half of this restaurant. You just met my husband, who is the star in the kitchen." She removed the charger plates sitting on the table. "Any dietary restrictions?"

Cole and Avery both shook their heads no.

Gail filled their water glasses. "Cocktails or wine this evening?"

Cole looked to Avery as though to say, "I'll follow your lead."

"I think that food and drink experts can make some surprisingly good choices if you let them," Avery said diplomatically. "Why don't you choose?"

"An adventurer! I like you already," Gail said.

"Wine or a cocktail?"

"Cocktail," they both said at the same time.

"So far, one hundred percent compatibility," Gail joked.

"Sweet or sour?"

"Sweet," said Avery.

"Sour," said Cole.

I'll be right back. Gail bustled away.

"What makes a cocktail sour, anyway?" Avery asked in a whisper.

"I think it means it has citrus in it, like orange juice."

"I was wondering if it meant a sour taste. Maybe I shouldn't have—"

Cole put his hand over hers for a brief moment. "Jake promised me anything they serve here is great. You can't go wrong."

This time, Frank returned with a silver tray and two cocktails. He picked the taller glass up and place it in front of Cole, saying, "For the gentleman—from Cuba—a classic mojito with lime, rum, and muddled fresh mint."

He placed a shorter glass in front of Avery. "And for the lady, a Grand Old Fashioned. It features Grand

Marnier, bourbon, and aromatic bitters. Guaranteed to warm you on a cold night."

"Tonight's menu honors America's First Nations. Dining begins with corn, blueberry and wild rice salad served with double cornbread muffins. The main course is bison filet mignon with fingerling potatoes and sweet potato mash. Dessert is Northern Cheyenne chokecherry pudding with sweet cornmeal crisps for dipping. Enjoy."

Avery looked at Cole in wonder. "Is this just a lucky coincidence or did you tell him?"

"I told him I might be bringing an expert on the Ute Indian tribes of Colorado. Was that okay?"

"It's more than okay. It's very thoughtful." She gave a shy smile.

Cole felt his heart skip a beat.

Avery continued, "The way this place operates, I'm surprised it hasn't got a waiting list."

"It does. Jake got us in."

"Naughty, naughty," Avery chided.

"Believe me, it was almost the end of Jake and Jaz's relationship. When he told her Frank owed him a favor, she accused him of being a dirty cop."

Avery's jaw dropped. "Dirty cop!? Where did she get that from? Did she even know what she was saying?"

"Not really. He explained it was a personal favor, not connected to the PD, but for a while there it was touch and go. He almost walked out on the date. Their first date, too."

Avery set her glass down. "That would never happen with two Quantico grads. We share too much common ground."

"Don't you mean combat ground?"

"Ha! Are you talking about that training day when you got *creamed*, and I was watching?"

"I didn't get creamed."

And so the evening went. Smooth, light, effortless.

Back at the bed-and-breakfast, Cole and Avery entered the common room, just to pass through it so they could access the hall that led to the guest rooms. There was Mr. Wilkinson sitting in a stiff-backed chair. They both stopped in surprise.

"Hi, Grandad," Avery began.

"Hey there, Mr. Wilkinson," Cole said. His mind clicked away, thinking how it was way past the older gent's bedtime. In fact, he looked like he was waiting up.

"Good morning," Mr. Wilkinson said, looking pointedly at his watch even though it was nowhere near midnight or the next day. "Where were you two? The Indie Music Festival?"

"Umm," Avery started. "There's no music festival in town that I know of. We were out to dinner."

"There's always one in town if you go looking," Mr. Wilkinson replied rather testily. "Ring on the finger first, granddaughter. Insist on it." He plucked his hat off a nearby table and plopped it on his head. "Goodnight."

He disappeared down the hall as Cole and Avery tried not to combust with laughter.

With Mr. Wilkinson on patrol, Cole felt he should end the evening on a gentlemanly note. This had been a business dinner, a thank you. The way to end it was with a polite exchange at the door to Avery's room with a handshake. Then, *exit stage left* as they used to say in the cartoons.

They walked down the hall and Cole was all prepared with a few polite lines when Avery said, "This is mine." They were outside the *Pine Grove* room. "It was a wonderful evening. So good seeing you again."

Cole almost flushed with pleasure. With effort, he kept it to a smile.

"I want to tell you one last thing about myself," Avery said.

"Sure."

"For next time, I'm a vegetarian. Mostly."

As his mouth fell open, she let herself into the *Pine Grove* and waved a few fingers goodbye.

Cole had to put a hand out to steady himself against the wall. He had fed a vegetarian red meat! Why hadn't he asked when he'd originally brought up the dinner with her? He was cringing inside with shame and remorse. Stupid!

But she said there could be a next time. So it couldn't be that bad.

Cole walked to his vehicle in the B and B parking lot like he was on a cloud.

The Next Day

The Colorado State Registry for Notable and Historic Architecture was housed in a stunning red sandstone mansion with a wraparound porch and a corner turret.

Built in 1892, it was a proud symbol of Denver's architectural significance. The people in charge of nominations to the state registry took their responsibility seriously, and so the Wilkinson application was given every scrutiny. Each page of documentation that Pat had submitted was reviewed by the committee to make sure every "i" was dotted and every "t" was crossed.

Now, on the day of their in-person interview, Pat and Mr. Wilkinson sat in the straight-backed, Victorian chairs that went with the design and decor of the Notable and Historic administration. The chairs looked great but offered little comfort to the body. This was not a place where you could forget good posture. Throwing a side glance at Mr. Wilkinson, Pat was sorry he hadn't thought to throw a suit in his bag before leaving Seattle so long ago. He was lucky he even had a dress shirt on hand. Mr. Wilkinson made up for both of them, though, in his tidy black suit, starched white shirt, and bowtie patterned with tiny American flags.

The administrator, a person of nonspecific gender and dress named Cecilu, peered over a pair of half-glasses at a printout of Pat's digital application. "I see you sent in a scanned copy of your notarized form with accompanying documentation."

"I also have the hard copy if you'd like to see it," said Pat.

Cecilu didn't answer, just kept peering. Eventually the half-glasses slipped an inch or two down Cecilu's nose, prompting a direct stare from eyes that were both bright and fierce. "We recognize properties that contribute to the understanding and appreciation of Colorado's architectural history."

"Yes," Pat and Mr. Wilkinson said in unison.

"If state recognition is awarded to your house, it means you are eligible to compete for state grants as well as tax credits."

Mr. Wilkinson broke into a broad grin. "That's the part I like!"

Pat quickly brought up a more serious angle. "We also thought that Elizabeth Wright Ingraham's association through her firm was an important point. The Wilkinson house was designed at that firm. She founded it in the 1950s in Colorado Springs. As the granddaughter of Frank Lloyd Wright, she brings the allure of the Wright cultural legacy to the home, as well."

Cecilu beamed approval. "We are well aware of the contribution of Wright Ingraham. It is the highlight of your application." Cecilu ruffled the papers into an elaborate fan and then shuffled them back into a precise stack. "Everything looks in order. The review board meets in two weeks. We will notify you first by text, and also in writing, of the board's decision."

The interview was over. Out on the sidewalk, Mr. Wilkinson was all smiles. "Son, you are the sharpest tool in my shed. I think they're going to go for it. What do you say?"

"I wouldn't doubt it, sir," Pat replied. "Let's keep all fingers and toes crossed. Meanwhile, we should pause the restoration just in case they come up with any last-minute modifications that we might have to make to qualify."

"Smart thinkin'. While we wait on those two weeks, I was thinking—"

"Sir, I had something in mind myself."

"What's that?"

"I was thinking I might go back to Seattle for a couple of weeks. Take a break from Independence."

"Ah." Mr. Wilkinson went to remove his western hat, remembered he wasn't wearing a hat, and settled for scratching his head. "It's that girl, Tyler Carter, isn't it? I haven't seen the two of you out and about lately."

"No, it's nothing like that—"

"Son..." Mr. Wilkinson faced Pat square on and his blue eyes were full of knowing, with a hint of sadness. "We're not supposed to gossip about what went on. I'm not going to bring that up. But I will say that hard times pull people together. Sometimes they pull people apart."

Pat dropped his head. Misery showed on his face.

"I'm afraid that if you go home, you might not come back."

"Course I'll come back," said Pat, with less conviction in his voice than he wanted.

The elderly man paused a moment. "When are you leaving?"

"Tomorrow morning on the ten forty-five out of Denver International."

The news reached Tyler the next morning that Pat was leaving on a flight to Seattle. The rumor on the street was that he might not be coming back. It was incredible to her that he would leave without a word after all they'd been through. At first, she was angry and hurt. But then she wondered if he'd been hit hard by the terrible experience they'd been through and wasn't in a good place. Maybe he needed someone to go in and rescue him. Just like he'd rescued her.

It was now nine in the morning. If she wanted to go on a recon mission and find out how Pat really was, there was only one way to find out. "Mom!"

"Yes, Tyler."

"Can I take the SUV for a while?"

"Sure."

The flight to Seattle was domestic and the airline recommended checking in an hour before departure. Pat was never early for anything so Tyler knew that the place to catch him was right at security before he passed through inspection.

The SUV ate up the miles to the airport. Everywhere, vehicles with roof racks strapped with skis, snowboards, and winter sports equipment whizzed past. At the airport, she threw the keys to a valet parking attendant and eased out of the driver's side with the dreaded cane. It was ten a.m. Ranger had been through many an airport and looked eager for adventure.

Seconds after they entered the terminal, they were approached by a uniformed woman wearing a security badge. Her uniform looked a little intimidating, but she had a nice expression on her face. "Good morning, ma'am," she said to Tyler. "May I check your dog's tags?

We don't allow animals in the terminal unless they are outbound on a flight or are valid service animals."

"Go ahead," Tyler agreed, jingling Ranger's leash. "He has a bunch of registrations."

The woman bent to look at the tags on Ranger's collar for a moment and then straightened. "All in order. Welcome to Denver International Airport. Have a nice day." She moved on.

The overhead electronic board showed arrival and departure gates. Frontier Flight 921P Seattle was on time, departing ten forty-five at gate eleven. The security station was on the second floor and there was no way she could make the stairs. But there had to be an escalator or an elevator. Down the hall, she found one. She and Ranger were inside and the doors were closing when a foot stuck out and a family of tourists piled on. Their rolling suitcases were enormous, and she and Ranger got squeezed to the very back. One of the kids started playing with the buttons so every time the doors started to close, they opened again. Finally, the mother dragged him back from the panel of buttons and the doors started their laborious effort to shut once again.

The trip to the second level was short, but this time one of the rolling suitcases got its wheel stuck in the floor space between the elevator and the edge of the elevator shaft. The family wrestled with the case until the open elevator doors started to buzz and honk.

"Pull the suitcase back in!" the mother said loudly.

"No, pull it out!" the father ordered the little kid stuck on the other side.

A wrestling match started while Tyler counted the seconds ticking by. Pre-boarding was likely starting at gate eleven by now. Outside, a burly attendant was making slow progress toward them. At least the honking and buzzing had attracted some attention.

"Help!" Tyler called. "Hurry, pleeeease!"

Ranger gave a short, sharp bark.

The attendant put some hustle into his step. As he reached them, the suitcase popped free, and the kid stumbled back into the attendant. They both went down like characters in an animated cartoon.

"Forward," Tyler commanded Ranger, and they dodged the flailing arms and legs to emerge into freedom.

"Which way to security screening?" Tyler yelled, louder than she meant. A few people looked up, eyeballed her cane and service dog, and helpfully pointed in one direction. Tyler headed that way.

The TSA station came into view, and so did Pat. Her heart did a flip-flop. He was in line, looking over his phone, reading intently. He looked tired, like he hadn't been sleeping. Much like herself.

Tension ran through her body like electricity through a wire. She wasn't ready for this. A restroom was a short distance away. She ducked inside and went to a sink. She ran water as cold as it could get and splashed some on her face. As she dried off with paper towels, the mirror confronted her. Ouch. Overhead fluorescent lighting washed out any color she might have had in her cheeks and offset dark circles under her eyes. The sight was almost enough to drain her willpower to see this through.

She dug a comb out of the little cross-body purse she'd taken to carrying since the injury. It left her hands free and held most everything she needed—keys, cash, driver's license. She fixed her hair. *Everybody looks better with their hair combed*, she told herself. *There's natural light from the glass walls at the boarding gate, too. It won't be as bad as what you're seeing in the mirror.* She pinched some color into her cheeks.

This is a public place. What if he makes a scene? What if he yells? What if I yell? What if I cry and make a spectacle of myself? The evil little voice continued, *Just let him go. It'll be less stress.*

Her more reasonable voice answered, *But then I'll never know. I need to have this settled and hear the words from his lips, "I don't want you."*

That seemed to shut the little voice up. But only for a second. *What if he tells you he's going to Seattle and the only way it can work is if you go with him? How would you like that? Life in Seattle.*

She was going to drive herself bonkers. When did she get so non-courageous, so un-courageous, so dis-courageous, whatever the proper word was for it? She abandoned the mirror and exited the ladies' room. Across the wide hallway she could see Pat moving through the line.

"Your attention, please. Remove shoes. Place hand luggage in one of the plastic bins," the public speaker system blared.

Pat heaved a carry-on bag over his shoulder and began walking closer to the checkpoint agents. Tyler stepped out of the entrance to the ladies' room and into the wide, tiled hallway. It had been clear just seconds ago, but now she was competing against people coming the other way. Ranger did his best to help weave through the people, but there were rolling suitcases to contend with and people much bigger and faster than Tyler hurrying in the opposite direction. Her cane got trapped between two rolling cases and gave her a painful yank before it wrenched free.

"S'cuse me. Sorry. Whoops. Ow," Tyler exclaimed as she hobbled along, trying to dodge people and luggage. She lost sight of Pat in the sea of people. A hulking man in a mixed martial arts jacket bore down on her. They were about to collide. *Eeek!* At the very last split-second, the man saw her and, instead of colliding, lifted her into the air before impact. She was pressed against his chest, but her legs, miraculously, sustained no impact at all. "I know knee injuries," he said in her ear. "This was better than letting your leg take the hit. I'm ready to set you down. All set?"

"Yes," she said as Ranger barked in alarm.

The man set her down light as a feather. He had done the correct thing. There was not so much as a twinge in her knee.

"Here, let me help you make it across this sea of humanity," he said. Putting both arms out, he acted as a human barrier and allowed her to finish walking across to the security line.

"Thank you so much," she said. But the big man was gone, swallowed by the crowd.

She strained to see Pat in the line of people waiting to be screened. *There!* He was showing the electronic boarding pass on his phone to the TSA agent. But Tyler was still too far away to reach him or even call to him. "Pat!" she called and waved. But no one that far away heard or even noticed. She was going to lose him. "Nooo," she moaned. The man who seemed her best bet for stability and support while she created a new future for herself was vanishing before her very eyes. "What am I supposed to do?" she said out loud to no one in particular.

"Miss, do you need help?" someone asked.

"Yes, I mean no!" she answered without even looking to see who was speaking. Ranger tilted his head at her. *What do you want me to do?* his eyes said.

The stranger moved on as Tyler's mind raced. Cole had said Ranger was trained in Germany. She didn't know a single word in German. But anything was worth a try.

Up at the screening entrance, Pat was reaching for his phone back from a flight official. He was kicking off his shoes, placing things in a grey plastic bin. It was now or never.

Tyler looked at Ranger. He had been watching her watch Pat. Did he recognize Pat? She couldn't tell. But Ranger looked watchful. Ready.

She didn't know the command to give the dog, so she just pointed at Pat and said, "Bring him back!"

Ranger seemed to register what she said. He leaped forward and crossed the area in four bounds, skirting the line of waiting people.

"Hey!" a passenger shouted.

Pat's back was disappearing as the TSA agent shrieked at the sight of Ranger.

"Help!" she screamed.

Ranger caught up to Pat and snapped his jaws closed on the back of Pat's winter jacket. He started to pull him backward out of the checkpoint.

Security guards rushed up. They drew weapons on the run. But when they saw Ranger's ADA vest, they paused. "Hold your fire," one of them said. The man looked around wildly and spotted Tyler, who was struggling toward them with her cane.

"TELL THIS DOG TO STAND DOWN," the man ordered.

"Ranger, come here boy," Tyler called.

Ranger let go of Pat's jacket and obediently trotted back to Tyler.

Pat eyed them both and said in a clear voice so everyone could hear, "It seems I have some business here. Guess I'll miss my flight."

CHAPTER TWENTY-TWO

AFTER DETENTION, an interrogation, a stern warning, and a call to Jake from airport law enforcement, they were let go. All three of them: Pat, Tyler, and Ranger. They walked out of the gate eleven area in silence.

"Let's just go sit somewhere before we get in the car," Pat said. "We need to get a few things out of the way." He led them to empty seats where no flights were scheduled incoming or outgoing for another hour. They were the only ones around. When Tyler took a seat, Ranger also settled down. They sat looking out a floor-to-ceiling glass wall at the tarmac where planes were taking off and landing.

"I'll start with the obvious question," Tyler said. "Why didn't you call me?"

His eyebrows shot up. "I've been doing nothing but calling you. I've called and called. I've left message after message on your old number and on the house phone number that Jake gave me."

"Granted, I haven't dealt with my old phone yet. The replacement is supposed to be here today. I have to get it up and running. But the phone at the house? It hasn't rung in days." The minute Tyler said it, a horrible look crossed her face.

"The phone hasn't rung in days, huh?" Pat said. "Has anybody checked if the ringer's off?"

"Oh no," she moaned. "Dad has a habit—"

"Now it's your turn. Why didn't you call me?"

"I DID!" she snapped. I left a heartfelt message. I begged you to come over."

"When?" His face reflected skepticism.

"A few days ago. Give me your phone."

Pat dug out his cell, tapped it, and handed it over, saying, "Here they are. All the recent calls. See?"

Tyler took it. "I see very well," she said. She pointed to a number. "See this number here? That's my mother's cell phone. It looks like my message has been deleted." She handed it back to him with a hurt look.

"Not so fast. There's no way I could recognize that number. I had no idea who it belonged to. When I listened to the message, it was nothing but static and droning. I couldn't make out one word."

The hurt look left Tyler's face. "We were both trying, don't you see?" she said in a small voice. "In Vegas we'd call this a French farce, an Italian comedy of errors."

"In case I was about to forget you're an artist, that just reminded me." He smiled for the first time.

"You get what I mean, though? We have no problem between us. There's nothing to be sorry for or forgive."

"Oh yes there is," Pat said quietly. "You were collateral damage to an old enemy out to get me." He shifted his body slightly away from hers. "Honestly. If I could undo it somehow..."

"Stop. I don't blame that on you. Did you send out invitation cards: Enemies from my past, please come and stalk my girlfriend?" She gestured dramatically with her hands for emphasis.

Ranger sat up to look at her with worried puppy-dog eyes.

Pat had a strange expression come over his face. He looked on the verge of a discovery.

"Stop beating yourself up," she pleaded. "Please. This is life. You take the good with the bad."

He leaned over and kissed her right on the mouth. He took his time and let her feel all his pent-up passion.

Ranger lay back down. He knew what this meant. The danger was over for now.

When Pat broke the kiss, Tyler asked in wonder, "Does that mean you can forgive and forget?"

"I want to. I'm ready to try."

"Please tell me you won't go back to Seattle. If we want to, we can push the reset button. Can't we?"

"Just push the reset button," he repeated.

"Why not?"

"Just like that?"

"Just like that. Let's go home."

"Home is the bed-and-breakfast right now," Pat reminded her.

"I don't care."

"We're going to have to swear Mr. Wilkinson to silence."

"I can think of something worse," she said. "We might have to promise we're not attending the Indie Music Festival."

"Let's not go overboard."

"Okay." She licked her lips.

They made it back to the B and B and into the *Cattle Rustler* without being spotted by anyone except a few disinterested tourists. Tyler took in the room with its old-timey burlap curtains and the analog clock on little feet with its 1980s design. "Nice place you got here," she said.

"The cow horns over the bed are the best feature, in my opinion," Pat replied. He hit the off-button on his phone and fell backward onto the bed. Tyler snuggled up to him. "What should we do now?"

"Shower," Pat said. "That session with airport security had me sweating bullets."

"Good point. Me first." She sat back up on the edge of the bed to perform her geriatric get-up-and-go maneuver. By now, she was able to hop a few feet without the aid of the cane. The doctor had advised her against this. If she lost her balance, her body would undoubtedly call upon the freshly operated leg, which would not help the healing process.

"By the time you make it in there, I can be out," Pat said.

"Go ahead, then."

True to his word, Pat came out, freshly showered, with a wet torso and wearing low-slung jeans. He stopped and pulled her toward him. "I'm so glad you're here," he muttered, biting her neck lightly.

A comforting shiver ran over her body, and she snuggled against his chest. He smelled heavenly, a bit like lemony shower gel, but mostly like Pat. The corners of her mouth lifted in a smile.

He began to spread feather-light kisses over her skin where her T-shirt had slipped over her shoulder. Feelings of all kinds rose in Tyler. Lust, of course, but also deep affection. She was tempted to blurt out all her thoughts, but bit her tongue. There was no time for that now. She would have plenty of opportunity later. It would be a shame to squeeze it in between kisses. Instead, she took his face between both hands and kissed him back. *Oops.* He had taken the opportunity to brush his teeth. But he didn't seem to mind the lack of mint on her breath, the way he returned her kiss. Then, with remarkable willpower, he broke away.

"What is it," she whispered. "What's wrong?"

"If we keep going, there will be no stopping. What about your knee?"

"What knee?" She pulled him close again.

Tenderly, he stroked her hair out of her forehead before giving her a playful slap on her rear end.

"Hey!"

But he only grinned devilishly.

Shaking her head and with a smile on her lips, she went into the bathroom. What could be better than having a handsome boyfriend standing bare-chested in the bedroom? Definitely a big enough incentive to take a shower as soon as possible before he put on a sweatshirt.

Later that afternoon, Tyler called Joe's Snow Removal and got a drive out to Jaz's place.

"How you feelin'?" Joe asked when she and Ranger were settled in the big cab. When she told him she was healing up, he had no further questions. Which was quite unusual for Independence. Jake must have gotten the word out about not airing the town's dirty laundry. Tyler made up her mind then and there that if Jaz had not heard about the incident at Denver Airport, she wasn't going to tell her. Yet. That was something they could all laugh about around a campfire down the road. Things were still new with her and Pat's reconciliation, and who knew which way things would go?

Joe pulled the snowplow as close to Rose McArthy's former house as he could get. "To save you steps," he explained. "Need a ride back?"

"I think I'll probably find one, thanks Joe." Tyler pulled a bill out and gave it to him. He rumbled off with a wave in the rearview mirror.

Inside Jaz's house, Tyler could spot a few things around the living room that betrayed Jake was living there. The place was looking more lived in with the signs of two young people living full lives. Not to mention a big dog with chew toys scattered on the floor.

"Tea?" Jaz inquired.

"I could use one," Tyler said gratefully. "No yoga at the studio today?"

"Even the boss needs a day off from time to time. Actually, it's an afternoon off. In preparation for the recovery yoga group coming here tonight."

Just as they were settling in, a call for Jaz came in. "It's Kat from Seattle," she commented, looking at her phone.

"Go ahead and take it. No problem."

Jaz put the phone to her ear. "Kat!"

"Jaz. Are you taking calls for once?"

"How nice. Don't act like you've tried me a zillion times to no avail," she countered, "because my phone tells me you haven't."

"Takes one to know one." The zinger came back as if it were shot out of a pistol.

"Ha ha. But it's good you called. I'm just talking to Tyler—you know, Paula's little sister."

"Does she even have time to talk to you? From what I hear, she's got her hands full right now with knee surgery, a crazy stalker, and last but not least, Pat. Our Pat, who you lured away from my Seattle with a juicy construction prospect. What a girlfriend you are! First you leave me head over heels, and then you steal our best buddy to boot."

Jaz winced. "Guilty as charged. When are you coming back out? I hope you'll join us. The snow is incredible. Beautiful, I tell you."

"Snow. Brrr." Kat didn't sound like that would be the deciding factor in visiting Independence again. "Forget what I just said. I'm having trouble with my landlord again. Rocky is only tolerated here. Actually, animals are prohibited in the building."

"Ah, the joys of the big city. How well I remember. That's why I brought Rambo to your dog salon most of the time."

"The landlord reminded me again today that he can terminate my apartment overnight if Rocky happens to have an accident in the stairwell. He never has. But the guy has it in his head like it's a violation of the Ten Commandments."

"It probably is in his little world. Today there were two totally nice customers with toy poodles in my salon. It made me think of Rambo right away."

"So, hopefully you realize you can't live without us and come out soon."

"Let's see. I still don't know if I want to give up my business here. It's doing so well right now. I'm sure I'd feel comfortable in Independence, with you guys around, but I wonder if people there get their dogs groomed? Aren't they mostly working dogs or guard dogs?"

Jaz thought a moment. "During ski season, you could take care of the vacationers' dogs. Lots of people have second homes in ski country and bring their animals. Maybe even the hotels and guesthouses would be interested in working with you and include it in their offerings."

"So what do I do the rest of the year?"

"I don't really know. On the other hand, Independence has grown quite a bit lately. If you did mobile grooming and worked a circuit between Breck and surroundings, there might be enough business. Life isn't as expensive here as it is in the big city either."

"That's the best news I've heard all day," Kat replied, a little wistfully. "I just need to do the math. Come up with new ideas on how I could make money. If you could ask around to see what properties are currently selling and what the prices are like, that would be great."

"All right, I'll do that. And keep both fingers crossed, because I miss you a lot."

"You too. See you soon and give Rambo a big hug for me."

"He'll need another hair appointment soon," Jaz purred into the phone.

"Yes, yes, I love that curly, fuzzy mop. Bye."

Jaz hung up, realizing how much she missed Kat. Sure, she had found an equally good friend in Paula. But one did not replace the other. They were too different for that. A clear goal was now in mind: Find a possible home for Kat, so that she couldn't help but move to Independence.

Jaz turned to Tyler. "Sorry about the interruption—"

An insistent banging started up on the front door. Ranger and Rambo started barking.

Jaz ran to the front and looked out. It was Paula. She swung the door open.

"Is Tyler here?" Paula said anxiously. Her auburn hair was sticking up more than usual, and she looked frazzled. I thought I saw Joe's snowplow earlier."

Tyler hobbled out to greet her.

"I need help," Paula said with alarm."

"What is it?"

"Leslie is missing."

"What? How long has she been gone?" Jaz and Tyler said overtop of one another.

"We had another fight about school." Paula looked helpless. "I know. What else is new? And when I insisted she go, she walked out to wait for the school bus. Only the bus never picked her up. She's gone."

"Go back home in case she shows up. We'll be right there."

CHAPTER TWENTY-THREE

Tyler noticed Paula's face was drawn with worry as she answered the door. Ranger pushed his way in and ignored Barns and Roo as they tried to engage him in play. Rambo was completely distracted and started to jump around.

"Out you guys," Paula said, and shooed them all away.

"The dogs couldn't find her?" Jaz asked.

"She's such a part of the place, they don't know what I'm asking."

Tyler noticed a package set to one side in the entryway. The logo on the label looked familiar. She squinted at it. It was show merchandise. "Hey, why's that just sitting here? I think those are the T-shirts I ordered for Leslie."

Paula made a face. "I didn't know what it was. I was going to ask you before opening it. There's been so much going on."

Tyler spun the box around and ripped it open. She held up a gorgeous pink T-shirt with crystals on the front that spelled Las Vegas. There were four more T-shirts in various colors in the box. "I think a few new clothes might make things easier for Leslie at school. That's why I ordered them."

"I'm willing to try anything at this point," Paula said.

"We'll get to them later, I guess," Tyler commented. She was disappointed that the "cool clothes" problem hadn't yet been solved for Leslie. With all the drama going on, Leslie had fallen through the cracks. That wasn't okay. Tyler decided the buck stopped right here today. "I'd like to give Ranger a crack at tracking her," Tyler said. "Give me something with her scent on it."

Jaz nodded approval.

"We might find her, Paula," Tyler said cautiously. "But what makes you think we'll have any success if we talk to her?"

"Not we, you," Paula answered. "She adores you. She sleeps at night with that owl you gave her." Paula got a sweatshirt from the dirty pile in the laundry room and handed it over.

Tyler gave it to the dog to smell. "Find Leslie," she said, leading Ranger to the door.

Outside, Ranger turned in circles, picking up many scents. He trotted around the back of the house and sniffed again in a number of places before he picked up the freshest scent. But it didn't lead to the road. He slipped under the paddock fence and trotted across the snow-covered area. Goats and horses watched with interest. Ranger continued to the barn door, sat down, and gave two barks.

"Leave this with me for a few minutes," Tyler said to Paula.

Jaz nodded in agreement.

Tyler made her way into the paddock and over to the barn door. She slid it open. "Leslie?" she called.

It was warm and quiet in there. The goats and horses were all outside. Tyler and Ranger went in. The door slid shut behind them. Ranger went to the ladder that led to the hayloft and sat down. He gave two short barks.

"You're busted, Leslie. I know you're up there," Tyler said in a kindly voice.

There was a rustling sound from above, and Leslie's face poked out over the platform of the loft. Her eyes seemed a bit red from crying. "What do you want?"

Tyler beamed a friendly smile up at her. "First, I wanted to tell you your new clothes are here. I saw the package from Las Vegas on the front porch on my way into the house. Those new T-shirts I ordered for you with the pretty crystals on them. They're here. Want to see them?"

"I'll look later," Leslie sniffed.

"I wanted to discuss something else, too. Want to come down and see Ranger?"

Ranger wagged his tail. He knew he was being discussed.

"What about him?" Leslie said.

Tough audience, this kid, Tyler thought. *I better cut right to the chase.*

"I wanted to ask you what you thought of the job he did protecting us and leading us to William's secret room at the house."

Leslie's head poked out farther. "He did a fantastic job," she said. "Why are you asking?"

"Come down the ladder and I'll tell you," Tyler replied.

Leslie looked at Ranger, wagging his tail with a big smile on his face. He bowed at her and whined. It was dog language for, "Come and pet me."

Leslie gave a groan of surrender and prepared to come down the ladder. When she got on the ground, Ranger gave her an enthusiastic welcome.

"If you think this is going to get me to go to school, I'm not," she said, after giving Ranger his love.

"I think it will," Tyler said.

Leslie thinly veiled a stubborn sneer.

Tyler said a quick prayer for the right words to express what she felt. "A dog like Ranger," she said, "he deserves the best care and treatment, don't you think?"

"Of course. He's a service dog. William might have hurt us without Ranger there."

"Exactly. So in return for protecting us, we should feed him well and treat him well and give him the best care. Right?"

"Yes. I agree."

"Who do you think gives dogs like Ranger the best medical care?"

"Vets, people like that."

"And who are they?"

"How should I know who they are?"

"Leslie," Tyler gave her a direct gaze. "*They are you.*"

As if on cue, Ranger sat down, ears perked and alert.

"The vet schools are looking for people who love animals and have talent for working with them. Everybody doesn't have that ability, you know that. Ranger and the dogs that come after him are depending on you to do your best, to learn how to be a vet, and be there for them."

Tears sprang to Leslie's eyes. "I never thought of it that way."

"I know you didn't. Imagine if Ranger got hurt in a rescue and there was nobody who loved dogs to treat him and bandage him? Because you weren't there."

Leslie cried quietly and stroked Ranger's fur.

After a minute, Tyler said, "Now can we go look at those T-shirts? Let's see if we have everything we need to send you back to classes. I'll order anything else you want for school clothes. Helping Ranger can start right now if you're willing."

Leslie put her arms around Ranger's neck and buried her face in his fur. Then she lifted her head. "All right."

An hour later, a grateful Paula surrounded Tyler with a bear hug. "You did it. I don't know how you did it, but you did it. She's agreed to go to school."

"Think she means it?"

"I think so. And thank you for the T-shirts. She's in love with them. I didn't know how important clothes are at school. It was never my thing. I have no experience. I'm learning this foster mother business one mistake at a time."

"You're doing great, sis."

Paula sank into a final, grateful hug.

Later that night, Tyler and Pat were in bed at the B and B. Tyler woke up and simply enjoyed his closeness. She traced the lines of his face with her fingertips. This amazing man was hers. At least for the moment. Surprised, she realized that this restriction didn't make her feel relieved, as before, but rather...well, what, actually? Made her sad? Since when was she looking for a permanent connection? Her *modus operandi* before surgery, or "BS" as she thought of it, was conquer and leave. But she had broken this pattern with Pat quite a while ago. She snuggled closer. Ranger, who was lying at the foot of the bed, lifted his head and made sure that she was still there. Then he lay down again.

Pat opened his eyes. As soon as he saw her, he smiled broadly. "Good, you're still here!" His voice was scratchy and somewhat muffled from sleep. With those words, he wrapped his arm around her middle, pulled her close, and fell back asleep.

If something permanent felt like this, she could get used to it. Careful not to wake him, she wriggled out from under, body part by body part. But even asleep, he wouldn't hear of it and tightened his grip around her waist. She tried to lift his arm. In vain. There was no choice but to stay put.

With all the commotion on the bed, the dog got fed up and jumped down to the floor. With a sigh, he settled on the rag rug lying next to the door.

That was all it took for the negative little voice to pipe up in her head. *Why in the world would Pat want to settle for a broken-down ballet dancer? Maybe he just came back, as Mr. Wilkinson put it, for the hanky-panky. Maybe he'd run back to Seattle again as soon as the restoration was done.*

Somewhere in the wee hours, she slipped into an uncomfortable, anxious sleep.

Early morning sunlight streamed into the *Cattle Rustler*. Even with half an eye open, Pat could see it was a morning with brilliant sunshine and blue sky. He slipped out of bed while Tyler lay asleep and checked his phone. A text had come in last night after they had gone to bed for the night. It was from Cecilu at the Colorado State Registry for Notable and Historic Architecture: *An unexpected Zoom meeting with the board last night resulted in a unanimous vote. The Wilkinson house has been approved.*

It was all Pat could do to keep from jumping in the air with a loud holler. It was a sign. Or at least he was going to take it that way. He slipped out of the *Cattle Rustler* and was back with a take-out bag before Tyler knew he'd been gone.

"Come on sleepyhead," he said.

Tyler cracked an eye open. "What?" she croaked.

"Picnic time."

"It's winter. We haven't even had breakfast yet."

"That's the point. It's a winter breakfast picnic. We have something to celebrate. Come on, quick!"

Halfway outside Independence, Pat turned onto a narrow road. Tyler already knew that the road led to one of the most beautiful viewpoints in the area. A spot that was also used by teenagers for whatever teens did alone in cars. She glanced at the man next to her. He could forget about that before coffee. Her knee may have made progress, but it was definitely not up for artistic contortions in a limited space.

Pat stopped the car at the lookout and got out, closely followed by Ranger. After getting something out of the trunk, a blanket, she realized, he held the door open for her. She hoisted herself out of the car as gracefully as possible and looked around. The view was truly breathtaking. One could see across the entire plateau surrounded by white mountain peaks. Actually, it was a pity that she often took her own area for granted and the beauty didn't always register. On the spot, she resolved to change that. She squinted into the sun. In the blue sky, high above, a hawk soared on outstretched wings. It seemed to be appreciating the view, too.

Tyler let Pat take her hand in his. The thought flashed through her mind how surprisingly well their hands fit together. Like two pieces of a puzzle. He led her to a wooden bench, sat down next to her, and wrapped her legs in the blanket. Then he got the take-out bag from the diner. Two large coffees with lids came out first. A little trail of steam came out the top opening of each cup. It smelled *incredible*. He handed one of them to her.

Tyler raised her eyebrows. "This is the breakfast picnic?"

He sheepishly held out the bag. "It's not summer yet, but today is warm enough to sit and have a snack. Picnic. Yes. You could call it that."

She glanced inside. Miss Daisy's famous cinnamon rolls. "What are we celebrating?"

"The most important thing is that you stopped me from making a big mistake yesterday." He held out his cell phone with the text from Cecilu. "I haven't even told Mr. Wilkinson yet. He's going to be delirious with joy."

"I'm so happy for you." Tyler threw her arms around his neck. "This is a dream come true."

Pat cleared his throat and shifted a bit on the bench.

She pulled away. "But what does it mean for us?" she said uneasily.

"Listen," he stammered. "I've been thinking about this for a long time." He spoke quickly, as though he were afraid she wouldn't let him finish. "You've been on my mind since the beginning." He laughed and ran a hand through his hair. "If you hadn't shown up, I would have started asking around Independence about that pretty blond ballerina."

She snorted and stifled a laugh.

"I know how that sounds. Pretty pathetic. But you came back and saved me from leaving the best thing I've ever had." He looked into her eyes and reached for her hand, as though needing a physical connection as he revealed his innermost feelings. When he felt her stroking the back of his hand with her thumb, he exhaled in relief. "When I think about the last few weeks, there's only one thing that ever comes to mind: how much I enjoy spending time with you, how I look forward to seeing you in the evenings, holding you in my arms. And when I almost lost you a few days ago, I realized that I love you."

She stared at him with wide eyes.

He swallowed and cleared his throat nervously. "I'll still be working on the Wilkinson house until spring, one way or another." He felt her body grow tense beside him. She still hadn't said anything. "After that, I'm going to look around the area for similar projects. If I can't find restoration jobs, I can take on new construction projects." He stretched and smiled at the clear blue sky. "I'm back to the snow-kissed Rockies, the pine-scented air of Colorado. It feels like home."

At last, a broad smile stretched across her face. "It doesn't have to."

"Doesn't have to? Does that mean you don't care if I stay or not?"

She wrapped her arms around his neck again and brought her face closer to his until the tips of their noses were almost touching. "No. It doesn't mean that. It means where you go, I'll go." When he didn't reply, she continued, "Because I love you too!"

"Thank God," he groaned in relief, hugging her so tightly she nearly lost her breath. "I was beginning to think you'd respond with a thanks, but no thanks."

She shook her head. "Not a chance. And you don't have to worry about your work for now. I'll just go with you wherever you go. I'm as free as a bird."

"Seriously? Did you talk to Sarah and Yuri?"

"Not yet, but that will be easy. The minute they know I'm out, there will be a hundred hopefuls lined up to take my place. It'll be a very short conversation."

"What's next then?"

"By spring, my knee should be healed enough for me to take stock and see what I'm fit for. Probably not enough for the big stages of this world anymore, but that's okay. I was really, really good once, if you don't mind me saying so."

He laughed. "I never doubted that."

"I'm sure there are smaller dance troupes that will take me in, even with a patched knee. As one prima ballerina said, 'If I can still walk, I can still dance.' Or I could restart Madame DuPont's retreats for professional dancers and performers right here in Independence. While you're helping old houses to their former glory, I could spend my time practicing and maybe teaching. I was thinking of community projects for disadvantaged kids, for example. Leslie inspired me on that angle. Even if I don't stay in one place forever, maybe it's enough to get something going and then hand over the reins."

"You've already thought about this," he marveled.

"I can't risk you moving on without me," she joked. "I have only one condition."

"And that would be?"

"I'm part of a team. Ranger has to come along."

The shepherd dog heard his name and trotted over to the bench to join the two humans sitting side by side. He was satisfied. Everything was as it should be, and he let the thick fur on his neck be scratched.

PREVIEW

*Don't miss the next book
in the Rocky Mountain Romances series!*

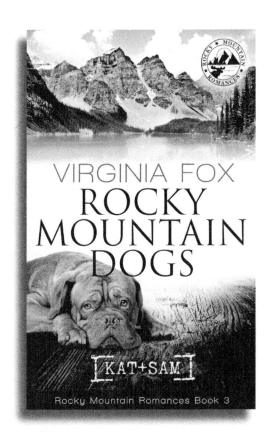

VIRGINIA FOX
ROCKY
MOUNTAIN
DOGS

KAT+SAM

Rocky Mountain Romances Book 3

CHAPTER ONE

It was a bright, blue-sky day and Kat chugged down the highway in her elderly but gently used recreational vehicle. The outside was painted white and polka-dotted with black pawprints. Electric-pink letters read:

Kat's for Dogs
Mobile Grooming

Kat and her traveling companions had just crossed the border from Utah into Colorado and were bound for Independence. *In more ways than one*, Kat thought, trying not to recall the turmoil she'd left behind. Independence Junction was a small town nestled not far from Breckenridge where friends and a pot of hot tea would be waiting to welcome her. Kat shifted her hands on the RV's steering wheel and stretched her neck from side to side. A chance to move her legs and chat over steaming cups of tea would be soooo welcome at this point after driving over a thousand miles from Seattle. Thankfully, the long road was behind her. Good times were just ahead in sixty miles.

She fumbled for her cell phone and called a number that went straight to voicemail. *Hi! This is Jasmine McArthy. If you are calling about classes at the yoga studio, please—*

Kat tapped her screen so the message cut off and started recording. "Hi Jaz! I'm just an hour away. I'll call again when I'm entering town. Love you! Say hi to Pat for me." She tapped *End Call* and brought up GPS again.

A quick glance into the back of the RV showed her traveling companions, two large dogs, napping contentedly in their crates. With a satisfied smile, Kat turned back to the road.

BOOM!

Distant thunder sounded in the distance.

Both dogs lifted their heads.

BOOM BOOM!

"Woof," went the dogs.

In a few minutes Kat was driving through snowflakes that got increasingly heavy the closer they came to the little mountain town. Wind gusted down from the rockies and buffeted the old RV. "Whoa, Nelly," Kat said out loud. Nelly was the vehicle's nickname. As if it understood, Nelly stopped rocking for a moment and drove steadily onward. But half an hour later the snow drove harder and the wind rose to a howl.

By the time a sign flashed past in a white bluster, *Independence 3 Miles*, Nelly was groaning against the wind as the dogs whimpered. Kat strained to see out the window in a near blizzard. Beside her on the passenger seat, the cell-phone GPS stalled. *No cell reception* popped up on-screen. The turnoff was just up ahead. Kat slowed to a near crawl and carefully steered into the turn. Blindly, she followed the road into town as the storm lifted a bit. Nelly no longer rocked in the wind. Kat breathed a sigh of relief. "We just might make it," she said out loud.

CRAAK!

The little RV lurched left as Kat hit something invisible on the road under the snow. Nelly started to slide. The dogs yelped, and Kat took her hands off the wheel, hoping Nelly could snap out of it. But with a sickening *crunch* the RV slid off the road, half on the pavement and half in a ditch. The engine rattled and died. The dogs whined, then cocked their ears and made no sound. Only the wind wailed outside.

Kat sat in stunned silence. Beside her, the cell phone still had no bars of signal. She was too scared to cry.

And then out of the cold and dark, a light shone. Was someone coming to the rescue? Kat's heart leaped with hope. "I'm here!" she cried, hoping her voice would carry through the windshield. "Please help me, I'm here!"

Two Weeks Earlier

"Won't you at least reconsider, Mom? I can order your ticket now." Kat turned up the volume on her cell phone and pushed a strand of curly hair behind her ear. Her light blue eyes were full of concern. "You just have to pack your suitcase and go to the airport with your passport. It would be so nice to see you again."

Her mother's voice was mournful. "It's not the right time for a visit, *luby*." Luby meant "dear" in the Polish language.

"Tell him I need to see you," Kat urged.

"Be patient. I'll plan a visit soon."

Kat bit her lower lip. Her mother had been saying that for a long time. "Soon" never seemed to happen.

"I have to go, Kathrina," her mother whispered into the phone. "I can already hear his footsteps on the stairs."

"But—"

It was too late. Only the dial tone sounded on the line. Frustrated, Kat dropped the phone and leaned against the headboard of her bed. A strand of hair fell into her face. Annoyed, she brushed the long brown curls behind her ear. Why didn't her mother see that she was out of date, a throwback? She preferred to stay home and tend a rocky marriage in Poland. As if two weeks in America would hurt it! Kat hated being thrown into competition with her father.

She sighed and drew her knees up to her chest. Her mother spoke excellent English and even had American citizenship. Kat had been born in America. But then, after more than twenty years, her father demanded they go back to Russia. Kat was eighteen at the time and refused to go. Good thing, because the return to Russia backfired and they ended up in her mother's hometown of Warsaw, Poland. That had been more than ten years ago. Since then, Kat had seen her mother only once, when she visited at Christmas a few years ago.

Kat's big male mastiff Rocky brought her back to the present by trotting over with a leash in his mouth. He rested his massive skull in her lap with a sweet clownish look on his wrinkled face. Kat stroked the short reddish-brown fur.

"Are you sure you want to go out?" She glanced out the window. Thanks to the dark clouds that had been hanging over Seattle all day, January was showing its bleakest side.

In response, Rocky nudged her with his nose.

"You're serious," she noted, unable to stifle a grin. Rocky was a huge charmer. His repertoire of facial expressions was expansive. Somehow his facial wrinkles took on a new landscape with each emotion he felt. Depending on what any situation demanded, he could be happy, sad, quizzical, wistful, pleading, or disappointed. He used all of them purposefully and as successfully as any professional actor. At least that's how it seemed to Kat.

"All right. Let's get the rain gear," she said out loud, and pushed herself up from the bed. As soon as Rocky realized that his tactic was successful, he scurried out of the bedroom and down the hallway, surprisingly light on his feet for his sixty-odd pounds of body weight. He skidded to a halt at the front door. Kat caught up with the collar in her hand and attached the leash to it. She slipped into a rain jacket and they were both ready to go. But she didn't move to open the door. Tension formed a lump in her throat. The landlord wasn't exactly Kat's best friend due to some bad timing. No sooner had she moved into this apartment than the building had been sold. The new owner hated dogs and banned all pet ownership. Kat and Rocky were "grandfathered" in, but only tolerated. It made for strained relationships all around.

Rocky refused to understand this and always tried to convince the landlord of his good looks and charm. Unfortunately, his enthusiasm and intimidating size were in the way. Kat prepared herself for a quick dash down the stairs and darted out. This time they were lucky and didn't encounter anyone in the stairwell. In this section of Ballard, in Seattle, many older apartment buildings were "walk-ups" with no elevators.

Outside, the heavy rain had stopped. Only the drizzle so typical of Seattle still hung in the air. She directed her steps to Golden Gardens Park. There she could let Rocky run freely among the tall trees until they reached the beach. Dogs weren't really allowed on the beach but Kat took him there only when it was deserted. She was careful to always pick up after him and leave no trace they'd been there. Her apartment building's close location to this park was one of the reasons she hadn't looked for a new place yet. It was perfect for a large dog needing daily exercise.

While she let Rocky sniff his favorite spots, her mind wandered. She really did need a new place to live. Her landlord asked them to leave at every opportunity. She was sure an eviction notice would have already been delivered except for the fact that Rocky was permitted by their original lease which had been signed by the previous owner of the building. But where could they go? Not far from here was her thriving dog salon. In addition to grooming, she cared for pets there during the day when owners needed doggos minded with love and attention. But after her two best friends, Jaz and Pat, moved to a small town called Independence in the middle of the Rocky Mountains last year, she often felt lonely. Without friends to confide in—and her mother's marital problems that never seemed to resolve—life wasn't getting any easier.

Rocky interrupted her thoughts by pulling on the leash. "Wait," she said, undoing it. After a few seconds she gave him a hand signal that he was free to go. She was always strict about not setting him free until he didn't pull on the leash. Otherwise, she'd find herself flying through the air behind him. *Kind of like kite flying*, she thought, amused. *Or dog flying*. She jogged after Rocky, who trotted on springy paws through the sparse woods toward the water.

Arriving at the beach, he placed a thick branch at her feet and looked up expectantly. "Of course," she said and bent down for it. With a practiced toss, she let it whiz across the water. Rocky dove enthusiastically into the beach water. Soon he had to start paddling. *Good. At least he'd be tired later.* Swimming was great for this breed, as was training and discipline. The mastiff was a working breed and too much downtime led to bad habits.

Kat put her cold fingers in her coat pockets and gazed out at Puget Sound. Only a narrow strip of light still illuminated the evening horizon. She had no idea if Rocky would even find the branch. But at least he was busy. *Busy.* She was grateful that her business was doing so well. She'd even hired an old friend of Jaz's who moonlighted at the dog salon when she needed extra money. Caitlin was reliable and trustworthy, and quietly admitted that she liked the dog salon better than the yoga studio where she usually worked. But something was missing. Kat just couldn't put her finger on where her own dissatisfaction was coming from.

Her eyes were drawn to movement at the shore. The big mastiff galloped out of the waves like one of Neptune's horses and spit the branch at her feet.

"I'm impressed," she said joyfully.

Rocky barked.

"Again?" she asked. A full-body wag was his response. She let the dripping branch fly back into the sea. That fleeting feeling she couldn't quite pin down suddenly came clear. She missed her friends. Jaz's attempts to persuade her to move to her small mountain town were tempting. So far, Kat had only explored the idea as a silly fantasy. Way too impractical. She was settled in Seattle! But missing her friends was a bigger deal than she'd let on.

One thing that was always keeping her tied to Seattle was the hope of convincing her mother to come out. But today's phone conversation made it abundantly clear that her mother was still not ready to leave her husband and might never be. Kat shuddered and pulled her coat collar higher. Maybe it was time to make decisions independent of Mom.

Rocky emerged from the surf without the branch a second time, busying himself by digging in the sand for crabs. Or anything else that wiggled. In reality he was mostly shoveling sand from one side to the other, much of it onto his nose and paws. His fun was going to be her mess to clean. She decided to stop by the dog salon on her way home. Luckily, everything was within walking distance.

Kat whistled to Rocky and started walking back through the park to the street. A block later she walked him through the alley where the salon's back entrance was located. As soon as she approached the door, Rocky stiffened and straightened up to his full size. A deep growl came from his throat. Uncertain, she stopped. What was wrong? Normally Rocky was so relaxed. Her eyes wandered from one corner of the alley to the other. But she could detect nothing that explained his strange behavior. She bent down and unsnapped the leash from his collar. If someone was hiding in there and Rocky needed to defend her, he needed to have room to do it. Rocky whined once, turned his head toward her as if to urge her to hurry, and trotted to the back entrance of the salon. Shaking her head, she followed. He'd probably scented a squirrel. She truly hoped it wasn't a rat.

Abruptly, he stopped and sniffed loudly. At his feet she could make out a shapeless shadow. What was it? Her dog didn't seem to be sure either. Again and again, he nudged the bundle with his muzzle. Kat pushed past Rocky and waved her arms in the direction of the outside light sensor. It came on but the low-watt bulb did a poor job of illuminating the darkness. It was enough to show what lay on the ground, though. A dog. It was tethered to one of the large dumpsters. And not just any dog. But a half-starved French mastiff, of all things, with mangy fur and bloody paws, because it had obviously tried to free itself. A wire was tied from the collar to the dumpster and the poor dog's paw had gotten wrapped up in it. *Who ties a dog up with wire?*

French mastiffs were uncommon dogs. Rocky was a French mastiff. How did one happen to end up tied to the dumpster outside her salon? She approached the animal carefully. Even the friendliest dog could bite if driven to it. She kneeled down and the mastiff weakly raised its large head. It seemed the struggle to get free had exhausted all his reserves. Rocky stood on guard with a worried look. It occurred to Kat that the first thing she had to do was get the dog inside. There she had enough light and an emergency first-aid kit to help.

THE UTE INDIAN PEOPLE

THE UTE PEOPLE EXTEND a warm welcome to all visitors interested in the Southern Ute Indian Reservation in beautiful Southwest Colorado, home of the Southern Ute Indian Tribe. The second weekend in every September is an Annual Southern Ute Tribal Fair and Powwow. The general public is welcome to attend the dance, drum and fair contests. *Máykh* means hello in Ute Indian language.

HISTORIC UTE

The Ute people are the oldest residents of Colorado, living in the mountains as well as the plains of Colorado, Utah, Wyoming, Eastern Nevada, Northern New Mexico, and Arizona. The word "Ute" comes from the word *eutaw* or *yuta*, which means "dwellers on the top of mountains." The number of Ute people left in the United States is few—they number in the thousands. The old ways and wisdom are precious, and we now realize it needs to be preserved. Cooking, hunting, medicinal plants, and a nomadic hunter-gatherer lifestyle were and still are samples of the expertise of Ute Indians.

FOOD

As expert hunters and gatherers, the Ute found food already growing in their environment to add to the meat of animals native to the region: buffalo, deer, elk, rabbits, and meat birds are just a few. Food was plentiful and nutritious. The Ute devised ways of drying and storing foods for the leaner winter months.

Chokecherry, wild raspberry, gooseberry, and buffalo berry were gathered and eaten raw. Occasionally, juice was extracted to drink, and the pulp made into cakes. Seeds from flowers and grasses were added to soups and stews. Earth ovens were made by digging four-foot deep holes and lining them with stones. A fire was started on top of the stones and food was tucked between layers of damp grass and heated rocks. Covered with dirt to hold in the heat, everything cooked overnight.

WAY OF LIFE

Historically, Ute families lived in *wickiups* and *ramadas* in the western and southern areas. A wickiup was a frame hut covered with a matting of bark or brush. Ramadas were shelters with a roof but no walls or only partially enclosed. Hide tepees were found in eastern territory.

Men and women kept their hair long or braided. Clothing clanged depending on weather temperature and seasonal conditions. They wore woven fiber skirts and sandals, rabbit skin robes, and leather shirts, skirts, and leggings. Baskets were woven to carry food and objects. Animal-skin bags were also useful for carrying goods. Tools were handmade from bone, stone, and wood.

TODAY

Very few Ute people are left and now primarily live in Utah and Colorado, within three Ute tribal reservations: Uintah-Ouray in northeastern Utah (3,500 members);

Southern Ute in Colorado (1,500 members); and Ute Mountain which primarily lies in Colorado, but extends to Utah and New Mexico (2,000 members). The majority of Ute people live on these reservations although some reside off-reservation. Tribal leaders and associations are developing businesses and securing outside opportunities for Utes now and in the future. These are a magnificent people who hold a meaningful and respected place in the rich tapestry of American life.

MISS DAISY'S RECIPES

THE DINER IS KNOWN FOR ITS DELICIOUS HOME COOKING!
THE RECIPES ARE EACH CALCULATED FOR FOUR PEOPLE.

———————————

Miss Daisy's
French Toast

INGREDIENTS

8 slices white bread

²/₃ cup milk

2 tbsp. sugar

1 tsp. vanilla extract

1 pinch salt

4 eggs

4 tbsp. butter

CINNAMON-SUGAR TOPPING

1 tbsp. cinnamon

4 tbsp. sugar

INSTRUCTIONS

Whisk together the milk, sugar, vanilla extract, salt, and eggs. Put the bread slices in the mixture until they are thoroughly soaked.

Heat the butter in a frying pan, and fry the bread slices until golden brown.

Mix the cinnamon and sugar together for topping. Then coat toast in cinnamon-sugar. The French toast slices can be kept warm on a plate covered with aluminum foil in the oven at about 200°F.

If you don't like the cinnamon-sugar version, you can enjoy the French toast with powdered sugar, maple syrup, bacon, or compote (for example, caramelized cinnamon apples; see next recipe). There are no limits to your creativity.

Miss Daisy's
Caramelized Cinnamon Apples

INGREDIENTS

8 McIntosh apples (or substitute Rome or Gala)

1 tbsp. cinnamon

4 tbsp. sugar

4 tbsp. butter

INSTRUCTIONS

Peel apples, remove the skins, and cut into slices.

Mix cinnamon-sugar in a separate bowl. If you like it sweet, you can double the cinnamon-sugar recommendation.

Melt butter in a frying pan.

Add the apples and sprinkle with the cinnamon-sugar. Slowly cook the apples on low heat, stirring occasionally until soft. The temperature must not get too high, or the sugar will burn and become bitter.

The cooking time is about 10 to 15 minutes, depending on the type of apple.

Miss Daisy's
Meatloaf

INGREDIENTS

2 oz wood oven bread or bread of your choice

⅓ cup milk

½ small onion (2.5 oz)

1 bunch fresh flat-leaf parsley

1 tbsp. butter or 1 tbsp. olive oil

1⅓ lb. ground beef

Herbal salt

Cayenne pepper

Oregano or sweet basil

⅜ cup cream

INSTRUCTIONS

Remove crust from the bread, pull it into pieces, and soak them in the milk.

Dice onions and sauté in the butter until golden. Mince parsley and add to sauté.

Season the meat with salt, pepper, and lots of oregano or sweet basil. Add the onion-parsley mixture. Fish the bread out of the milk, and squeeze the milk out a little. Add the bread to the meat mixture. Then mix everything together thoroughly.

Form a small ball of the meat mixture and fry. Taste the sample and re-season the mixture to taste.

Form 1–2 equal-sized roast pieces and place in a roasting pan. Bake at 300°F until it reaches a core temperature of 150°F.

Remove and let stand for ten minutes wrapped in aluminum foil.

Melt butter in saucepan on medium heat. Add drippings and cream, whisking together constantly. If it starts to clump, turn up the heat. Add cornstarch or flower if need to get the preferred consistency.

Serve with mashed potatoes (see next recipe) and vegetables of your choice. Carrots or Brussels sprouts go well with this.

Miss Daisy's
Homemade Mashed Potatoes

INGREDIENTS

3 lb. Yukon Gold potatoes

4 tbsp. butter

1 cup milk

Nutmeg

1 cup cream

1 pinch salt

INSTRUCTIONS

Peel potatoes. Cut into 1½-to-2-inch cubes and boil in salted water until soft.

In a separate saucepan, add the butter to the milk and warm on low heat.

When potatoes are soft, drain the cooking water out of the pot and return the potatoes in the uncovered pot to the still-hot stove on low. Allow as much liquid as possible to evaporate. Keep shaking the pan gently to prevent the potatoes from sticking to the bottom. When there isn't much steam rising, remove the pot from the stove.

Use a potato masher to mash the potatoes.

Season with nutmeg to taste.

Add the hot milk butter mixture to the potatoes.

Now add the (cold) cream a little at a time until you reach the preferred consistency. The 1 cup is an approximate guide.

At first, this may sound like a lot of work. But once you've made the recipe a few times, it takes only 20 minutes. And it's so much tastier than anything out of a box.

TIPS FROM MY EDITOR MONIKA POPP FOR ADDING COLOR:

Depending on your color preference, add peas, carrots, or beet. This gives the mashed potatoes a completely different color. For Halloween, you can also experiment with food coloring.

Miss Daisy's
Fluffy Chocolate Cake
(Gluten-free)

When I stumbled across this recipe, it immediately appealed to me because the ingredients are almost the same as my favorite chocolate cake.

(Like I desperately needed a second recipe for the same cake... but lo and behold, trying it out paid off!)

The only real difference is that the egg whites are beaten and folded into the batter. The result is a very moist yet very light cake.

Warning: the risk of addiction is high.

INGREDIENTS

9 tbsp. butter

5.3 oz dark chocolate

¾ cup sugar

1 packet or 1½ tsp. vanilla sugar

1.75 oz peeled ground almonds (in case of almond intolerance, use oat or spelt flakes)

1 pinch salt

2 tbsp. cornstarch

3 eggs

¼ cup cocoa powder or powdered sugar

INSTRUCTIONS

Preheat oven to 350°F.

Melt butter and chocolate slowly in a hot water bath or slowly in microwave. Careful not to burn the chocolate.

Separate the egg whites. Beat them until stiff and refrigerate.

Mix sugar, vanilla sugar, almonds, and salt into the liquid chocolate. Leave to cool slightly.

Mix in the cornstarch and then the 3 egg yolks.

Gently fold the beaten egg whites into the mixture.

Pour the dough into a buttered springform pan. Bake in the middle of the oven at 350°F for about 30 minutes. I prefer to take the cake out a few minutes earlier to avoid it becoming dry.

The cake will be quite flat. If you want, you can double the quantities to get a higher cake.

Serve as-is, or sprinkle the cake with cocoa powder or powdered sugar.

BOOK CLUB QUESTIONS

1. Author Virginia Fox spent time in a similar Colorado town and the warmth of the people and the sense of community is what inspired her to write this series. How would the folks in the fictional small town Independence Junction greet you if you walked into the local coffee shop? Would you blend in? Stand out? Make new friends there?

2. The main characters shift within the Rocky Mountain Romances series, but the setting stays the same. Which characters are you drawn to the most?

3. Many people dream of a rural life and making a homestead where they can grow food and raise animals. Do you have any interests along this line? Would you like to live in a similar Rocky Mountain town?

4. Did you feel Independence Junction and the setting was realistically portrayed? Were the weather, geography, and winter sports true to life?

5. What did you think of Tyler leaving the Vegas show to "go out on top"? Was that a career choice you might make if you were a ballerina with an injury?

6. Did Tyler remind you of anyone? Did any of the characters remind you of anyone you know, or other characters from other books?

7. There was an infestation of martens (weasels) in the bed-and-breakfast. What did you think about how the animals were handled? What would you have done to ensure they never came back?

8. Do you have any thoughts on the intergenerational tension between Mr. Wilkinson and the younger generation? Does he have points to make? Or is he hopelessly out of date?

9. Everything stated about the life and career of architect Elizabeth Ingraham Wright is true. She really was the granddaughter of Frank Lloyd Wright, and she designed houses in Colorado beginning in the 1950s. Was adding this information a good use of local history? Did you enjoy this element? Why or why not?

10. Were you knowledgeable about the Ute Indian tribe before reading this book? Was Avery's character believable? Thoughts about the information added to the back of the book about the Ute people?

11. If you were to write a story set in this Rocky Mountain town, or fan fiction about these characters, what kind of story would you want to tell?

ROCKY MOUNTAIN ROMANCES

Rocky Mountain Yoga

Rocky Mountain Star

Rocky Mountain Dogs

Rocky Mountain Kid

Rocky Mountain Secrets

COLLECT THE ENTIRE SERIES!

ABOUT THE AUTHOR

AUTHOR, MOTHER, HORSE WHISPERER, and part-time healthy food cook, Virginia Fox is a woman who cares deeply about family, animals, the environment, and friendships.

Creative from a young age, she turned her love of books into a prolific career as a writer. Her German-language Rocky Mountain series saw every volume enter the Top 50 of the Kindle charts on day one of launch. Now the bestselling Rocky Mountain Romances series breaks onto the US scene.

Virginia Fox lives on a small ranch near Zurich with her family, her Australian cattle dog, and two moody tomcats. When she isn't writing, she delights in caring for her horses and cooking for her family. Discover more on her website:

WWW.VIRGINIAFOX.COM

Printed in Great Britain
by Amazon